I0687510

ROSE STAR GHOST HOUSE

Book #4 (and final book) in the
Four Families Series

Merry Brown

Additional books by Merry Brown

Fiction
The Four Families Series:
      Gold Manor Ghost House
      Crimson Hall Ghost House
      Silver Tree Ghost House

The Exiled Trilogy:
      The Knowers
      The Second Fall
      The United

Nonfiction
How to Be Unprofessional at Work: Tips to Ensure Failure

The Food Addict: Recovering from Binge Eating Disorder and Making Peace with Food

YA Books imprint
ISBN: 978-0-9899934-8-7
December 2024

Front and back cover design by Merry Brown.
Front and back cover photographs, shutterstock.com

This book is dedicated to my sister,
Melinda Hill

Chapter One

I sat in the emergency waiting room with time to burn on my hands.

Meg was being treated for a concussion, her multiple cuts already bandaged. I'd been sitting quietly by her side until the hospital staff decided I had to go.

The IV delivering a cocktail of relief, Meg rolled her head to the side. "Don't leave me."

"She'll just be in the waiting room, dear," one of the nurses assured her.

Meg was in distress, which was nothing new for the ER workers. That was their life. But none of them knew what had just happened to Meg. And Meg didn't know what I'd seen after she was knocked unconscious.

I could use a little mind-numbing painkiller right now I thought as I left her room, trying – and failing – to give Meg a reassuring smile. I couldn't help laughing when I realized no drug would make the trauma of the night go away. And besides, I didn't need a drug to zone out. I already felt nothing.

Turning the corner to the waiting room, I was startled to see Sylvia, our director and all-around keeper. I wasn't surprised she was at the ER, checking on her injured star. I was surprised I hadn't sensed her. Guess I really was numb.

"Were you just with Meg? The doctor said I couldn't go back, they're running tests," she said, annoyed.

"Yeah, I just got kicked out."

It was a slow night in the ER. There was only one other person in the room. An elderly man filling out paperwork at the front desk.

We sat down, two vinyl chairs between us. "They think she'll be fine. Just a concussion," I reported, hoping rather than knowing it was true. Hoping I hadn't been too late.

"Let's not discuss this here," Sylvia replied, eyes cutting to the old man. "I spoke with one of the doctors. I'll take it from here. You're free to go."

"She asked me to stay," I replied.

That was the end of that.

Within the hour, Sylvia was called back to Meg's room. The old man had gone, and I was left alone. And finally, I began to feel it. 1 a.m. in a vacant emergency room, the shock of the evening starting to wear off, the images of the night coming back.

The woods.

Dom hurt Meg, he'd tried to *kill* her. Colby had tried to kill *me*.

Finn killed Dom, and now he knew he wasn't the only Family present.

Corey killed Colby.

Dom and Colby dead, Meg and Finn out cold, and the tree from my dreams, in the waking world, left behind so I could get Meg to safety.

I shook my head. I couldn't think about it anymore. I had to come up with a cover story.

Ha! How in the world would this be cleaned up? No way. No way through it. *No way, no way, no way.*

I pulled my knees up and hunched into a ball, repeating my mantra, rocking.

"Anna?"

I lifted my head, confused to see the pair of them here.

Chapter Two

"Anna, are you okay?" Katie asked.

Why were Katie and Andrew, her magical boyfriend I wasn't close to figuring out, in the ER? Were they part of the cover story? Should I have been checking my texts? How did they get roped into this?

"Peace to you," Andrew said, laying his hand on my shoulder, halting my meltdown. It was no greeting; it was a command. He was very strange, even by my new standards.

"Are you here for me?" I asked, confused, unfurling from my fetal position.

"Uhm, do you need something?" Katie winced, answering my question. Coincidence. They were at the ER for medical reasons.

"Why don't you sit. I'll tell them you're here," Andrew said, easing Katie into a chair and going to the desk.

I felt like an idiot. "What happened to you?"

"It's so dumb. Andrew was cooking for me. He was telling me about his 'clean living' versus his months-long binge on junk food. It was a sad story, and he could tell he'd made me sad, so he told a joke. It wasn't funny, but it was funny that he tried. Unfortunately, I was mid-bite and started choking. He saved me by performing the Heimlich, but it *hurt* my ribs. He insisted we come in and get me checked out."

I looked up at Andrew. His bulky frame was hunched over, filling out paperwork on the narrow countertop. He was huge. Hercules like. No doubt he could cause serious damage, even when he didn't intend to.

"Are you in much pain?" I asked, trying to act like a normal person.

"It's not too bad," she lied.

Andrew came back. "It'll be a little while," he said, irritated.

"Strange. It's completely empty in here except for us," Katie replied, trying to take short shallow breaths. Her long explanation for the ER visit had winded her.

"Apparently, their resources are temporarily diverted for all non-life-threatening cases. Anna, care to tell us why?" Andrew inquired.

"There was an accident. Meg was knocked unconscious. She's awake now. I'm sure that's it."

"Is she going to be okay? What happened?" Katie asked, forgetting about her ribs for the moment and swiveling too quickly to face me. "Ow, shoot. Ouch."

"Hang on." Andrew placed his hand on her side and closed his eyes. What was he doing? Was he praying? "A little help, please?" he asked, looking at me.

"Sure. Anything. What do you want me to do? Get a nurse?"

While I was sad Katie was in pain, them being in the ER was the perfect distraction from my waking nightmare. I wondered, yet again, at their strange relationship. They clearly were super into each other, but there was something just beneath the surface, some awkwardness they couldn't get around. At least thinking about them was a relief from my screaming mind until Andrew demanded, "No, you. You heal her."

"I don't understand," I said, scanning the room. "What do you expect me to do?"

"I've seen what you can do. Take away her pain."

"I would if I could, but I don't know what you're talking about. I don't know what I can do," I added in a whisper. Surely we shouldn't talk about this here.

"I don't care about your secrets," he bit out.

"Stop it," Katie chided.

"I don't know why you'd want to be with me. I am utterly useless," he said to her, running his hand down her side.

"Stop it," Katie said with a shiver, in a very different tone. Andrew, distraught, dropped his hand. She took it, giving it a light kiss.

"Andrew, if I could help her, don't you think I would?" I said.

"I don't think you've ever given it a thought. You are a selfish creature."

"That is so not true! You don't know the first thing about me, what I've done and been through." He was pissing me off.

Andrew gave me a glare that said he really didn't care. If I couldn't help Katie, he was done with me.

But I wasn't done with him. "What a hypocrite! You waltz into the middle of some really crazy evil stuff with the ability to help us, and *you* refuse. You hung your lifelong friend Ewin out to dry. And you call me selfish, like you're not?"

He cryptically replied, "I am now."

Our exchange was cut short when Sylvia reentered the waiting room.

"Here for moral support?" she asked Katie.

"No. I had an accident. I think I'll be okay. Just waiting to be seen."

"I can fix that," Sylvia said. Walking back the way she came, she muttered, "What is it with this production?"

"Sylvia will get you taken care of. She has a way about her," I said to Katie, whose brave façade was fading. I looked at Andrew who was watching her. I wanted to help, wished I knew what he was talking about. I had healed my leg once, but it hadn't been intentional. I rarely did things intentionally when it came to understanding my relationship to manipulating energy.

It was only a matter of minutes before Katie's name was called at the admissions desk. As Andrew helped Katie up, I said, "I hope you feel better soon. I really wish there was something I could do."

"If you wanted to help her, you would've been preparing and practicing," Andrew said.

I was about to defend myself when he added, "You have no idea how frustrating it is to see all the power you possess, and yet you play with it. You're dripping in it."

"Drowning," I said to his back.

He turned around and looked at me. I felt instantly naked, exposed. "Yes. Maybe you are."

Katie let out a whimper and I was instantly forgotten.

"Oh good, you're still here," Sylvia said to me as Katie and Andrew disappeared behind the automatic double-doors of the ER. "I know you're not my PA and can say no, but would you mind going to Meg's house for these items?" she asked, handing me a long list.

As I read it over, Sylvia added, "I don't need to say it, but I will. This should not be leaked. Only Meg has the right to say she is here if she desires."

"Is she? I mean, is she going to be here for a while?"

"They plan to keep her for at least twenty-four hours. Dr. Glass is with her now."

"Oh. I guess I would've thought she could just be watched at home for a concussion," I said.

Sylvia didn't move an inch. The giveaway. It might not be "just" a concussion. "Your discretion is much appreciated."

"Sure," I nodded, as Sylvia handed me the list and key code to Meg's house.

On my way out Sylvia asked, "By the way, do you know how it happened?"

"Meg didn't say?" I deflected.

"Says she can't remember."

"I'll be back as soon as I can," I called over my shoulder and got out of there as quickly as I could.

Chapter Three

In the short trip from the hospital to Meg's house, I began to freak out all over again. Where was Adam? How was Corey?

My mind was completely preoccupied as I grabbed a bag from the hall closet and began filling it with the normal and completely unnecessary items on her list. *Bath bombs? Why does she need bath bombs?*

My scary night and inner turmoil were the only reason she caught me off guard. Hovering above the shower floor was the green Gold Ghost.

I screamed, dropping to my knees on the cold tile. The contents of Meg's make-up bag scattered. My heart stopped, stuck in my throat. I slowly raised my head as my phone lit up. It was Adam.

"The ghost is here," I whispered into the phone.

"Sylvia said you went to Meg's. Is that where you are?" His voice hard.

"Yes," I mumbled.

"I'm on my way. Don't engage her," he said as the ghost began to hum.

I pushed the speaker button and lifted my head.

"Fifth, more will come looking. Go to the grave, to the tomb. The third from the third. Find and know or she will die, and all is lost."

Adam's disembodied voice was warning me. "Anna, don't talk to her!" But he wasn't here. He didn't see what I saw. She wanted something. She wasn't giving up.

"Why do you call me Fifth?"

"Eyes that shine in the desert, hungered for and rejected. The storm of the sea and the murky ropes tossed.

The tomb beneath the ground. The tomb of storm and sea. You are not, and you are. Finder, seer, server, binder."

"Anna!" Adam warned.

The Gold Ghost was becoming translucent, as if she were dissolving. Maybe it was the adrenaline, I don't know, but I asked, "Is the tomb the tree?"

She immediately came into focus, her size shrinking to almost human. Her voice lost a bit of its ethereal edge. "The silver tree where Iris hides."

"Iris?" I asked, puzzled.

"Iris," the ghost replied, unusually clear, as if I were having a conversation with a friend.

In the moment I turned my head toward the sound of the front door opening, the ghost was gone.

Adam smacked into me, sending the things I'd gathered flying out of my hands again. I began to defend myself for engaging the ghost, but he didn't want to hear it. Instead, he held me. Tightly.

At first, I thought he was comforting me. Then I pushed past myself and saw him. He needed me.

"Come on," I said, taking his hand.

We went downstairs, out to Meg's back porch. It was an all season sunroom, facing a secluded wooded area. We both needed a serious time out. For one glorious hour he rested his head on my lap, and I played with his hair. We didn't talk, we just were.

It was a little past two in the morning when Meg sent us back in motion with a text. "You ok? Lost?"

"Taking a break. Sorry. Be right there," I texted back.

"Body pillow, chenille."

"Sure."

Adam sat up. "All good things must end."

He meant it to be light, but it came out wrong.

13

"Help me get Meg's stuff and then let's crash. Is that okay? Can everything else wait until tomorrow?" My worries were coming back. How was Corey? Why hadn't he called? And what about Suzanne and Finn?

Adam could feel my rising anxieties. "It has to," he said, which wasn't reassuring. But it was the truth. This night was nothing short of a living nightmare.

We gathered Meg's things. On the way to the hospital Adam observed, "We need to add Meg to the list."

"Isn't she already?" I replied automatically. Then it dawned on me I didn't know what he was talking about. "Oh, no. List of what?"

"Exactly. What kind of person does a ghost stalk?"

And that was all the brainpower we had to spend on that idea. Adam helped me bring in her items. A nurse showed us to her room, telling us to be quiet. If Sylvia wasn't there, Meg might be alone. If so, I'd stay with her. Meg shouldn't be by herself.

As we drew closer, I could feel she wasn't.

Meg and Corey were both trying, though failing, to sleep in the dark hospital room, lit by the nurse holding the door open just enough for us. Adam set her stuff down and I laid her pillow at the foot of her bed.

As we tip-toed out, Meg rolled over and extended her arm to me, whispering, "Thanks."

14

Chapter Four

My alarm went off at 5 a.m. I was slated to be in hair and make-up by 5:30 a.m. Scheduled for the week was a wide variety of exterior shots. The guys were shooting half of their football games for the season and most of their practices. I was shooting tennis matches, cheerleading scenes with the football team, and at the end of the week, more running through the woods.

But this was October in Northwest Tennessee. Nature didn't answer to our schedule, we had to work with hers. And this morning it was pouring rain.

I dragged myself down to the basement with two minutes to spare. The text came as I sat in the make-up chair. "Due to weather conditions, no shooting today. Take the day to recharge."

"Back to bed, ya'll," Lucy laughed. "See, I'm starting to talk like the locals!"

I yawned, setting off a chain reaction. I was prepared to be an adult and put the horrors of the night behind me. Denial was a great place to visit, and work an excellent way to get there. But sleep was my fate instead.

As soon as I fell back asleep, I was pulled into Mr. Seacrest's dreamscape.

I mechanically recited the events of the evening. All of it. I was too tired to censor my words properly. Mr. Seacrest took notes, nodding, shaking his head occasionally, alternating vibes of being pleased and displeased.

I awoke when I felt Corey enter my room. His heavy heart would've shaken the coldest person.

"I didn't mean to wake you," he rasped.

It was still raining outside. My room was lit with a soft bluish-gray hue from the overcast morning sky.

"What time is it?" I mumbled.

Corey pulled out his phone. "Just after ten."

I sat up and patted the space next to me. He slumped down.

"Have you even been to bed yet?" He looked like hell warmed over.

"Sometimes, when it rains here, I get the feeling we need to get on building Noah's ark or we'll be washed away," he said, staring blankly out of my bedroom window.

"I'll take that as a no."

Corey sat motionless. "Anna, I killed someone. How am I supposed to live with that? I don't think I'll ever be able to sleep again."

I got up on my haunches and held his shoulders, making him look me in the eyes. "No. You saved my life. He was about to kill me."

"Maybe he was, maybe he wasn't."

"You listen to me, Corey. He was going to kill me. I know this because he told me, and I quote, 'I'm gonna snap your little neck.' Secondly, you know that I know things. I can tell the difference between what people say and what they mean, and what they're about to do. Especially when they're touching me."

"I took his head off," he said mechanically.

"I know, and I'm sick for you. I am. But I'm glad to be alive. If he'd killed me, if you hadn't stopped him, you'd be sitting on my bed, staring out the window, wishing you had saved me. Right?"

"Anna," he groaned, his heavy burden shifting, lifting slightly.

16

"Don't you "Anna" me. I'm glad to be alive! Thank you. Thank you for always having my back. I'm the one that is sick to death that you were even in that situation in the first place. I wish I could take away your pain. I wish I could take away what you had to do for me."

But we both knew I couldn't. That neither of us would've asked for a different outcome. Well, that wasn't true. I wished I could've de-escalated the situation. I also wished Corey could've simply incapacitated Colby. And if he had to kill him, maybe in a less gruesome way.

Some things are better left unsaid.

As I got out of bed, I felt the weight of the night. The deaths and discoveries. Corey was still zoned out.

"I'm going to take a shower. Why don't you get some rest," I suggested.

"I don't want to move."

"My room is yours. No need to leave," I said, gathering my things.

Corey fell over, his giant tree trunk legs hanging off the side of the bed. I put my towel and shower caddy down and lifted his legs onto my bed, taking off his shoes.

"Thanks," he mumbled, closing his eyes.

"Stay as long as you'd like. It's going to be okay. We'll get through this."

I gathered my things and left for the shower. Before I closed the door behind me, Corey said, "It changed me. I'm not the same anymore."

This I knew. Even with so much of my energy spent, I could read Corey. It felt like a dormant part of him had been activated. "I know. We'll figure it out."

Chapter Five

It was noon when Adam found me in the library. I was half asleep, but still reading. I would have been completely asleep if it weren't for the stupid book I was trying to lose myself in.

"What have you been up to?" I asked as he sat down, draping my legs over his.

"Fires, you know, love. Lots of fires to put out."

I stared at him for a long moment, trying to put into words the numbness and terror vacillating through me. "I feel … so awful."

"They deserved it. Both of them," he said through gritted teeth.

"I don't think that matters. If what happened in the forest last night doesn't turn your insides out, something's wrong."

Adam looked at me. "Stop it, Anna. War is hell. That's what happens. You kill the enemy. They were combatants, not innocent civilians. They were here to kill whoever stood in their way. Dom, well, we're working on that one. Colby, because he liked to kill. He wanted to kill you just because he was a sick psychopath. Stop trying to work your head around this, any of this, like it's normal. As if we were on a normal stroll in the woods last night. We weren't. We were following killers and ghosts. You can't make it through a war with peacetime mentality. You can't."

"I…."

"Look. Look at the death around you. Look at what you're in the middle of. Wake up, Anna!"

His words were harsh. I thought I was doing a fair job dealing with murderers, death, ghosts, and being hunted. I didn't have the energy to fight with him.

"No, don't do that." He'd stopped rubbing my legs.

"Do what?" I asked, picking my book back up.

"That. Retreating. That's my gig. Don't close me out."

"I can't deal with "us" drama. Can we not do drama?"

"Sorry, love. I love you too much to not press this point."

I put my book down and pulled my legs back, sitting up. "And the point is?"

"The point is, you can't go to pieces when an enemy falls."

"I'm no killer. If you think that's going to change, you don't know anything about me."

"Anna, stop it! This is me. Why are you intentionally twisting my words? You know I'm trying to help. Here's the truth. Those two died because of their own actions. Not all the Fourth are bad, so Colby chose. As for Dom, insofar as he wasn't possessed, it was his choice to lure Meg out to the woods. He was going to kill her. That was all him. If you want to feel bad for anyone, it should be Meg. She may not remember what happened right now, but she will. And Corey. You know this changed him."

"I felt it. The moment it happened. Something in Corey. What was it?" I asked.

"The curse. The dreams will now kick in for him. Not all at once. But now that he's killed, it will reveal just how much Fourth is in his blood. Up until now it has all been a guess."

"And the more Fourth, the worse it will be for him?"

"The closer a relative is to the Four Families, the stronger the curse. Both of my parents account for what I can do. And you, well, you're our unicorn," he teased, patting his lap for my legs again.

I clicked off the reading lamp and sank into the sofa, plopping my legs back on top of his thighs. "I'd rather be a Pegasus, if it's all the same to you."

"Why?" he asked, lightly rubbing my legs.

The room was dim, lit by the soft light filtering through the rain into the study through its two entrance doors. The steady stream of rain continued. Would it stop any time soon?

"I like the idea of being free. I want to fly."

"Don't worry. No one can tether you." There was an ache in his voice.

Chapter Six

I awoke with a start. I had just been in the middle of a wild dream, being chased through Crimson Hall by something. When it had been about to grab me, I'd screamed, pulling myself out of my dream.

It was a terrifying dream. It felt so real, like I was actually there, in Crimson Hall. *Had* I been? My heart, still running crazy, believed I had. Adrenaline was rushing through me. I couldn't seem to calm down.

I got off the couch slowly, feeling cornered and watched. The energy running through me wasn't going to stay in my body. I had to dump it quickly because my scream had brought the inhabitants of the house running.

Almost out of time, I flung my arms out, commanding the doors to slam shut. *Calm down, Anna, Calm down. You're in Gold Manor, you're okay.*

I closed my eyes and planted my feet firmly on the ground, ready to get rid of the crazy amount of energy pulling through me. I reached out to find Adam in the sea of people pounding on the door. He'd help me center.

But he wasn't there. Neither was Corey.

I opened my eyes and looked around the room again. I pushed out. I felt the bodies in the house, their mass; I heard their voices; I felt who they were *supposed* to be. But they were not my people.

"Let me in, love," fake Adam purred from the other side of the door. "What's wrong? Are you okay?"

"I...bad dream. Just give me a minute," I called back, hoping not to give away that I knew this wasn't right.

The first thing I had to do was figure out if I was in a dream. If so, was it mine or someone else's? Or was I now awake and had somehow been taken?

Mr. Seacrest engrained into my head his mantra: don't show your hand. He said the oldest trick in the Family bag was to push and trick someone into exposing themselves. Only a rare few could perceive the kinds of hidden powers that sometimes accompanied being a Family member. He'd drilled into me to always make the other show first.

I sat back on the couch and looked around the room. Did this feel like a dream? Not really. If it were, it was like no dream I'd ever been in before. Therefore, maybe I should assume I wasn't in a dream.

Okay. Kidnapped? Had someone made an elaborate set of Gold Manor's library? Possible.

"Anna, please, let me in," fake Adam called from the hallway.

Was he a fake Adam? Now I wasn't sure. Would it be the dumbest thing I'd ever done to open the door and find out?

"Just a sec," I answered. Energy still plentiful, I raised my hand to open the doors, but thought better of it. Instead, I ran the energy through my hair, soothing it and sending it back down to allow gravity to take it.

I went to the entrance and opened the door as normally as possible. The wide hallway was crammed with a dozen bodies, all trying to get a look at me.

"Uh, sorry, guys. Like I said, bad dream. Go back to whatever you were doing."

Those from the prop and lighting crew returned to working on the house, and those from craft services continued setting up dinner. Adam came up to me and held me.

"What happened to you? I woke up and you weren't there," I asked him, trying to act casually, but he wasn't letting go. "I feel weird," I whispered, almost completely certain it *was* my Adam I was hugging.

He held me tighter.

Why didn't he ask me what I meant? Why didn't he ask me about my dream or tell me where he'd gone off to?

"Are you...?" he trailed off, not finishing the question. But I knew what he was trying to say. He was asking if it was really me.

Was he experiencing the same thing?

"Adam," Suzanne's voice a question, Finn standing beside her. Him, I could feel. He felt the same, though maybe more pungent than usual.

"Not now," Adam ordered.

"Don't address her like that. Ever," Finn said calmly, his tone assuming he would be obeyed without question.

Suzanne uncharacteristically shifted her weight nervously and took a deep breath. "Finn is ... awake."

Chapter Seven

I saw it.

We had two full-blooded princes who were used to being in control. For all of Adam's talk of being a "foot-soldier" and Finn's decision to not follow the Family's way, Finn was still Lilian and Dane Varga's son. They were direct descendants of those who massacred the innocent. They had more in common than they'd like to admit.

More in common... like extra powers?

"Now, gentlemen, let's all have a seat?" I said, stepping out of Adam's arms. But before I turned away, I whispered, "It's him."

Adam and I sat on the loveseat across from Suzanne and Finn. Before we got started, I realized I hadn't seen Corey.

"Is Corey okay?"

"He's asleep in your room still," Adam answered, smoothing my hair. "I'd gone to check on him."

"Oh."

The room was quiet. There was a steady buzz of movement around Gold Manor. Crews were at work here and there and Lucy was downstairs working with Drake on her costumes. Since production had suddenly fallen into a holding pattern due to the unrelenting rain and our ill lead, there was a push to take advantage of the rare lull in the shooting schedule to check off those little things that never seemed to bubble to the top of the to-do list in the swamped days and nights of a living set.

But here we were. The four of us. Whereas yesterday at this time Finn had been blissfully ignorant that he was in hostile territory, today he knew something was very wrong.

Just how much he knew, I couldn't tell. I couldn't read him in the same way anymore.

"You need to tell me what's going on," he said to Adam.

"The manor is full. Not a great place to talk," Adam replied, as if they were discussing dinner plans, not a war.

"We can go to my place," Finn smiled. Adam laughed.

"Third floor?" Suzanne offered, her voice small. She was really starting to freak me out. Whatever Finn was doing was disrupting my intuitions of everyone. Suzanne was scaring me.

"No," Adam said, running his fingers down my back.

I was having a hard time concentrating, not letting on that whatever Finn was doing was affecting me. It was like a vibration crawling up my spine, and it was increasing. Soon it would reach my skull and rattle my teeth.

Suzanne grabbed her head. So, it was affecting her too.

"What's wrong? Are you okay?" I asked her.

"Don't talk to her, Anna. I don't know what the hell you all are playing at, but I know what you are," he said, looking at Adam. "I can dial it up, if you'd like."

"Please don't," Suzanne whispered.

Finn looked down, torn. He wanted to hurt us, not Suzanne.

"Then tell them. All I want is the truth," Finn said to her.

My head was rattling now, it was hard to think. I saw my phone light up with a text from Echo.

"What the hell is going on?" his message read.

I could feel that he was upstairs.

"Stay there. It's Finn. Make certain Corey doesn't come down," I texted back.

All eyes were on me. "What? Just someone I needed to respond to."

My phone lit up again, this time with a message from Mr. Seacrest. "What's wrong?"

"Wow. I'm popular," I said aloud as I texted back.

As if on cue, just to make this moment perfect, a Gold Ghost made an appearance. She materialized, larger than life, in the space between us. She said nothing, her gaze held by something on the ceiling.

"Follow me," I mouthed to the Fourth sitting across from me, putting my finger to my lips to emphasize the need for quiet. I yanked on Adam's hand. It was inconvenient he couldn't tell what, or rather, where I had in mind.

They followed me silently to the front porch, leaving the ghost behind. The dreary day and steady rain echoed our sentiments. I dropped Adam's hand and held mine out, expecting him to give me his keys. He gave me an odd look, so I fished them out of his jeans.

"No," he said.

"Trust me," I said as confidently as I could, my brain now vibrating, thanks to Finn.

Finn and Suzanne got in the snug back seat of Adam's sports car, Adam and I in the front.

"Turn it off," Adam said to Finn.

"You will tell me the truth," Finn insisted.

"I do as I want. You are alive because I decided to leave you as such."

"You've got it wrong. I'm letting you live. For now," Finn answered, his vicious heritage rising to the surface for the first time.

Maybe I had made a grave mistake. Maybe these two were going to rip each other up. I had assumed that once we got Finn alone, and Adam had shown his hand by acknowledging Finn was messing with him, Finn would back down. But Finn refused to stop doing whatever it was that was harming us.

"You're hurting me, Finn," I said to him, hoping that would make him stop.

"I'm sorry, Anna. I wish you weren't one of them."

"You don't know what I am. I am going to give you a chance. A chance Adam won't," I warned.

Finn didn't like the threat. My teeth were now rattling. Suzanne was holding her head. Gritting his teeth, Finn reached out to her and traced an x on her back. Suzanne immediately sat up, freed from his invisible control.

"You can trust them," she said to Finn. "Please."

Suzanne couldn't interfere further without facing horrific consequences from either one of them. It was up to me.

I didn't need intuition to know Adam had decided Finn was going to be eliminated. He knew too much. He had power. But his bodyguard was now food for worms and Finn was alone. There were more of us.

I could either let Adam kill Finn or try to bring him into our strange group.

Finn had dismantled my reading abilities, but I could still manipulate matter.

I didn't know how much longer I could hold on to consciousness. The world felt wrong. My vision was fading, everything in sepia. I hated it. I saw Adam flex, readying to take Finn out, by hand, in the car.

"Stop!" I commanded, willing everything to cease: the rattling in my body and mind, Adam's fist, Finn's reaction. The rain around the car slowed. I reached out with my mind and enveloped all of us.

Chapter Eight

We were thousands of miles from where we'd been.
My first instinct was to take everyone to my father's home.
But would that put him in danger? I opted for Huntington
Beach in California. Again.

The day was beautiful, bright, and clear. The tide was
low yet relentless, the sun instantly warmed my soul.

The "trip" had shaken off Finn's hold on me and
Adam.

Free to feel the world again, I focused on Adam. But
he wasn't focused on me. I could clearly read his intention to
kill Finn. Right then.

I stood up, but both Finn and Suzanne were dazed
and completely confused.

"First, Adam, you are not going to kill Finn."

That little pronouncement sobered them up.

"Second, we are on my favorite beach. People can see
us, kind of. If anyone were to look at us, even closely, we'd
just look like generic people."

"How…" Finn began.

But Adam, finally divining my purpose, cut him off by
turning on me. "No! Absolutely not!"

"This is his only chance. Don't you see that? We are
going to lay it all out. For Finn, and for you too, Suzanne," I
said, smiling at her.

She was blank, hard. She was trying to cover what
was going on in her heart. It was fracturing. She knew Adam
was going to kill Finn. Kill the man she loved. And she wasn't
going to fight him.

"He's dead either way," Adam said to the sea, certain
my words would change nothing.

"What are you? How is this possible?" Finn gasped, astounded, looking around. I could sense him, still in fighting mode, working up to fry us again.

"Now that I know what you can do, Finn, don't. It won't work. I am your only hope. Listen to me. Will you? I want you to live."

"Don't worry about me. I'm stronger than I look," he said.

"So am I," I replied, pushing off lightly from the sand, levitating a foot off the ground.

"This is a dream. You are a Dreamer. You've trapped me," Finn said, shaking his head.

"No." Suzanne took his hand. "Listen to her."

"I am what you think is impossible. I am a ..." I began.

"Don't," Adam pleaded, trying to stop me.

"It's time," I said to him. Turning to Finn and Suzanne, I repeated, "It's time. You will listen to what I have to say, yes?"

I kneeled on the sand in front of them and closed my eyes, allowing the contacts to burn away. I leaned closer.

"I am Family, just not what you've met before," I explained, opening my eyes.

"Holy crap!" Suzanne yelled, backing away from me. Others on the beach looked our way, curious. Finn fell back on the sand.

"Did I break them?" I asked Adam, trying to lighten the mood.

Adam got up and offered me his hand. "Let's give them a minute."

Together, we walked down the shore toward the pier. While I could feel the world again, Adam wasn't coming in clear. I tried to shake off the buzz still in my ears from Finn's handy-work and looked at Adam. I squeezed his hand as my eyes ran over his body. He was looking down at the shoreline, but a smile finally crept onto his face.

"What are you thinking? You seem so far away," I said, breaking the silence between us.

"A few thousand miles?" His smile vanished.

"Are you mad at me?"

He didn't answer right away. As we walked, the buzz continued to fade, allowing me to see that the barrier between us was Adam's wall.

"Are you?" I asked again.

"You don't know what you've done. That, over there? That mess on the sand? The Fourth will know he's not where he's supposed to be. They've probably tried to contact Colby by now. Guess what? They won't be able to find him. Because we killed him. They'll come. Finn will either tell them what you are voluntarily, or they'll force it out of him. Or Suzanne. Unless I do what needs to be done and kill them now."

What was he saying? I was getting a whole new kind of headache.

Adam continued, but he was talking to himself now. "She'll forgive me. Better I do it than *them*."

"I… I…." I floundered.

"I love you, Anna." He slid his arms around my waist. "I don't blame you. You are good. Too good for us. You didn't know." He drew his knife. "Please forgive me," he whispered.
I stood, stunned, as he took off running.

My mind reached Adam before Finn and Suzanne even saw him coming. I willed him back to the car in Martin, where we'd started.

I ran back to Finn and Suzanne. They were both visibly unnerved by my unveiled eyes, but unwilling to look away.

"This is it. We are going back. Finn, is your place empty?"

"Yes," he replied, his voice barely audible.

"You are going to call your handlers, or whatever, and tell them Colby attacked you. You killed him. Got it?"

I didn't wait for a response. I grabbed them both and took us to Finn's house.

"Call," I demanded, not giving space to catch their breath.

Finn looked at me. "You will protect Suzanne? Do you swear it?"

I nodded, looking at him square on. "I will, as best as I am able. I swear."

We were standing on his threshold. Finn punched in his security code and went in the house. I wasn't sure if I should follow, and since Suzanne hadn't moved a muscle, I stayed with her. We stood there for five long minutes in silence. It wouldn't take long for Adam to figure out I was back in town and where I was.

Finn emerged from his house. "It's taken care of. We need to talk. Not here."

"Not the manor," I said.

"Let's get dinner," Suzanne suggested.

"Yes. Public might be best. It's early yet. The Grind won't be too busy, and we can walk there. Do you have any umbrellas?" I asked Finn. It was surreal to ask such an ordinary question of the guy who had just caused me a lot of pain and who my boyfriend was determined to kill.

"On the back porch. Just a sec," Finn said, leaving us for a minute.

I took out my phone and dialed Adam. "Want to get dinner?"

"You are safe?" His relief washed through me.

"Yes. We're headed over to The Grind."

"We are on our way," he said, tires peeling.

"No. Wait. I need a pair of contacts. Would you please?" I asked.

"Certainly," Adam replied too cordially.

Chapter Nine

"How many?" the waitress asked.

It was only the three of us and I wasn't certain who was coming with Adam. I did know, however, I needed to hide out in the bathroom until Adam arrived with my contacts. I nudged Suzanne to answer and went looking for the bathroom, head down.

Not expecting to run into anyone I knew, I was surprised when I rounded the corner and saw Andrew standing at the bar. Caught off guard, I jerked my head up to say hi.

Andrew didn't normally walk around with a grin or anything, but his usually impassive demeanor turned dour. I ducked my head back down, hoping he hadn't noticed my eyes. I thought about rushing past him, but there was something about Andrew. He was centered and wise. I craved a little wisdom.

He put his hand on my shoulder. "I am sorry for you, this burden you carry."

I looked up at him, my eyes swirling and searching for answers. "Do you know what I am?"

"My *sister* was there, in the days following the tragedy. I heard a way had been made, a mercy, and hoped it would be found. For all those souls. Yet how sad it is that hearts harden."

As a waiter approached with Andrew's order, I closed my eyes, wishing desperately I understood what he was saying.

While Andrew was talking to the waiter, I felt Adam enter the restaurant. A moment later the contacts were in my hand, but he was gone. No words, no feelings. As I feared, he had shut me out.

"So long," Andrew said, beginning to walk away.

"Please, Andrew. Please help me."

He shook his head. "This isn't my fight."

"Won't you, please? I'm so lost." Knowing he could help us somehow made me all the sicker at his refusal.

"I'm struggling too much with my own issues to be able to help you," he answered, clearly pained.

"I don't need you to be perfect. Please, just your insight. I'm drowning."

"If you're headed to the bathroom, you might want to do something about your hair," was his only answer.

"Thanks," I said, defeated. As he turned to go, I asked, "Is Katie okay? I'm really sorry I couldn't help her."

"Better, thank you." And then he was gone.

I got to the bathroom, barely, before the tears came. Andrew was right. My hair was doing its crazy anti-gravity shtick.

Okay, pull it together. You can save Finn and Suzanne. No falling apart right now. Stop crying so you can get these damn contacts in!

I could fall apart after dinner.

Sobs under control, contacts in, hair smoothed, I found our table in the small overflow room at the back of the restaurant. To my surprise, Andrew was sitting next to Echo.

"You're staying?" Slightly cheered, I took the empty seat next to him. It wasn't lost on me that Adam hadn't saved me a seat. "So, Katie's better?"

"She's at the hospital, in Meg's room. Meg kicked me out."

"And you left?" I hardly believed even Meg's strong will could keep Andrew from Katie.

"Katie's fine. The doctor is keeping her another night for observation. Meg heard she was there and insisted they share her private room. Katie thought it best if I left them to rest. Meg made a pronouncement about me being unwelcome after that."

That was the longest speech I'd ever heard from Andrew. He wasn't acting like the person I knew, yet he seemed more in control of himself than usual.

"So," he continued, "I decided I'd hear what you all have figured out." He pulled his food from his to-go bag and started eating.

"I don't think we're that far along," I smiled, glad he was here.

Surveying the table, I was struck by a sudden realization. I was in the presence of great courage, fierce loyalty, and love. From both sides. This was going to work.

"Not to be rude, but what is this random guy doing here? I thought this was all clandestine. Aren't you just Katie's boyfriend? Are you First or Second?" Finn was trying to work out the dynamics of the table.

"Hardly," Echo scoffed, offended for Andrew, though Andrew took no offense.

"I'm here at Anna's request," he replied. Andrew wasn't the kind of person who would be pushed into revealing anything about himself – or anything at all.

"Okay, then. Fine," Finn said. He had kept his defenses off, but he was feeling cornered, and I could feel that he was about to turn them back on.

"There's no need for that, Finn," I said to him.

"Mind reader?" he accused.

Everyone looked at me, slack jawed.

"Come on, all. We are at a lovely restaurant. We are going to dine and get this all out and, I predict, survive to fight the real enemy," I said.

"Love." Adam caught my attention, shaking his head.

"Then what do you propose?" I waited for his response. We all waited.

We received a temporary reprieve from the tension when the waiter came for our drink orders.

He left and Andrew spoke up, surprising me. "In a former life I was well-known for my negotiating skills. Call it divine intervention, but I am here and at your disposal."

"I doubt it. No talking out of this," Finn dismissed.

Echo confirmed, "It's true. Andrew's skills are world-class. Adam?" He deferred to his leader.

"What do you propose?" Adam asked Andrew.

"You must each swear that my work will remain secret."

Andrew got up and went to each person, clasping their forearm, asking for their word. All willingly gave it, even Finn, who was the lamb in danger of being sacrificed if this strange experiment with the expert negotiator failed.

"If you break your word, I cannot save you from the consequences. Understand?"

"Who had the Sprite?" our waiter asked, distributing the drinks and taking food orders.

"Maybe we shouldn't be doing this here," I said, now concerned we were too public for whatever soul-searching or soul-crushing plan Andrew was about to enact.

"This is the best atmosphere," Andrew countered. "We are tucked away, out of view of the other patrons. Suzanne and Finn should feel safe in this neutral territory. All language should be vague enough that the casual observer

36

won't understand what we're talking about. Let's start by identifying according to Family. Echo, please begin."

He looked uncomfortable, but answered, "Second."

Sitting next to him was Adam. "First," he said with pride.

Across the table was Finn. "Fourth, of course."

Suzanne coldly said, "Fourth."

Then it was my turn. Would I say it?

"Anna? This will only work if we're honest," Andrew coaxed.

"Fifth," I said, exhaling.

The group at the table did its best to act like that was as normal as apple pie, though Finn's neck muscles looked like they were trying to exit his body.

"And what about you?" Finn asked Andrew through gritted teeth.

"I belong to no Family. I am older than the Families and am familiar with them, you, all that has transpired through your terrible history."

"Then what are you?" Finn demanded. "If I'm going to trust you, you've got to give me a reason. I don't trust easily or often. Just so you all know, I've done my part, my olive branch. I don't know why Anna would take me so far away, but I can tell from your face, Adam, you know what that triggered. When my people checked in with me to see what was going on, I told them I had to take Colby down and that it messed with the charms around me. A new guard is on his way, but no army. Yet."

"That was a wise decision, Finn," Andrew said, keeping his place as head of negotiations. "As to the kind of being I am, well, it's not relevant and I can't say without breaking covenants *I've* made. I am not what I once was, though I realize that means little to you. However, since I have a unique understanding of this situation, I see that I can help. I can help because of what I once was, but more importantly, the time is right because you have found Anna."

Chapter Ten

"The Fifth doesn't exist anymore than the boogeyman does. The Fifth *is* the boogeyman. Even my kind like to scare their children." Finn looked around, incredulous. He was waiting for the punchline or the metaphorical analysis.

"This is happening. I can see what she can do," Suzanne said.

"If this is the crap you're going to feed me, don't bother. How about you leave me alone and I'll do the same. Deal?" He was on his feet, pulling out his wallet.

If only this were a real offer. A real solution. But it was impossible.

Andrew stood up too. "I'll see you out."

I watched as they walked off, defeated. Did Andrew know the stakes, what would happen if Finn wasn't made to listen?

The server showed up and began distributing food to our silent table. I felt out towards Adam but couldn't feel a thing.

"I'm not hungry," I mumbled to my mute friends. I was too worn out to be mad at their indifference to Andrew's failure and Finn's imminent demise.

"Don't give up so quickly," Adam said, unconcerned. He was adding salt to his fries, looking carefree. I, on the other hand, was starting to feel sick to my stomach. I couldn't do it. I couldn't be the savior, solve the problems. I was screwing everything up.

I laid my fork back on the table and took a sip of water, trying to steady my shaking hands. I was imploding. Lack of sleep, lack of insight, lost, and the shock finally reaching me.

My elbows on the table, head in hands, I didn't feel him until he was touching me, soothing my hair back in place. He leaned in, arms around me. "I've got you. Always. Don't leave me over this. We will find a way. You are mine, my love."

Adam kissed my cheek and took the napkin from my lap to wipe away the tears.

"They're back." Adam straightened up and went to his seat.

Andrew sat down and began again. "Okay, now that we're clear who's at the table, the problems are obvious. Mortal enemies and such. I am not with any Family. My only concern is for peace and reconciliation."

"There can be no peace with their kind," Echo said. "You know this."

"What I *know* is that Beauty will redeem us all," Andrew replied.

"What does that even mean?" I asked. Half the time I couldn't follow what he was talking about. It seemed like he was always referring to something else, older, when talking about the present.

Ignoring my question, Andrew pressed on. "Finn, before you knew there were First and Second on the set, you liked them, yes?"

"Sure," Finn agreed.

"And Anna?"

Finn hesitated. "I'm still not convinced she isn't a witch. I mean, there are ghosts – actual ghosts - roaming around here freely. But if you aren't a witch, I'm big enough to admit I like you, Anna. I thought we were to the actual friend level, which is rare for me."

"There are many elements at play. I believed I was of no use since I was … changed. But it seems I have been brought here for a purpose. Anna, after we finish eating, do you think you could take us all somewhere very private?" Andrew asked me.

I closed my eyes, thinking of the perfect place. "I'm spent, but I can do it."

"I don't feel comfortable taking Finn into any dreamscape of Anna's," Adam said.

"Neither do I," Finn agreed.

"I knew you two could get along," I sighed under their withering looks. "Actually, I have a better idea."

I pulled out my phone, caring little my food was almost room temperature. I sent a message and heard back right away.

"Okay. I found us a local place that's empty. I still have Meg's code and she said we could use her house tonight."

The mood of the table lightened considerably. The decision had been made, the location found to figure it all out. Everything would be out on the table. And whatever happened next, well....

Chapter Eleven

No one seemed in a great hurry to finish dinner. When the bill came, my phone flashed in my lap. It was Corey.

"Corey's awake. Should we have him meet us?"

"He shouldn't be alone, but I don't think he needs this on his plate right now," Adam answered.

"Right," I said, sending Corey a text asking him to go back to the hospital to see Meg. She had Katie, but Corey and Meg had been through the same horrific night. They could use each other's company.

When it would've been weird to put it off any longer, we made our way to the front to pay the bill. A new energy surged through me. I must have been on my sixth wind.

Meg's house was just a few miles from the restaurant. I rode with Adam, Echo, and Suzanne, while Andrew took Finn.

Suzanne had been quiet all evening. "I choose you," she declared, firmly in a flat tone.

"I know," Adam affirmed.

I wanted to protest unfair choices, misplaced loyalty, and the idiocy of needlessly broken hearts. That's what I wanted to do because I was used to speaking my mind. But now, I wondered, to what end? Suzanne hadn't decided to keep her allegiance to Adam on a whim or without thought. It would cost her, greatly. But not everything. What was left if she couldn't be with who she loved? She was left. She had her integrity.

She had turned her back on the Fourth. There was no way forward in her relationship with Finn. He could not leave his Family as she had. They would *never* let him go. So, she would do what was right for both of them.

It was awful, and unfair, but that was just the way it was.

Pulling into the driveway, Adam looked over at me. "You're awfully quiet. How are you?"

I took inventory. "Sick, excited, and very, very tired."

We sat in the car, waiting for Andrew and Finn to exit theirs.

"Let's get this over with," Suzanne exhaled.

We filed into Meg's spacious living room, settling in. My people took spots on her navy leather sectional. Finn took the funky gold, fuchsia, and turquoise loveseat while Andrew stood in the middle, facing us.

"I'm going to begin with a story. Remember your oaths. This is not to leave this room." Andrew waited for nods of consent. "Long ago I was working on a project with some of my kind. It brought us to your ancestral village. In that region, there had been a particularly nasty wraith infestation. Your village had yet to be affected. We stayed for a few weeks. I remember doing magic tricks to delight little Violet." Andrew paused, looking at Adam. Everyone knew the names of the children who'd been murdered, sparking the retaliation and subsequent curse. Violet was Adam's sister, whom he'd never met.

"I knew Samuel." He looked over at Finn. "I knew Lilian and Dane when they loved each other. We'd been gone from the village for such a short time when we heard what had happened. We came back to mass graves and the curse."

"It was our mission to help those who would be helped. Those in what you call the First and Second Families repented. Those in the Third and Fourth Families hardened their hearts and doubled down. It did not take long for them to see the curse was not the muttering of an old man, but

43

terrifyingly real. The Families couldn't live together, the village torn apart. All those who took part in the massacre had to deal daily with what they'd become, receiving no peace, no escape in their dreams.

"But Beauty always finds a way," he said with pride in his eyes, "always seeking sanctification and redemption. Beauty will provide a way out. From the beginning of the curse, the path was made. The Families must reconcile with themselves, each other, and the world. The way this will be brought to pass is through the Fifth. A child from the lesser Families, the servant classes. Of Second and Third. When this child is brought forth, the curse will be broken."

I was on the edge of my seat, enraptured. "How? How am I supposed to do that?"

Andrew looked at me. "It is not in your actions or your life. It's in your death. When you die, those of the original Family die. When you die, all others will begin aging."

"But that doesn't make any sense. If the Fourth knew she existed, they'd capture her and kill her. They think she's a weapon," Finn countered.

"But she is," Andrew said. "Why do the Families have such different tales about the Fifth? Where did they come from?"

"They are burning in Uncle Seacrest's library," Adam murmured.

"There has been a very successful misinformation campaign, from the beginning. Can you think who would want to mislead the Families?" Andrew urged.

"The First and Second," Finn said, without thinking.

"The Third and Fourth!" Adam pushed back.

"No. The one who placed the curse," I realized.

Chapter Twelve

"No...." Finn shook his head, trying to put it all together.

"That can't be. Dom was going to kill Anna!" Adam agreed, his fists balling.

"And what about Dom? How does he fit in with what he was doing with Meg?" Echo added.

Soon, everyone was talking, Andrew trying to answer this question and that, continually cut off with another question or reason as to why his explanation wasn't right.

"Hey!" I yelled. "Cut it out! Everyone stop it." All eyes were on me. "Andrew, please continue."

Quiet returned. Andrew stood silently for a moment before continuing. "As I was saying, there have been different stories about the Fifth, and they all have truth. The First and Second see her as a deliverer, and she is. She will stop the suffering. The Third and Fourth see her as a weapon. And she is. She will stop them. The end began when she came into the world. If she'd contracted a childhood disease or been hit by a car, the elders would be dead, and Echo, you'd look older.

"However, what the Medicine Man who placed the curse did not anticipate was his influence on his new tribe. They took up his cause, became his people. His intent was suffering for those who'd murdered his kin, but he knew all things would come to an end. The people saw what he did. They coveted the immortality side of the curse. They are now known as the Seers and Immortals, living in a parasitic relationship."

"Vampires?" I gasped, grabbing my neck.

Despite the situation, no one could suppress their snickering.

"What!" I asked, slightly irked. "What else is immortal but vampires?"

Adam put his hand on my arm. "The world is a mysterious place, Anna. The Immortals of the Se- "

"Mermaids?" I cut him off. "There are mermaids? They're immortal?"

"No, no," he laughed, as did they all. "Not mermaids. The Seers."

"Seers? What's a Sea...? You've got to be kidding me!" I jumped up. "Mr. Seacrest is some kind of a... an... immortal monster?"

"Well, yes, but only of the Second Family variety." Adam smiled up at me. "But now that you're here, I guess none of us are immortal. Shame, really."

"What?" I gasped, confused. "I thought you wanted a cure."

"I was, actually, looking forward to living forever with you," he said, taking my hands, speaking peace to my heart.

"Oh," was my brilliant response.

Finn spoke up. "Mr. Seacrest's ancestors hailed from the immortal village. The Seer people who left the village became known as the Seacrest clan. But of the Seer people, only few are changed."

I was lost. Changed? Changed to what from what? I looked around, expecting to see puzzled faces, but this made some level of sense to everyone else.

Finn continued. "And they are known as the Leviathan Immortal. Mr. Seacrest's family has always been among the servant caste, first in that region, and then they migrated to serve Adam's family."

It was a little unnerving how much Finn knew about Mr. Seacrest. "He's no servant now," I said under my breath.

He was one of the most successful and powerful people I could think of!

"You are mistaken. He serves the Queen, as do we all. What he does, he does at her bidding, by her will, for the Families," Adam said.

"Hold up," Finn said, rising from his seat as I sat back down. "Our best intel on the Seers is that they haven't made any immortals in well over a hundred years."

"And yet two of their devotees show up here," Echo said.

"I'm obviously missing some information," Finn said, looking at Suzanne. Suzanne looked over at Adam.

"Dom's sister, Emma? Did you meet her? She was on the show last season, killed off in the first episode," Adam began.

"I don't remember meeting her," Finn replied.

I took over. "Someone was trying to break into my dreams. I thought they needed help, turns out it was Emma, and she was trying to kill me. I don't think she knew I was Fifth, just Family. And they really thought they were getting Meg."

Finn was a bit too still.

"I know that was confusing. I…, well, I'm a dreamer…." I wasn't sure how to explain it all to Finn, or even if I should.

Finding his voice, he said, "You're loaded with gifts. Yeah, yeah, let's leave it at that. So, go on."

"Someone was reaching out for me in my dreams. They were kinda nightmarish and unusual. I thought someone needed my help. Finally, after months, turns out I was being lured into a trap laid by Emma and Dom. It was Emma in my dreams. She thought I was like a normal Family member, didn't know what I could do. In the dream, which was part of the waking world too, she tried to kill me. When I resisted, I am certain it killed her. The weirdest part, is, they got me mixed up with Meg."

"How is that even possible?" Finn shook his head. Meg felt nothing like a Family member of either side.

"I know. Weird. I think they were inexperienced. The Gold ghosts come to Meg sometimes. I guess they thought that was a sign. And, given some of Dom's last words, I don't really think they were here looking for Family to kill." My mind was rolling, and I saw it. Saw it all laid out.

Adam could all but hear the gears grind in my mind. "Tell us," he urged.

"If Emma and Dom were here for another reason, what could it be? If they really are part of this community Dom claimed to fight for, the Seers and the Immortals, was he looking for something? How long ago was the Gold Massacre? What, a hundred and twenty or so years ago? And what the gold ghost said to me in Meg's bathroom so clearly. She mentioned Iris, which is the name of Jade's great-great-grandmother. Maybe the tomb is Jade's super-great grandmother? I mean… it must be. The ghost basically said it! 'The silver tree where Iris hides.' Maybe she was buried with something the Seers want. Buried beneath *the* tree."

"Wait," Finn stopped me. "You 'talked' to a ghost today?" Finn ran his fingers through his hair. "This is some crazy, crazy…. I need a break." He got up and drifted off towards the kitchen.

"We did hear the Immortal clan lost their ability to make more like them. To change them," Andrew confirmed.

I asked just a few of the million questions I had. "Is it a *thing* that they lost, like an artifact? How does someone become Immortal? Why only make a few? Are they good?

No, they sound bad. Can they be killed?" My mind was running wild.

Andrew put his hand up. "Peace, young one. Peace to you."

"No! No," I said trying to calm down. "I'm finally getting the answers I've wanted from the beginning. Don't stop. Please," I pleaded.

"The Seers, when they become Immortals, are insidious. Evil. Not like the Fourth, though," Echo said, answering one of my questions.

Andrew agreed. "True. They are closer to wraiths. They have given up this mortal coil and achieved immortality, or so they believe. They are wrong, of course."

"Is everything he says such a puzzle?" I asked Echo.

"Usually," Echo shrugged. He had a lot more patience than I, in addition to a greater tolerance for ambiguity when it came to stuff like this.

"Wraiths are bad, yes?" I asked for clarification.

"Think demon," Adam nodded.

"Okay. So, Immortals bad. But the Families don't fight them?" I asked the room at large.

"What makes you think that?" Adam asked.

"Well, I've never heard any of you mention them."

"There are many creatures in this world," Andrew replied.

"Now that, that I've heard," I nodded to myself.

"And wars and feuds," Echo added.

"We, for the most part, stay out of the way of those who aren't our sworn enemy. If we got in it with every monster, we'd attract too much attention and never accomplish our mission," Adam explained.

"Which is taking out his kind," Echo said, looking at Finn as he came back into the room.

"That's not true. You love Suzanne. I love Corey. We don't want to kill them." I hated it when they made it sound so simple. "It's not Us vs. Them. It's good vs. evil."

"You put me on the good side?" Finn asked, head cocked.

"If she hadn't, I would've killed you the day you came to town. No offense," Adam said matter-of-factly.

"None taken. I'd say ditto, but I'm out of the killing game. I gave it up for show business. I'm not sure what I would've done if I'd spied you first," Finn mused.

"No one is killing anyone, at least in this room," I said, drawing their attention back. "Agreed?" I asked pointedly, looking around the room for agreement. I only got tacit consent.

"Anyway, back to the Seers," I said, trying to get more information before someone decided enough was enough.

Adam answered. "I think you want to know about the Immortals. The Immortals and the Seers are not the same. They live in a kind of parasitic symbiosis. The Immortals feed on the Seers, on their fears. They live below, in the sea."

"They live in the sea? And you're sure they aren't mermaids or mermen?" I asked.

"No, no." But this time Adam didn't laugh. No one did. "They live in tombs, embalmed."

"Forever?" I asked. "That sounds awful. Is it a punishment? Like hell or something?"

"No. It's a choice. One their servants, the Seers, aspire to. The Immortals live in a kind of disembodied state. They have given up the use of their body for an illusion of …." Adam trailed off, reluctant to finish his sentence. He didn't want to scare me.

"Please, tell me. What is it?"

"They are forever in a dreamscape. They make their own universe and live in it."

"It is a sad fate for a once proud people," Andrew said.

"Sad? Sad how?" I asked. Being in a tomb sounded bad, but dreams could be good.

Andrew explained. "They have trapped themselves into believing that who they are is not connected to their physical body. They live only in their minds, which has crippled them. They are no longer human. And with each passing year, as they continue, they poison themselves, the sea, those who aid them. They have become greedy, spiteful. And their dreams, their imaginations, reflect what is in their minds. They are full of bitterness, not goodness. But because they are as they are, they cannot see it. Their decay continues."

"Why would anyone want to be one?" I wondered out loud.

Andrew answered. "Immortality, or at least the promise of it, is seductive. It is hard to resist. Harder still if those to whom you are closest tell you lies about what it is. False, vile promises of beauty. As if they knew. They never knew. They have my pity."

"Do you know? Do you know how someone becomes immortal?" Finn tried to ask Andrew casually, but we were all burning to know, unsure if he would share.

"The Immortals have the knowledge to turn a patron," he responded darkly.

"But I thought they weren't able to move?" I was confused.

"They don't use their bodies, they choose hosts from time to time to do their bidding," Andrew explained.

"Is that all?" Adam asked, pushing Andrew to say what he was leaving out.

"Before they became Immortal, they were alchemists. They dug deep into the earth and took what should have been left. This is needed to perform the death ceremony, and it is what they're now missing."

"What's been missing for over a hundred years," Suzanne summed up, bringing us full circle.

"Now we know. Emma and Dom were sent here by the Immortals, looking for this object, whatever it is, and stumbled across a Family member," Adam said.

"And I am the end of the curse, one way or another," I said.

"Only if you die." Finn's voice was quiet. Too quiet and deeply unsettling.

"*When* I die," I retorted, my heart taking off, the realization hitting me. "If I'm not dragged into an immortal watery grave."

"No one is going to take you, Anna. No one." Adam's eyes were hard.

Suzanne looked at Adam. "Did you hear what Dom said? They don't want the curse broken. Maybe they know Anna, or the Fifth, is somewhere in the world and they want to find her, to control her, change her so she will always live. Be Immortal. And the curse never lifted."

"The Fourth would also want this," Finn said.

"Would the Fourth and the Immortals work together?" I asked.

"Doubtful. Not impossible, but doubtful," Andrew said, looking at his watch and then at me. "Anna, has this been helpful? Is this what you wanted?"

"Yes. Exactly. You don't even know. Thank you so very much."

Andrew's countenance lifted. "I don't think I've ever been thanked so kindly for being the bearer of exceedingly bad news. It's usually a 'shoot the messenger' scenario."

"I am grateful to be out of the dark. Or, less in the dark." I smiled at him.

"I will leave you then. Remember your promise to me. I will hold you to it. Violent ends come to those who carelessly speak," he warned us.

I watched Andrew leave, a sense of relief settling over me. It wasn't until I'd gotten off the couch, had a nice long stretch, gotten myself a glass of water, and returned that I realized I was the only one in a good mood.

Chapter Thirteen

"Anna," Adam breathed my name. I saw exactly what he was about to do. What every single person in the room was about to do.

"No," I snapped. "I feel good. You can tell me later, tomorrow, next week maybe, why I'm wrong. But I think I will actually be able to sleep tonight."

"You don't get it," Finn disagreed.

"Let her be." Adam was too tired to muster enough hostility to tell his sworn enemy to piss off properly. "For practical purposes, I call a truce."

"Can you do that?" Echo, who never questioned Adam in public, let his question slip, uncensored.

"I know there has never been a truce before. But we are at the end. I feel it. Isn't it clear? We are sitting here in this living room, having a rational conversation with a First, a Second, two Fourths, and the Fifth. New rules apply, and we shall make them together." Adam got up and walked toward Finn, extending his hand. "Truce?"

Without hesitation, Finn clasped Adam's forearm. "Swear."

The two were on their feet, swearing a cease fire. But it was more than that. A new alliance was being formed. I was no longer the only Fifth in the room. I was Fifth by blood. They were Fifth by choice – princes of First and Fourth working together, mixing for a common goal.

Back at the manor, I barely dragged my tired body up the three flights of stairs. It wasn't even nine p.m., but I couldn't keep my eyes open. Adam kissed me goodnight and was off to make plans.

"I should come," I said through a huge yawn.

"Sleep. I'll fill you in over breakfast."

I climbed into bed, forgetting to protest. It was the strangest sensation, feeling Adam and Echo moving outside my door, going toward the third-floor landing, meeting their new partner, Finn. As ever, I was aware of Finn's Fourthness, the fire in him, but it felt different now. I fell asleep trying to understand this new sensation.

I wasn't visited by anyone in my dreams since I'd made the last-minute decision to take the sleeping draught. For once, instead of fearing the oblivion of sleep, I welcomed it. I awoke, if not refreshed, at least ready to get back to work on both my actual job and figuring out what our plan of attack was going to be given our new understanding and alliance.

Stretching, I cocked my head to the side and noticed it was still raining! How was that possible? Where was all this water going?

Turned out, some of the water went into the tunnels, which meant no outdoor or underground shots. And since most interior scenes involved an unavailable Meg, another day of shooting had to be canceled.

After reading through the notice by Sylvia, I realized I had a full free day in front of me. I was relatively rested and clear-headed with a peace I hadn't had in a long while.

I listened out, looking for who was in the house. My people were all here, asleep. I didn't feel either ghost, but they usually showed up unannounced. I also didn't feel any of the crew. The only other person I sensed was Sylvia.

The house held the first chill of fall. I pulled on a sweatshirt and tiptoed downstairs. I found Sylvia in the kitchen drinking coffee. More accurately, holding a mug of coffee tightly as she stood staring blankly out the kitchen window.

"Good morning." I startled her and she spilled her coffee.

"Ow, uh, I didn't hear you," she said, putting her mug down to fill it up again.

"It's so quiet."

Sylvia didn't respond right away. "Do you ever try to remember something? Something you know you know… but you don't know what it is? You know it's vitally important, but you just can't remember?"

"I'm not sure," I said, trying to make sense of her pensive mood.

And just like that, she pulled herself back, the question gone from her face. Back to the woman in charge. "I gave the crew the day off. Even craft services. You can fend for yourself, yes? The kitchen is stocked."

"Of course. Sure," I said, getting a glass down for water. "Update on Meg?"

"She's in her house. Released early this morning."

"So, she's better?" I asked hopefully, but I knew Sylvia wasn't going to say yes.

Ever the diplomat, she answered, "It's a good sign they released her. But she isn't fully recovered."

Sylvia pulled out a stool. She let it scrape the floor, barely able to lift it, her body heavy with sleep and worry. "She still doesn't know what happened. Or… isn't saying." Sylvia looked back at me, with accusing eyes. "I don't suppose you can shed any light on the subject."

"Well, I got a text from her that she was with Dom. Maybe he knows," I said, feeling conflicted about the lie I was spinning.

Sylvia's face went white. "Meg said she saw Dom, in the woods. That's all she remembers."

"Have you asked Dom, then?" I said, pulling up a stool.

"No one can," she said in a whisper, "because he's dead."

Chapter Fourteen

"I don't know why I'm telling you this, but I feel I can trust you. I see you can keep a secret," Sylvia said to me.

My hands had covered my mouth in genuine surprise at Sylvia's knowledge of Dom's death.

"I ... I'm happy to listen."

"About two hours ago I got a call from the police. They'd found a body and they wanted me to identify it. We give the hotels our actors' schedules. This helps us both. You never know about crazed fans, so it's good to enlist all the security we can. It also helps them so they can know when to send in housekeeping. Anyway, sometimes we forget to forward shooting updates to the hotels. Today was to be an early shoot. Dom was scheduled to be in hair and make-up. When housekeeping when into his room, they found him."

"What did they find?" I gasped, truly captivated. How was this going to play out?

"There was no forced entry. They think, at least their initial assessment is ... suicide. Anna, they think he killed himself."

"What?" How could they conclude that? I had seen Finn jam a krim right through Dom's back! How would someone commit suicide by putting a knife in their own back?

"I know. It's unbelievable. Maybe... maybe Meg broke up with him and he hit her? Maybe he went to his hotel room thinking he'd killed her. They found drugs in his room too. Maybe he was desperate?"

"Wow. That's just... too much." My head was spinning.

Spin was exactly what had happened here. I'd known the Families killed, I'd just never really considered the cleanup side of the equation. They were probably very skilled at making the death of a Family member, or an innocent who got caught in the crossfire, look non-supernatural. I mean, Dom had been killed with a hexed knife!

"I know. This shoot. And you know I'm not a superstitious person at all. Not one superstitious bone in this bony body, at least, not until I came here." Sylvia looked up at me. "I probably shouldn't be saying this to you, but this show feels cursed."

"My mom died. Kayla and John, dead. Dom." I left unspoken thoughts of Emma and the two Fourth who had been killed in this sleepy little town. "Too much death."

"If you were me, would you pull the plug?" Sylvia asked for a rare piece of advice. I'd never seen her ask advice from anyone.

"Well, if you're asking if people are more important than this TeenTV show, one hundred percent yes. My mom is worth more than all the shows ever made." I took a beat. I was getting a little heated. "But that's not the question."

"No." There was real compassion and reflection in her voice. "If… if the deaths are going to continue, then we can't. I'll have to pull the plug. But that's unreal, right? We're doing make-believe here." She was trying to convince herself.

I didn't confirm or deny her claim.

"I thought maybe it was this old house. Maybe take the show to L.A., film on a lot. But then again Meg's injuries didn't occur here, and Dom was in a hotel. Still, it could be this town," she said into her mug.

"The security measures you installed since Finn came here seem a step in the right direction," I offered.

"Agreed."

"Maybe we could institute a buddy system?" I suggested.

"Realistically, I don't see how. We are all grown adults. I can't tell people what to do in their spare time."

"You *can* talk about studio liability and old houses. And I don't know if you know this about me, but I'm pretty good at reading people. I'm happy to help you, if you'd like, in vetting new people on set." I was being light, but Sylvia looked up from her coffee.

"Why do you think I'm telling you these things," she smiled, turning reflective. "I watch everyone, and not only through the camera. You are observant. I was like you when I was your age, until... well...."

"Yes?" I prompted. Sylvia was on the verge of telling me something about her past. What I got from her was her mind trying desperately to understand her own muddled memory. It was like watching someone slog through a field of thick mud. I could practically see the flicker of images in her eyes. There was something from her past she periodically tried to recall but couldn't. Something she wanted to talk about, but she couldn't remember it. Whatever it was, it was powerful.

She shook her head, her fuzzy thoughts still incoherent. "You have solid instincts."

"Thanks," I said, though I didn't feel grateful. I didn't like the idea of being watched as closely as I always watched others.

"I've got to let everyone know. We won't shoot again until his parents take his body," Sylvia said casually.

I choked on the water going down my throat. "His parents are coming here?" I asked, trying to keep my surprise and terror out of my raw voice.

"I'd just called them before you came in the kitchen. They are planning to come out and fly back with the body. No funeral here. I didn't speak with them too long. They

60

requested no autopsy, due to their religion. I told them that was outside my purview, and that they needed to talk to the local police since I was under the impression they were doing one right now. I don't blame them."

"For not wanting an autopsy?" I was puzzled. I didn't think Sylvia was religious at all.

"No. For yelling at me. They were livid. I mean, wow. But their son... Anna. Their son is dead. I feel awful for them."

"Me too." Even if Dom had been evil, he was still a person with family. Family who were coming here.

"When will they be in town?" I asked, trying to act nonchalantly.

"I'm sure they'll be here as soon as they can." She finished her cup and poured another. "No rest for the weary. Back to work for me."

"Is there anything I can do for you?"

She was back to her usual distant mode. "As a matter of fact, yes. We are halting production for at least a week. I don't mean this to come off as unfeeling, but when we have properly mourned for Dom, we need to be ready to go back at it. I need Meg to be well, Katie too, though her injury wasn't as severe." Sylvia was now talking to herself. "If Meg doesn't recover in time, maybe it's a sign." She closed her eyes, clearing away whatever dark thoughts were there, then refocused on me. "What can you do? Help them get better."

Help them get better? Was she asking for a supernatural aide like Andrew had? "Do you want me to play nurse?"

"No, and it's not really Katie I'm worried about. Her boyfriend is an unusually attentive individual. It's Meg. Her physical injuries are healing just fine, but it's as if she doesn't have the will to get better. She doesn't want to get out of bed. That's what I want you to help her with. Her mind."

"Her mind," I echoed. "Got it."

Sylvia topped off her coffee, saying as she left, "I know you do."

Chapter Fifteen

I made myself a bowl of cereal and took it to the dark and empty dining room. I moved the cheerios around the bowl, dunking some, watching them turn soggy. I finally pushed the bowl away. I had no appetite.

I laid my head on the cool wooden table, thinking. Maybe Sylvia was right. Maybe it was time to pull the plug on this production. It wasn't like we were making high art, we were just adding needlessly to pop-culture. Maybe it was wrong to have others around, non-warriors. If production was halted, would we stay and fight? Is all of this happening because TTV is here... or is it just because of us, or me, specifically?

"On second thought," I heard her walking through the kitchen looking for me. "Anna?"

"I'm in the dining room," I called.

"On second thought, I'd rather Meg hears in person about Dom before I send out the message. How soon can you be ready?"

I looked down. I was decent enough, my favorite comfy sweats and Ghost House swag hoodie, tank underneath. "I could go right now. I'll get some shoes."

I gathered my breakfast items, rinsed them quickly, and put them in the dishwasher.

"You don't have to do that, Anna. You're not the housekeeper."

"That's how we do it in my house," I shrugged.

"Let's get going, okay?" She was trying to hurry me along, but her "let's" had me confused.

"No, I got this. You don't need to come," I assured her.

"I should," Sylvia persisted.

"No, really. I've gotten to know Meg. I think it really will be okay coming from me."

Sylvia was relieved to be off the hook, though she would have done it. She always did the right thing, the necessary thing.

"Okay. I plan to send out the message in thirty minutes. Will that be enough time?"

"Sure," I said, going up the stairs.

I went to my room for my purse and shoes and was about to leave when I realized I probably should bring someone with me. I stood still long enough to notice Suzanne and Echo were awake. Focusing on them, I knew they were in her room.

"Hello," Suzanne answered my knock.

I would not ask her for anything for a while. She felt wrong.

"Can I talk to Echo?"

She dropped her hand from the door, pushing it open.

"I have to go out. I probably shouldn't go alone. Mind coming?" I asked Echo.

"No problem. We'll finish this later," he said to Suzanne, walking past her.

While my hair was in a messy bun, my teeth were unbrushed, and I'd just taken off my slippers, Echo was dressed for the day.

"Thank you," Sylvia said as we passed her in the foyer.

In the car, engine running, I turned to Echo. "Aren't you going to ask where we're going?"

"Does it matter?" His tone wasn't rude, but it was withdrawn.

"Are you mad at me?" I asked.

"No." But I could tell that was only half true.

"I thought we were friends," I said, throwing the car in reverse. When he didn't respond, I told him our destination. "We're going to Meg's. Sylvia didn't want Meg to hear about Dom's death in a group text."

"They found him, then."

"Guess so. They think it was a suicide. But I saw Finn ram that krim through Dom's back. How could the police think suicide? What, he fell on it intentionally?"

"It's part of what we do. We kill and clean it up," Echo said, confirming my suspicions.

"You know, Meg's going to freak out. The last thing she can remember is the ghost and Dom acting psycho. I'm not sure what to tell her. Hell, I don't even know the story. What's the cover story?"

"You'll know. You're good at figuring out people and what they need to hear."

"You mean I'm a good liar?" *Thanks a lot, Echo,* I thought.

"Why would you think I meant that? You can read the respect I have for you."

"And the distance you're keeping me at," I added.

"You are an odd creature, it's true. I don't know what to do with you. But it doesn't really matter. I decided long ago my allegiance. You are to be protected."

"Because of Adam?" I asked.

"Partly. It's much larger than one person. It has to do with what I believe."

Turning my gaze on him, I noticed something different. "But you've changed, recently. Yes?"

"I think that's due to you. Remember when Adam pardoned Suzanne a second time? When she'd tried to hide who Finn really was? In the past, that would've been the end of my respect for the First I followed. In a different time, I would've sought a reassignment or even reported Adam's action. But watching you has taught me to look again."

"But you're still not sure what to do with me?" We were sitting in Meg's driveway now.

"Do you know what you are?" He answered my question with one of his own.

"I know the word, 'Fifth,' and what Andrew says I'm going to do. But, no, I don't really know."

I cut the engine and we sat there, both in our own thoughts.

Finding the resolve, I was ready to face Meg. "Enough about us. Let's go."

Chapter Sixteen

When we returned to Gold Manor, Sylvia was still sitting in the foyer.

"That didn't take long," she said. "How is Meg?"

"She said she's feeling better," I answered. "Katie and Andrew were there. Meg asked Katie to move in with her."

"Andrew too?" Sylvia's voice colored with disapproval.

"No. I think he'd just gotten there. Brought them breakfast."

"The company will be good for her, but I'm surprised," Sylvia mused. "Meg values her privacy. She's only just met Katie. I'll talk to her about it. But, how did she take the news about Dom?"

"She's shaken, of course," I said. "But she's not falling apart. I don't think she will, either."

"I think you're right," Sylvia agreed. "Did you tell her how he died?"

"She knows."

It was the truth. I'd told her what had happened. Meg knew Finn had killed Dom to save her, that Adam and Echo had staged the scene in Dom's hotel room. She asked if the ghost had tried to hurt her. I told her, in complete honesty, that I believed the ghosts had been asking her for help. Dom had been the real threat to her.

When I'd sat down beside Meg on her bed, I hadn't been certain what to say. I'd had Echo, Andrew, and Katie wait downstairs. I'd wanted to focus on Meg and what she needed. She'd wanted lies in the past, to bury her head in the sand. But was ignorance what she *really* wanted, needed? Was it practical, since she was tied up in what was happening?

"I've got something to tell you about Dom," I'd started.

"That sonofabitch. I never want to see his face again!" She pulled her covers higher, clutching them.

"He's dead, Meg."

It was her instant reaction, both sadness and relief, no note of shattering, that decided me. Leaving out "Family" talk, I told her the truth.

"There's more to the story, more you don't know. Maybe later?" I half smiled.

She clasped my hands. "Thank you. You don't know what it means to me. To not be constantly 'protected for my own good.' Whatever that means," she scoffed.

I understood more than she knew. "I'm glad you're safe. But, if you don't want to live here alone, come back to Gold Manor. Your old room awaits."

"I've asked Katie to move in with me," she said, surprising me. "I know, weird, huh?"

"Maybe a little," I agreed.

"I like her. And her boyfriend. I don't know… I feel safe around him. Does that make sense?"

"Perfectly."

I didn't hang around. I told her I'd be back later, but I had other fires to put out. Echo was with Katie and Andrew in the kitchen. Before I left Meg's house, I needed to clear up a certain matter of privacy.

"Andrew, um, I have a few questions. You mind?" I was certain Katie knew what was going on and knew more about the mysterious Andrew than all of us, but I wasn't going to break my bond and blurt anything out.

"You can ask what you'd like," he answered. "I keep no secrets from Katie."

The way his voice landed on her name was almost reverent. It made me wonder what she'd done, or was it what he'd done, to warrant such devotion.

I cleared my throat. "I know we'd all agreed to tell no one what you told us last night. I was wondering if we could widen the circle to include Mr. Seacrest and Corey."

Andrew put down the glass he was drying and looked at me. "The oldest of the Family are aware of my kind," he answered cryptically, true to form. "I, however, am not what they remember."

"So, it's okay to tell those two?" I asked for clarification.

"I do not pretend to see the future, nor am I a great reader, as you are. I will leave this to you, Anna. Do not stop thinking. You must listen. You must train."

"Mr. Seacrest is my trainer."

Andrew looked down and unconsciously leaned into Katie. Katie's face turned a lovely shade of pink.

"I cannot tell you about him. I know what he once was, but then I was another thing, too. Watch and listen."

Katie got up on her tiptoes and whispered something into Andrew's ear. He shook his head. "We will leave them out of it as long as we can," he responded.

I tucked that into my mind for another day.

I was about to thank him and leave when I realized Katie still didn't know what had happened in the forest.

"One more thing. I'll make it quick. Katie, has anyone told you what happened in the Gold Manor forest two nights ago?"

Andrew shook his head, warning me to be gentle, but not asking me to stop.

"I don't know how to say it other than to just get it out. Finn killed Dom. And Corey killed Colby, Finn's

69

bodyguard. Dom had a krim, a cursed knife, and he was trying to kill Meg. And Colby attacked me," I paused, the words caught in my throat. Taking a deep breath, I finished. "Echo and Adam took Dom's body back to his hotel room and staged a suicide. I don't know where Colby's body is."

"Is that why you came? To tell Meg about Dom?" Katie asked, shaken.

"Sylvia wanted it to be broken to her gently, instead of hearing about it in an impersonal message."

Andrew crossed his arms. "What did you tell Meg? The official lie or the truth?" The question felt like a test.

"I left out specifics like Family issues and why Dom was really here, but I told Meg as much of the truth as I could. She sees ghosts. In fact, just so you know, I encountered a Gold Ghost here yesterday."

Andrew's demeanor signified I'd passed his test, though I couldn't always tell with him.

Chapter Seventeen

The week that followed was as gloomy as the wet and windy October weather. Everyone felt it, all of us slightly off and damp down to our souls.

It wasn't the hardest week I'd had, but all the turmoil and uncertainty was rough. Meg had decided to give herself a vacation from the rest of us, completely endorsed by Sylvia. She communed only with Katie and Andrew, no one else, which sent Lucy into spasms.

Lucy, for all her selfishness, genuinely felt awful for Dom. For that, she rose slightly in my esteem, though she still didn't make it easy to like her. Once she got her shock and mourning under control, she turned to how the show was going to deal with the sudden death of a principal player.

Meanwhile, for those of us involved with Family issues, there was an entire herd of elephants in the room. Were we not talking about how Corey was changing? Or how Finn and Suzanne were clearly in love but refused to look at each other? Or maybe it was that I might well be a weapon of mass destruction? That Dom's Family members were on their way, at that moment, to claim his body? Were we not talking about the insane ghosts who clearly wanted something? We certainly weren't talking about our plan.

Our not talking began the day Sylvia announced Dom's death. Jade had come over to the manor to express his sympathies. Adam, Suzanne, and I had been eating lunch when I felt him enter the house. I don't know why, but I could feel myself slightly relax.

"We're in the dining room," I called to him.

Jade walked in, followed by Corey.

"Hey, you're up!" I said brightly to Corey. He glared at me through swollen eyes, not appreciating the cheer. He grunted back at me and walked into the kitchen, appearing seconds later with a cup of coffee.

Jade cleared his throat. "Uh, guess I caught you at a bad time. Just came over to say I was sorry about Dom. I had no idea he was depressed."

"You believed that crap? You must be dumber than you look!" Corey scoffed.

"Corey!" I gasped, astonished. Corey was many things, but not mean. Ever. While I didn't want Jade treated disrespectfully, it wasn't him I was worried about. He didn't have a fragile ego. It was Corey my heart was breaking for.

"Not really," Jade said, simply. "It didn't seem right."

"What didn't seem right?" Finn asked, joining our non-merry luncheon.

No one answered Finn. Instead, Corey went up to Jade and put his hand on his shoulder. "Sorry, man. I'm not myself. And if I were you? I'd turn around and walk the hell away. While you still can." Pain and desperation dripped from his voice.

He put his undrunk coffee cup on the table. "Sorry, A. I don't think I'm fit for company right now."

We all watched in silence as Corey stormed out of the dining room, followed by the front door slamming.

"What was all that about?" Finn asked, sitting down.

Suzanne began to answer. "Corey's in the beginning stages. That was his first-"

But Jade cut her off. "I... just stopped by to see how you were doing, Anna. I'm going to get going."

Suzanne's face flushed with mortification as she realized she'd begun to discuss Family business with someone outside our circle. Just another sign we were all barely keeping a grip on reality.

"Are you sure? You just got here?" I slid my chair out to go over to him. Adam gently put his hand on my knee. He was telling me to leave Jade alone, give him space.

"Yeah. I, uh, I'm gonna take that advice and just walk right back out."

"Well, if you need anything, let me know, okay? "I said.

"Sure thing," he nodded.

Chapter Eighteen

With Jade gone, quiet settled over the house. I'd been ready to jump into it, figure out our next plan. Plan, plan, plan. We had to be ready for the next attack. But no one said a thing.

Finn got up and made himself a plate. Echo wandered in soon after and did the same, unaware of the spectacle he'd missed. I picked at my food, my anxiety growing as I waited for the meeting to begin. I settled the acid rising in my stomach with some bread.

And that was it. We had this nebulous knowledge of brewing war hanging over our heads, but… we didn't voice it. We did normal instead. That afternoon I went running with Echo. The next morning Finn joined us. It didn't take long for our old habit of chit-chat to resume. By the end of the week, I barely felt the strain between us. Echo had only slightly warmed to Finn, but I counted it a victory.

The only conscious decision I made to not deal came when Mr. Seacrest demanded to know what was going on. I told him I was on hiatus from training. He was furious, but he'd come to know my stubbornness. Besides, he was industrious. I wasn't one bit surprised when Adam casually mentioned he'd spoken with his uncle.

"Good," I said.

"Good?" he smiled. "I thought this was all a no-go right now."

"Isn't it wonderful? Wonderful, and morbid. We get a week off because of a death. I'm sorry to say it, but better you than me when it comes to your uncle. I just needed…."

"A break," he finished my sentence.

I rewarded him with a kiss. "Yes. Thank you. And you can tell me all about it when we finally start talking about what we're currently not talking about."

"All this time you've been relentless. Who could've guessed the straight-up truth would stop you in your tracks!" he teased.

"I know, weird. That's certainly not what I would've guessed. But seeing as how we are breaking our unspoken rule to not discuss crazy stuff, can we get back to the TV? This show won't binge itself. Only two seasons left. Ready?"

"Always," he whispered, his sweet breath tickling my ear.

"Hey!" I jerked back. "I thought you were committed to getting through this series."

"Sure," he purred.

"Then stop distracting me with your..." But I was suddenly having a hard time using my words. He had turned towards me, eyes ablaze, focusing his full attention on me. Warmth rolled off him in waves, settling around my chest.

"You were saying, love," he prompted, sliding his fingers through my hair.

He'd caught me completely off guard. I was usually the one tugging at him, testing his resolute will. But he was normally a fortress. He would kiss me and cuddle, but he was always aware of the wheels that would be set in motion if he allowed himself to get swept up physically with me. I was also aware of the danger, but given all the trouble we'd been through, I just didn't care. "What more could the queen really do?" I'd argue. He'd kiss me back and say, "Plenty." But he never gave in.

But now, in the middle of a Thursday afternoon, I saw it in his eyes. I felt it in how his body was attuned to mine. His defenses were gone, nowhere to be seen. He was entirely open to me, mind and body, and I was stunned. How could I be so fortunate?

As had happened so often before, he seemed to read my mind.

"I'm the lucky one, Anna. I still expect to wake from this dream, this lovely vision of you." He caressed my cheek, slid his fingers over my jaw.

There had been times before, though rare, when our physical proximity caused a glow to be emitted between us, from us. I recognized it now as flowing from my excess energy. But it wasn't coming just from me. It was a current, a push and pull between us.

"Beautiful. You're... too much," he whispered, closing the little space between us.

When his lips touched mine, my brain...stopped. Was this what it was like to have an out of body experience? Such joy and pleasure? To have all of Adam. All of him with me, fully committed to the moment. No scheming or planning. Just him and me. Just us.

I wrenched myself away with a second to spare before Corey entered the room.

"What are you watching? Oh, what season?" he asked, flipping on the lights. He was oblivious to what he'd just interrupted.

"Season four. Hey, could you get the lights?" I asked, squinting.

"Oh, you're gonna love it. That's when – "

I cut him off. "Don't even think about spoiling it!"

"Yeah, sorry. Mind if I join you?" he asked hopefully. It was at that moment he realized we maybe wanted to be alone. "Or, not," he said, dejected.

"Of course. The more the merrier, right, Adam?"

But Adam had pulled out his phone and was tapping away. The moment he looked up, my heart contracted. There he was, again. My normal, guarded Adam. If Corey hadn't been there, making me scoot over, I would've started sobbing.

Seven episodes and two pizzas later, it was time for bed. We said goodnight to Corey, whose room was on the second floor. Walking up the third flight, hearing Corey's door close, I asked Adam, "What was that? And, more importantly, why can't I have that all the time?"

His playful mood dimmed, replaced with defensiveness. "You know why. It's dangerous."

"I wonder if maybe you're being a tad dramatic," I protested, standing in front of my bedroom door. "Besides, it's so ridiculous! Why should anyone else care what we do in private?"

"We've been over this," he groaned. "I know you think it's stupid, but I've seen the punishments before. Ever wonder why my sister is the way she is?"

I let that information sink in as we walked into my room. Lying on my bed, I snuggled against his chest and he wrapped an arm around me, one hand playing with the ends of my hair, the other behind his head.

"I won't risk it. And now that we know who you are and your role in the Families? I don't know how we can ever..." he trailed off.

But I knew the rest of his sentence. He believed we could never be together. It would never be safe. There was no getting over what I was. If our relationship became official, word that I was a Fifth would get out, painting a target on my back. We would no longer be able to control the story; it would be in front of us, and we'd be on the run until I was dead. Adam would never do that to me.

"So, you see? I apologize for this afternoon." He was now drawing patterns on the side of my arm.

"Don't you do that!" I pulled up to look at him.

He wasn't flustered. "Ever since Finn messed with my mind, it's been harder to judge others and keep my thoughts hidden," he calmly explained.

"I'm glad it happened," I said. "I'd been feeling…cut out. Like what I am, it's too much work for you. Too high maintenance."

"You think you're high maintenance?" he said, shaking his head. "You're the most even, most trustworthy person I know. I'm sorry we haven't been talking."

"We usually don't need to. We just know what's going on with each other."

"I suppose we shouldn't take that for granted right now, love," he said, drying a tear on my cheek.

I lay back down, and a wave of self-consciousness rolled through me.

"Now *that* I feel." He spoke of my silence, my reluctance.

I wasn't sure how to say what I was thinking, how to voice it.

"Anna?" he prompted after a long moment had passed.

The longer the silence continued, the more butterflies gathered in my stomach. I could see the approaching storms. I felt we had a reasonable chance of pulling together our motley group and figuring out what to do, how to survive. But to what end? Adam had maintained that Family life was half duty, half private. It had to be. But…

Adam sat up. "Just say it, Anna. Talk to me."

I sat up too, my hands in my lap. "Well, you just said it. How can we ever really be together? It won't work. I will always be the thing to protect. But what kind of life is that? You'll always have to be the warrior, never the lover. Never just you."

Adam placed one of my hands on his heart. The layer he kept between us fell away, the room immediately illumined by the blue energy running through us. "I am all in. I was in when I met you in my dreams years ago. I was all in when I laid eyes on you at the table read. When you walked into that room, for my reaction I deserve an Emmy, Oscar, Tony, BAFTA, all of them. No one has acted like I did on that day. That day...." He stopped midsentence.

The intensity of his gaze coupled with the intimacy of his words began to work on me in a new way. I began to see what I hadn't before.

Adam felt the shift. "I keep this in, Anna. How can I not? How could I function if ... if...."

I shook my head. He didn't have to say another word.

"No," he continued. "I want you to understand. I want you to know. When you question how I feel or if I'll leave for this or that reason, you don't see me. I want you to see me."

He put his hand on my heart. The current between us changed from a steady blue stream to a pulsing white. It took a moment for me to realize that it pulsed in time with our beating hearts. Together, they made a rhythm, a music of our own. Our own language.

"This is why I think we are, usually, able to see each other so clearly. Why you are able to use my dreaming abilities to amplify your own," he said quietly.

It was amazing.

We sat there, watching the dance of light. The house creaked, breaking the spell, and I dropped my hand, but Adam did not. The stream changed back to blue.

"I want to tell you one more thing," he whispered with a smile. "My great secret is my peace. You bring me peace."

"I do?" I laughed. "I'm a walking weapon of mass destruction. Literally!"

"Are you laughing at my heart?" he teased. "I mean it, love. Before you there was only bitterness, chaos, war, death. Meaninglessness. Now? Sure, there's danger and war, but there has been and will be until I die. Only now, there's you. There is love. I understand what Andrew always talks about," he said more to himself.

"And what is that?"

"Beauty will redeem the world. Andrew speaks of Beauty as if it is a being or a tangible thing. But if it's love, I understand. You make the fight worth it. I don't want to fight without you, and I'll gladly, gratefully fight every single day because of you," he said, pressing firmly on my heart. "Do you see?"

And I did. In my own mind a door had opened, and I saw Adam in a different light. He was showing me what he held close, what was most precious to him. What he was afraid he'd lose, if he voiced it. And it was me.

He slid his hand down until it rested in my palm. The current was gone and so was the door, his inner self tucked safely away. But his eyes were full of love and desire.

The look on his face now told me I'd be in charge of putting on the brakes tonight. It didn't matter what I thought of the Family rules about physical intimacy; they were what they were. And it would be easy, because I loved him. If our bodies couldn't be intertwined at present, I now saw that our hearts were. They busily hummed out a tune that was always there, just below the surface.

Chapter Nineteen

It was a risky week with the possibility of Dom's Family arriving to claim his body, but we still spent most of it just hanging out and recharging. While the idea of his clan coming to town was disconcerting, it would've been foolish not to rest.

All week I waited for the news that Dom's parents were in town. Sylvia had informed us of a wake planned in their late son's honor. We were told to be ready and flexible, as she wasn't certain when they were coming.

By the end of the week, when they still hadn't arrived, we all received a short message from Sylvia stating that his parents would not be accompanying their son's body home. No reception.

I ran in to Sylvia soon after she sent the message. "So, they aren't coming?" I asked, hoping for more information.

"Every family grieves in their own way. His family had his body prepared and sent home Wednesday."

"Have the writers decided what to do next?"

"Honestly, Dom's character was being written out. He only had a few episodes left. His family has asked for no memorials, nothing. While Dom and Emma enjoyed the spotlight, apparently the rest of the family does not," Sylvia surmised. "We will, of course, respect their wishes. But the reactions of fans and the media isn't up to us. We can ask that the family's privacy be respected, but that courtesy is rarely extended to anyone anymore. Not even to those who grieve."

And so, Dom's character was quietly erased from the narrative of Ghost House.

Bright and early Monday morning, all principal players, recurring extras, and crew were called to the school gym for a meeting. Sylvia started with a few words in memorial of Dom and told us of his parents' requests.

"This shoot has suffered missteps and tragedies unparalleled by any production I've ever worked on or heard of. There were serious discussions as to whether this show would continue. Let me tell you, it was *not*," Sylvia paused on the word for emphasis and looked around the gym, into the eyes of all present, "*not* a unanimous decision to continue. But that was the decision. The full order of twenty-two episodes for this season stands. This is a testimony to the hard work and professionalism of every single one of you. If you weren't as good as you are, our product wouldn't be what it is. And it's good. Our ratings from season one went through the roof, and streaming platforms are renewing their licenses for our content. Season two, episode one was the highest rated show of the year, in our category. The network wants us to succeed, I want us to succeed, and so do you.

"So, what can we do about the tragedy that continues to plague our set? Your mental health comes first. Know that. I will use Anna as an example. I'm sure you remember that a few weeks ago she became exhausted and, in the middle of a busy week of shooting, had to take time off. Yes, it was inconvenient for the rest of us. But here she is today, healthy. Let's allow ourselves to be inconvenienced for each other. It's called being decent. This is a hard business. We work insane hours. Only you know what is going on with you. Pay attention to yourself. Know when something isn't right and speak up. Know the people you work with day and night. If they start acting off, talk to them. Speak up for them. Talk to their supervisor. Hell, talk to me! Believe me," she chuckled, "we are going to continue at a break-neck pace. Most of us can handle it. But you can only handle it until you can't. Take what you need."

Sylvia stood on the court while her PAs distributed binders. Inside was the schedule for the week and a script with revisions due to Dom's death. In the back was a section on mental health with tips, numbers to call, and websites.

"I trust everyone is ready to get back to work. I expect all of you to familiarize yourselves with the resources in the back of your binders. While you may never need them, you might. And if you don't, your co-worker or friend may need you to see their warning signs and get them the help they need. Any questions?"

The only sound was from the PAs shuffling through the crowd. Despite Sylvia's words, she wasn't what one would consider an approachable person. If anyone here had a question, they'd ask whoever they'd buddied-up with on set.

Sylvia gave it about twenty seconds before ending her meeting with, "Okay, people? Let's get back to work!"

Many of us went straight from the gym to do table reads in one of the old classrooms that functioned as a meeting space.

Seated at the table, Sylvia asked if we had any questions.

Lucy, whom I hadn't seen for most of the week, asked a good one. "Has anyone heard from Emma? I've been calling her, but she won't pick up."

"I spoke with her parents. They said she doesn't want to talk to anyone right now," Sylvia answered.

"Okay," Lucy said, unsatisfied.

Every other person at the table, even Jade, knew why Emma wasn't picking up her phone. She was dead.

And then it dawned on me. Lucy was living in a totally different world. She was living the life of an ordinary starlet – how strange the rest of us must seem to her! Maybe that was why she was snarky, cold, and distant. She was completely out of the loop. She was here with us every day but had no idea what was going on around her. She was easy to dismiss, but maybe that wasn't all on her. Maybe I'd act out too if I were marginalized by the people around me.

The scripts distributed, Sylvia began. "Before you open what's before you, I want to tell you what's different."

"Besides no more Dom?" Lucy snarked.

Sylvia continued as if Lucy hadn't spoken. "We are pulling the storyline through the end of the season. We already have eight episodes in the can. For the remaining fourteen episodes, we are adding another layer of narrative. One that's been hinted at since the pilot, the backstory of the ghosts and the manor. We're also going to be giving direction to the overall arc of the season, the chase to the end game."

"No offense, Sylvia, but is this the right time to add more principal players around here?" Meg asked, rubbing her head. She was back at work, but not totally back to her old self.

Lucy chimed in with her agreement, her face souring as she did the math. More players potentially meant less screen time for her.

"This is what we're doing. If anyone wants out..." Sylvia trailed off. The end of the sentence was clear.

The script was another winner. My character was still possessed, causing my relationship with Jade's character to fall apart. But at the end of the ninth episode Meg's character discovers it, prompting a search for the cure.

The worst surprise was finding that there would be a scene with Keith Prater, the actor who played Corey's dad on the show. He was a truly awful man.

I don't know why that was the moment I could no longer keep silent, but I had to speak out. I interrupted Jade's reading.

"I'm sorry. I know this isn't the right place, but I just have to say something." I could feel my hair wanting to drift upward as my feeling intensified. I tugged at my ponytail and worked to calm my heart. "When Keith Prater was here last year, he made inappropriate advances towards me."

"What? Why didn't you say anything?" Sylvia put her cell down, giving me her full attention. I had *everyone's* attention.

"I… I was new and he's a veteran. He said no one would believe me. I'm not going to file a formal complaint, but I thought you all should know. He is welcome to defend himself, but I know others here can corroborate my story."

"What a…" Corey trailed off in strangled anger as he rose to his feet. "Why didn't you tell me?"

"Because I didn't want you to punch him. But I did. He got in my way and threatened me. So, I hit him. He said I'd regret it. I don't."

Adam placed his hand on my back for support.

"Then why are you even saying anything?" Lucy asked in genuine confusion.

"Not everyone has the self-defense skills I do. I don't think we should have to be around people who act that way, who threaten us. He made it sound like if I didn't do what he wanted or if I reported him, I'd be out of a job. I didn't really believe him, but I wasn't sure. You know, his word over mine."

"You've got to be kidding me," Sylvia shook her head, livid. She already didn't like the guy, but from her response, it was clear she hadn't known he was a predator. "Has this happened to anyone else?"

"He tried it with me," Meg said, head up, only looking at Sylvia.

With Meg throwing her hat in the ring, I wondered if Lucy would follow suit. But she was uncharacteristically quiet.

"Thank you, Anna and Meg, for letting me know. I can assure you, I take this seriously," Sylvia said quietly. "Anyone else have something to say on this matter?"

"Fire the bastard," Jade said under his breath.

"I will not fire anyone without allowing them to defend themselves. Even Keith Prater will get a chance to defend his sorry ass," Sylvia said firmly. "But this is exactly what I was talking about earlier this morning. We've got to look out for each other. If you have anything to say to me on this matter or any other, please come to me. If you don't want to talk to me, contact human resources," she urged. "Whether or not you intended to file a formal complaint, Anna, I will. This is serious. He will not be back if your story is corroborated."

"Thank you," I said, and meant it. Part of me wished I hadn't said anything. I didn't want the hassle or to be labeled weak. But if Keith Prater was a predator, he shouldn't get away with it.

"On a brighter note," Sylvia deftly changed the subject, "the rain has finally stopped. We have clear sunny skies forecasted for the week and beyond. We've got to get our exterior shots for football and tennis. That's top priority. Once we have those, we will move on to the shots in the woods and other exteriors. You know I don't like to shoot out of order, but here we are. I need you to be flexible, professional, and attentive to the changes in your own personal schedules that are bound to come up. We are at the mercy of the weather gods."

As soon as Sylvia was finished, I had to hightail it over to the costume department for a fitting. None of us had time to sit around and chat. As Sylvia said, our schedules were booked solid.

Gathering my things, I sighed. Looking over at Adam, I saw his usual pensive expression turn to stone as we both registered his uncle's presence. He quickly shifted back, tucking his feelings away as he turned towards me. "Let the fun begin," he said, kissing the top of my head.

Adam departed for his trailer and Suzanne and I were headed toward wardrobe when Mr. Seacrest approached us.

"May I walk with you?" he asked. It wasn't a real question.

"We've got an appointment in wardrobe and we're late," I informed him.

"I've come all the way here. Let's meet for dinner," he persisted.

"Can't. I'm booked until late tonight. I'm not intentionally putting you off. I'll forward you my schedule," I said conversationally. Suzanne stiffened next to me. She did not approve of the way I interacted with Mr. Seacrest. She thought I should be deferential, but I'd explained to her that I didn't see him as my superior.

"Nonetheless, we need to meet. It will have to be later, then."

He meant in my dreams.

"Can't it wait?" I asked.

"I have allowed you this time, but it's over. You will keep your part of our arrangement as I have kept mine," he threatened. For him, the conversation was finished. "I will see you tonight."

Work was intense, but a great relief. And yet, there was something in Mr. Seacrest's manner that had me on edge.

As day gave way to night, a sense of foreboding settled in my heart.

"Can you explain it to me?" Adam asked, playing with my hair. We were shooting a football scene, he in his gear and me in my cheerleading costume. Several takes in, the sun had set so the lighting had to be rearranged. We sat on the sidelines in our official chairs.

"He's hiding something."

"Nothing new. Uncle's always hiding something." Adam gave a hard laugh.

"I know, but it was like he wanted to tell me and couldn't. Do you know what it could be?"

"Orders, sounds like," he said, nodding to himself.

"Orders?"

"If he was told to do something by his superior, even something he didn't like or disagreed with, he'd be duty-bound to do it."

"Oh."

The only person Mr. Seacrest answered to was Adam's brutal mother.

"Will you come with me tonight?" I asked hopefully.

"Wild horses, love, couldn't keep me from it. You'll need to collect me first, in case Uncle tries to pull a trick," he warned.

"But he's not a Dreamer."

"No, but he knows his way around. Bring me with you, but hide me until you need me to be seen."

It was a relief to know Adam would be with me. In the real world, here, we had our own little army. I trusted Echo, Suzanne, Finn even, to take up arms to defend me. Corey would join in. Adam's bandmates, and perhaps even Andrew. Maybe all those loyal to Adam would show up on the battlefield and we'd stand a chance.

But in dreamscapes, everything was different. And even though Adam would be with me, I was scared. I had a lot of power in both places, but it was all still so overwhelming. I knew the basic rules people played by in the waking world. Few people could do stuff out of the ordinary here. But in the dream world, especially if you knew what you were doing? There were seemingly endless possibilities.

Adam told the rest of our circle of Mr. Seacrest's request/demand. I promised a full report in the morning.

"It's a trap," Finn said.

I wanted to dismiss his intuition as the prejudice of a Fourth. But when he said it, the nebulous idea forming in the back of my mind crystallized. It *was* a trap. But I had to go anyway.

In bed, I longingly eyed the vial of untouched herbs on my nightstand. What would happen if I took them and didn't show up to meet Mr. Seacrest? The idea brightened my mood. I allowed myself the fantasy of safety and peaceful dreams as I prepared for sleep.

Adam, lying next to me, squeezed my hand. "You've got this. We've got it. You know what to do if Finn is right? You know who to bring, yes?"

"Yes."

We kissed goodnight. The next time I opened my eyes, I was blinking away the bright sun.

Chapter Twenty

"You are on time. That bodes well," Mr. Seacrest greeted me on the steps of Crimson Hall.

I had completely expected to be in his cave meeting room. I was so off balance at finding myself at Crimson Hall that my heart stuttered to find its rhythm.

"What are we doing here?" I asked. But it was a silly question. Whatever the answer was, it was nothing good.

"Reports have been made to the queen. She has requested a firsthand account from you. You have been summoned." Mr. Seacrest was a stonewall, hiding his feelings.

Looking around, I saw that the grounds were empty. It was just me and him.

"Where is everyone? Why are we doing this in my dreamscape?"

"Are we?" he asked, his cryptic words giving me some vital information.

One: We weren't in my dreamscape; we were in someone else's.

Two: Mr. Seacrest had my back.

"Shall we go in?" he asked, extending an arm toward the stairs leading to the great doors.

"Give me just a moment, please." With this new understanding of the situation, I had to adjust my focus and power expenditure. Whoever had decided to trick me into their dreamscape was in for a nasty surprise. I was *more* powerful in other people's dreamscapes, provided I knew that's where I was. I siphoned power from the dreamer and didn't have to expend any of my own in creating and maintaining the space around me. This was a spot of good news, but I didn't want to tip off whoever was waiting behind those doors, so I wiped the smile from my face.

I straightened up and noticed I was in a light blue dress. Going up the stairs, I pulled at the fabric. "You are dressed to see a queen," Mr. Seacrest simply stated.

The hall was empty and silent, our footsteps echoing down the corridor. I followed Mr. Seacrest, a lump growing in my throat. He led me to the throne room.

Flanking the entrance were two huge warriors. One a First and one a Second. Entering, he stopped and bowed to the queen. She was seated on her throne, her daughter, Maggie, to her right. Her faithful bodyguard stood behind her, hand on his sheath. Mr. Seacrest walked to Queen Cora, knelt, and kissed her ring. She spoke quietly to him, then he rose and took the lesser throne to her left.

In the throne room was a large round table, every chair filled with unfamiliar faces of First and Second in equal proportion.

"Come," the queen summoned me.

I felt pushed by an invisible force, which irritated me. I would've come forward of my own volition. Though I was scared, I was filled with raging curiosity.

I was stopped at the foot of the stairs to the three thrones. Behind me, I heard the scraping of a wooden chair on the cold floor. A woman who appeared to be in her early twenties, full-blooded Second, approached.

"A report has reached us. There is a claim you are Fifth. Defend yourself."

The woman stood there, like a schoolteacher waiting impatiently to hear the report she'd assigned weeks ago. But I was unprepared. What was I supposed to say?

"Not so brave now?" Maggie sneered, misreading my irritation as fear.

Adam and I had talked about what to do next. We all had. What was our next move, given the knowledge we had? We didn't have an answer. We had to wait for the universe to play her hand and go from there.

Echoing in my head were Finn's words, *no one will believe you*. I looked up at Maggie, Mr. Seacrest, and Queen Cora. An enemy, an ally, and a madwoman, respectively. What of the others? How would they react? I looked behind me to read the room.

"Up here, girl," Queen Cora snapped. "Answer her."

"My mother was of Second descent," I said.

"Liar!" Maggie shouted and the room filled with murmurs. The queen gave her a withering look.

Behind me, someone asked, "And what else?"

I knew that voice. It was Ewin, another friend. I reached out through my mind, drawing strength from his confidence in me.

"My mother was a Second, and my Father was Samuel Perry. He was Third," I said. I dissolve my contacts, exposing my eyes and unleashing mayhem.

The room erupted in shouts of denial, calls for more information, and an all-around frenzy. The queen jumped to her feet.

"Quiet!" Mr. Seacrest boomed. Everyone stopped, rooted in their spots. "I hold the keys to the histories. What Anna says is true. She was found first by our beloved Diane." At the mention of her slain child, Maggie's twin, the queen stumbled back into her chair.

"Anna is Fifth, but not as we thought," Mr. Seacrest continued. "She is the cure, the end of the curse. The Fourth are afraid of her, and for good reason. When she dies, so will they. So will all the originals. And the rest of you, our children, will fade, as it should be."

"Not possible," someone in the back gasped. I felt Adam tugging at me mentally, willing to be uncloaked. He emerged behind me, already speaking.

"It is possible," he said firmly. "It is *confirmed*. By Alistair Seacrest, the highest ranking Second, and by me. Anna is not the threat. The Fourth are. And the Leviathan. They are on the move."

"Speak quickly, boy," a woman said, her sword drawn, within striking distance of me.

A man to my right extended his hand to the woman to put the sword down. "This is good news, Alistair. Why the spectacle?" he asked hesitantly.

I could feel the division and confusion in the room. Some thought I was a miracle, and others regarded me as the devil incarnate.

"We encountered an anomaly in the New World," Mr. Seacrest began to explain. "Our young prince, Adam, was drawn there. You were all so outraged when he left us for the silly nothings of the world I watch. Yet have you ever questioned why I watch it? What *I* was looking for? Which of you pretends to know what I do?" he boomed, now towering over the gathering, commanding the room.

While Mr. Seacrest made his speech, I'd been trying to locate the Dreamer responsible. I couldn't figure out who it was, until I opened myself wider to other possibilities.

And then I saw it. It wasn't a person, but an artifact. The sentries stationed at the hall entrance weren't guarding the court taking place, but the globe allowing the meeting to be in the dreaming world. Smash the globe, the dream ends.

Thankful we'd had the foresight at the last minute to bring Echo with us. He was watching me and saw what my gaze landed on. I felt minutely relieved knowing our exit was secured.

"There is an object in the New World that ghosts have been protecting. Members from each Family have been drawn to that location. Even the Fifth, herself. And now Leviathan servants. Anna is no threat. She is the key. She is found. We should be celebrating!" Mr. Seacrest growled, growing frustrated.

"Enough," the queen commanded.

More nimbly than I would've thought possible, the queen reached behind her, yanked her bodyguard's dagger from its sheath, and charged down the stairs straight towards me.

As the court looked on in shock, she knocked me to the ground and raised the dagger above my heart. "For all who have endlessly suffered, I finish this now!"

Adam rushed towards me, but Maggie beat him, tackling their mother. She ripped the dagger from her mother's hands and plunged it into the queen's heart, giving it a savage twist.

A shockwave hit the room.

Adam fell to the ground beside his mother, his hands applying pressure on her wound, desperately trying to stop the bleeding. Maggie stood, blood running down her arms, her eyes crazed.

"We have the upper hand. We have her, the weapon. We will use her to destroy them all," Maggie growled. She was met with stunned silence. "I am your queen now!" she shouted as her people stared at her in horror. "You will bow. You will do as commanded. You have sworn allegiance to this seat," she said, pointing behind her, "which is now rightfully mine."

She turned back and pointed at me, a frenzied smile on her face. "Take her!"

I closed my eyes, telling Echo to smash the globe. Nothing happened. I looked to Adam, panic taking over. Bent over his dead mother, he tenderly kissed her cheeks. He pushed up to his feet, clinched fists, and nodded in the direction of the artifact.

Chapter Twenty-One

I didn't even hear the glass break.

I shot out of bed, trying to contain my screams of horror. Echo, who had been sleeping in a chair in my bedroom, jumped up, dagger at the ready. But Adam just rolled to his side.

"Adam," I cried, sinking back down on the bed, my arms awkwardly closing around him.

He didn't respond. He remained catatonic.

He had lost his mother tonight. Cora had tried to kill me, but she was Adam's mother. I felt no relief that she was dead. And she had been viciously murdered by his own sister. He had lost them both, because now we knew what Maggie's plans were. I felt no gratitude for her saving my life, because she didn't actually plan to spare me. She was on the side of the Immortals, and she wanted me entombed in a living hell so she could live forever.

After a moment, I got up and went over to Echo. I wasn't sure what to do, I was in shock.

"Give me a minute," Adam said, his voice thick with grief.

"We need to regroup," Echo said, checking the hallway.

Adam, knowing he wasn't afforded the luxury of grieving now, sat up. "Get Suzanne and Corey."

Echo was out the door in a flash. A flicker of light outside my third story window caught my attention. I looked into the backyard, but only saw the brilliant stars.

I didn't want to push Adam, but the urgency was real. "Our circle is wider. Let's use it."

He looked up at me numbly, a tear rolling off his chin. "Do what you think you must."

I called Andrew, Finn, and Jade. No need to contact Mr. Seacrest. I was certain he was already in his car, breaking every speed limit this town had.

I dragged Adam, Corey, Suzanne, and Echo downstairs, shushing them as we hurried on to the front porch to wait for the others.

"What are we doing out here?" Corey asked, rubbing his eyes. He was blissfully unaware of what had happened.

"We can't meet in the house. Sylvia will wonder what we're up to. Besides, do you know what time it is? It's almost four in the morning." I swung around at the sound of an old truck sputtering into the drive. "Here's Jade." We watched as his headlights illuminated the front of the house.

Within ten minutes, Andrew arrived with both Katie and Meg, followed by Finn. We'd assembled our entire team, save Mr. Seacrest.

"Follow me," I instructed.

I led the group around the side of the house and through the backyard, holding the white gate open for them as we walked into the vast field separating the manor from Heaven's Gate cemetery.

"Lucky ten," Corey said, passing me, catching up to Meg.

"Eleven," Mr. Seacrest amended, walking briskly from the shadows.

"I knew you'd come," I said to his back.

I quietly closed the gate, Adam and I in the rear of our little war party. In this situation I normally would've deferred to Adam. But he was like the living dead, going through the motions, putting one foot in front of the other out of habit alone.

When Suzanne had reached the spot I wanted us to be at, I called out, "Okay. Stop."

The party turned and looked at me. I took Adam's hand and advanced to the front, our path lit by the moon. I smiled up at her, thankful for her reflection of eternal sun on us.

"Let's sit in a circle, okay?"

There was no resistance. I made a mental note that calling a pre-dawn, clandestine meeting in the back forty seemed to be the best way to get everyone's cooperation and rapt attention.

"What we've been waiting for has happened," I began.

"What have we been waiting for?" Corey asked, struggling with his weariness and cantankerous nature.

Meg patted his knee, settling him. I noticed her hand remained there.

"I was summoned, in a dream-like state, to Crimson Hall. The main grounds of the First and Second Families," I clarified for Jade, Meg, and Katie's benefit.

"Mr. Seacrest was there," I said, nodding at him, remembering the surprise I'd felt at seeing him take his place on the dais.

I knew I needed to tell them the whole story, but I was still in shock. Subconsciously, I touched the bruise forming from being violently knocked aside by Maggie.

"Peace to you," Andrew spoke, sensing my turmoil.

"Thank you." I couldn't help the tears. I squeezed Adam's hand, unsure if it was to comfort myself or him. He squeezed back. "Okay," I took a deep breath, regaining my composure. "Somehow they'd heard I was Fifth."

"They?" Finn prompted.

I set the scene for them, describing who all had been there. "I told them what I was. Mr. Seacrest explained it to them. The queen grabbed a knife and shoved me to the ground. She tried to kill me, said she would end it all. But Maggie took the knife from her. She killed her own mother," I finished, my voice breaking.

Adam finally spoke. "Maggie claimed leadership and ordered Anna taken into custody. That's when we left the dreamscape."

Corey was no longer sitting cross-legged in our circle. He was pacing, and he was livid. "You *left*?" he asked challengingly.

"Escaped," I amended.

"I am sorry for your loss, Adam. May she rest in eternal peace," Andrew said.

"This all happened in a dream?" Katie asked quietly, trying to understand.

"Yes. All dreams affect the waking in some way. Anna and Adam are Dreamers; what happens in their dreams can have real-world consequences. And there are some rare artifacts that can extend a dreamscape to others, making a dream communal," Andrew explained.

"And so it was," Mr. Seacrest confirmed. "The ancient artifact used for this dream was destroyed on Adam's command. That will neither be forgotten nor forgiven by some."

"Add it to the list," I said dismissively. A smashed globe was the least of our worries.

"So, the cat's out of the bag. And now the First and Second want to kill or imprison Anna? Typical," Finn sneered.

That's when the wispy beginnings of a thought began teasing the edge of my mind. "But they don't know everything," I mused. I turned to Mr. Seacrest. "What did you leave out, when you told them about me?"

He looked at me severely. His world was unraveling. "Nothing. I swore to tell them all I knew, and I did."

"No. You didn't tell them about Finn. And if that wasn't intentional, then it was a small mercy. They don't know that some things have changed, that we are all allies. They are still playing at the same old war and we are not. I know this is significant."

Before I could follow this thread in my thought, Katie pointed towards the cemetery. "Look!"

Skirting the edge of Heaven's Gate was a ghost. It was close enough that I could feel it wasn't a Gold Ghost. This was something new.

As we all watched, it drew closer to our circle.

"No, no, no," Meg said, shaking. "This can't be happening."

Corey put his arms around her.

"You know her?" Andrew asked.

"Not another ghost," she rasped, shaking her head in disbelief.

This ghost was different from the twins. She was dressed in strips of dirty linen. While the Gold Manor ghosts seemed trapped in a cloud of malice and madness, this one seemed lost and confused. It had been drilled into me that ghosts were dreadful, bad creatures. But she just seemed...sad and tired. She walked into the middle of our circle, slowly making a full loop before stopping in front of Meg.

"Can we help you?" I asked.

It wasn't clear if she hadn't heard me or was ignoring my question. Jade cleared his throat, drawing her attention. She moved toward him, her feet barely hovering above the blades of grass.

"Kin. Will you help me?" She bent down, eye to eye with Jade and gripped his forearm.

I jumped up, ready to spring into action. To do what exactly, I didn't know. It wasn't like I could push her off; she wasn't solid – mostly.

A distant bird screeched, breaking the moment, and she disappeared. Jade shuddered, wincing.

Speechless, I realized I'd been holding my breath. I looked him over. What had she done to him?

"Kin?" Corey turned over the word, sparking something in Suzanne.

"Could that have been Jade's *dead* great-great-grandmother?" Suzanne asked.

"I think so," I answered, just as Andrew said, "No."

"No?" Adam asked.

"That woman is not dead," Andrew replied.

Chapter Twenty-Two

"What do you mean?" Adam asked.

"I know what a ghost is, and that was not one," Andrew replied.

It was clear he wasn't going to volunteer any information unless we asked.

"Okay, then what was she?" I prodded.

"That was an Immortal."

"Not possible," Finn disagreed. "They can't project into hosts this far from the depths where they live. They can project into hosts locally. But not this far."

"I believe she's the result of some sort of experiment," Andrew responded. "Do you not see? Anna, you're the daughter of Samuel Perry, correct?"

"Uh, yes." It had never been put to me that bluntly. "Biologically," I added, because he wasn't who I considered my real dad. He was a horrible original Third who was a seducer and murderer.

Somehow, I was brought to this tiny town, where Samuel Perry had lived, seduced, and murdered over 150 years ago. We'd discovered his secret lair in the caves, with the help of the Gold Ghosts. My head was swimming, but a picture was forming.

"Tell me, what did you find of Samuel Perry's?" Andrew asked.

"In a cave we came across a bunker with a bed, desk, newspaper clippings, clothes, and tools," Corey said.

"What kind of tools?"

"Old-timey tools, you know. Like saws, hammers, that kind of stuff."

"And medical instruments," Suzanne added.

"Medical instruments," Andrew repeated, as if he'd stumbled upon something important. "What else can you tell me about Samuel's place?"

"It's in the tunnels that run through this property. The tunnels were hidden until recently," Echo answered.

Andrew thought for a moment. "Have you seen the ghosts down there?"

"That's how we found Samuel's stuff. The ghosts took Emma into the tunnels, and we followed them," Echo said.

"And the less crazy ghost repeated what she always says," Adam said. "'Go to the grave, to the tomb. The fifth from the third. Find and know or she will die, and all is lost. Stay and die,'" he recited. "I still remember the expression on her face. She seemed devastated, she was pleading with us."

"I got sick to my stomach the two times I was there," I added.

"You did? Let me think about that," Andrew said. "What I can tell you is what I know. I know the creatures in this world. I know what we just saw wasn't a ghost. She is one of the Leviathan."

"You're absolutely certain?" Adam asked.

"Not possible," Mr. Seacrest interrupted, confidently. "There has never been an Immortal Leviathan anywhere else. No. And the way to make one has been lost. No," he said, shaking his head, "Just no."

"Yes," Andrew countered. "Accept it, Alistar."

"Explain," Mr. Seacrest asked, his mind wanting to cling to his rejection of this possibility, but warring with his trust in the knowledge Andrew held.

"Did you notice how she moved, as if submerged in water?" Andrew answered.

"But, I mean, that's how the Gold Ghosts move. Their bodies are always in motion, like they're treading water," Adams said, totally engrossed.

"The way ghosts appear and move isn't always the same. Maybe what you call the Gold Ghosts aren't actually ghosts," Andrew mused. "But I do know how the Leviathan Immortals are made. This immortal – "

"Iris," Jade cut in reflexively.

"Iris," Andrew acknowledged, "is here, in a body of water."

I couldn't help my gasp.

"In actual water, like a pond?" Katie looked up at Andrew, wrapping her arm around his more tightly. He nodded.

"Is she still alive? Can we save her?" Jade asked Andrew.

"She is not dead. While she lives, there is always hope."

"I have never heard of an Immortal anywhere else, or returning from their sea tomb," Mr. Seacrest said, mulling over the real possibility that Andrew was right.

"Nor I," Andrew conceded. "Nonetheless, that is what Iris is and she has asked for help. At the very least she deserves to be found and set free. The Leviathan Immortals have an awful fate."

Jade drew in a ragged breath. "I'm in. Whatever you need."

"Where do we start?" Corey asked gamely.

"We won't have long to figure things out," Andrew warned. "Crimson Hall has a new queen. She will be coming for Anna."

"She will be coming for you, too, Adam," Mr. Seacrest added. "You know that."

"Yes," Adam conceded, his raw emotion and fractured heart breaking my own.

Echo and Suzanne rose. "Let them come," Suzanne challenged.

"They won't get far," Echo predicted. "They won't touch a hair on his head. We have many allies." His devotion for Adam was fierce.

"Have a seat, friends," Mr. Seacrest said. "We'd stand a greater chance of weathering this coming war if I understood what Maggie is up to."

"I understand," I muttered. The swirling pieces had settled into place, presenting to me the full picture of what was going on.

Corey nudged me. "Do you care to share?"

"The queen tried to kill me not because she hated me, but because she wanted to end her own suffering. She couldn't take it anymore. And there was still part of her that knew her duty, to stop the Fourth and end the curse. Killing me would accomplish both."

"Yes," Adam nodded. This wasn't new information for him, though it did spell it out for the others. "What else?"

Now came the hard part, confirming his worst fears. The betrayal of his sister. "I'm sorry, Adam. I... I know you love her. I know what you've lost. But..."

"Just say it," he said harshly, angry because I was the messenger. Mad at the world because it was the truth.

"Maggie doesn't want me dead. She doesn't want to die. She wants to hand me over to the Leviathan. She wants to make me one of them."

"How can you be sure?" Adam asked, looking for a way out.

"When she killed the queen, it was written all over her. She was entirely open, like reading a book. It wasn't

105

premeditated, but as soon as she saw a way to ensure her own immortality, seize power, and get rid of me? A plan solidified. I don't see any reasoning with her. Her plan is to capture me, hand me over to the Leviathan, help them find what they lost, and then turn me into an immortal so the curse will never be broken. She can guarantee her long life and rule."

"This cannot stand. It is treason. I will not follow a traitor," Mr. Seacrest said.

"What do we do?" Corey asked, looking behind his shoulder, assuming they'd be here any minute.

Mr. Seacrest drew himself up, going into action mode. "She will not strike immediately, but soon."

"Soon?" I asked.

"It will take her time to get what she needs. She believes she's invincible and calculating. But we don't have long. A week or two? I believe this group will do what is necessary to protect each other. All are vulnerable. Do not underestimate Maggie. I will call in my favors, which are many and great. I'm leaving, but before I go, take me to Samuel's cave."

He stopped and looked around. "Does anyone else smell blood?"

Chapter Twenty-Three

That's when we saw the blood seeping through Jade's jacket.

"Are you okay?" Katie asked.

"Fine, I'm fine," Jade stammered.

Even in the pale light of the stars and waning moon, I could see he was losing color. I knelt, gently pushing up the sleeves of his jacket.

"Jade!" I gasped. There were open, bleeding wounds on his forearms where the immortal woman had touched him. It instantly took me back to what happened to me on the plane when Emma was trying to kill me. All that blood.

"Anna, you can help him," Andrew said at my side. Jade looked moments away from losing consciousness.

"I don't know how!" I cried, frustrated. I pressed Jade's jacket to his wounds, trying to put pressure on the deep cuts.

"Call an ambulance!" I cried to Adam.

"How can Anna help him?" Adam asked Andrew, trying to decide if he should carry Jade out of the field on his back.

"Anna can manipulate matter," Andrew explained.

This I knew. Or at least it was in the back of my mind, but still seemed impossible. Having Andrew say it out loud felt equal parts empowering and violating.

"It's her gift. She hasn't fully understood what she is capable of, and she is woefully untrained," he said matter-of-factly, making my heart sink. "But that has served her well. It is the only reason she has gone undetected by your feuding Families and others who would covet her skills."

He turned to me. "Anna, visualize what you want. Focus your energy and make it so."

All eyes on me, Jade bleeding out, his life in the balance, I sided with the feeling of empowerment over being unwillingly exposed.

"Jade, why didn't you say something?" I whispered, wishing he'd spoken up sooner.

His lips were white, and he made no response.

I didn't want to treat Jade as a science experiment. But Andrew believed I could do this, and if I didn't at least try, Jade might not make it out of the field.

Attuned to my desires, Adam cleared the space for me. "Please, everyone, over here. They don't need an audience."

I wasn't sure where to begin. Andrew put his hand on my back.

"It may help to know the cause," he said. "Immortals work through the mind and attach to a body."

"She did this intentionally?" I asked, looking at the lifeless Jade.

"Possibly. However, she didn't seem malicious. She was trying to get his attention. Unfortunately, whatever her intent, Jade is dying."

"I think something similar happened to me," I said. "Emma tried to bleed me out once, on an airplane. I fought back."

Andrew sat in silence beside me, giving me the mental space to figure out what to do. I reached back to that memory.

"Adam," I called. I needed to lean on him. "Please stand behind me."

His legs snug against my back, my energy rose. I placed my hands on Jade's bloody arms and concentrated. I wanted his blood loss to reverse. I wanted his skin to knit back together, leaving no trace. I wanted the light in his eyes to return. I wanted him to walk out of here on his own, whole.

Repeating what I wanted softly to myself, I kept my hands and eyes on Jade. I felt energy flow, from Adam, through me, to Jade. Once I figured out what to do, I arched my back, unlinking from Adam. He was operating on fumes as it was. The push he'd given me was enough.

I was lost in time. It could've been seconds, minutes, days, but the sun was making an appearance when Jade opened his eyes.

"How are you feeling?" I asked.

"Tired." he said, dazed. I helped him sit up slowly. He looked at his arms, turning them over.

"Amazing," Adam marveled.

Instead of gashed and mangled flesh, Jade's forearms were whole. Almost pristine, save a few silvery lines.

I stuck out an arm and pulled up my sleeve, pointing to the lines I'd received from Emma's attack. "We match."

Everyone gathered around us.

"How are you? What can we do for you?" Katie asked.

Jade pushed himself off the ground, brushing the dirt and grass from his clothes. The blood wouldn't be so easy to get rid of. "I'm fine. I feel normal," he said, taking stock of himself. "I'm tired, but I was before we came out here."

I had been outed as a true freak. No one was intentionally gawking at me, but it was hard to hide their shock. It was one thing for them to know in their minds I was different. But to see with their own eyes what I was capable of? My status of "other" was set.

With little time and even less energy to explore what had just happened, we turned to the practical.

We couldn't very well traipse back in the wee hours of the morning without calling attention to ourselves. Finn needed to get back before his new bodyguard, Ned, noticed he was missing, and most of us had to be in hair and make-up soon.

Mr. Seacrest walked up to Adam and me. "I do need to see Samuel's cave. I'm leaving in a few hours," he frowned. "I'll be back as soon as I can. By week's end. Arrange it."

Adam nodded. "Friday afternoon a few of us are shooting in the woods by the tunnels. Can you arrange to be there?"

"I can be back by then. If not, if I don't return, you know what to do," Mr. Seacrest said darkly.

I was taken aback by his intensity. "There's a good chance we might attract some ghostly presence. And we want to keep the crew out of it," I added.

I was worried about unsuspecting cast and crew becoming collateral damage and didn't expect them to be on his radar. To my surprise, Mr. Seacrest agreed.

Meg had walked up, scrolling through her phone until she found the shoot schedule. "Friday at three in the afternoon I'm shooting out at the barn with Corey. Sylvia and most of the crew will be there. That should give you the window you need," she suggested.

"How will you explain my presence?" Andrew asked.

"Andrew, will you come with us into the tunnels?" Mr. Seacrest addressed Andrew with deference, which increased my curiosity as to who or what in the world Andrew was.

Andrew thought for a moment, nodding his head in consent.

"Katie, will you stay with Meg and the crew while we descend beneath the ground?" Andrew asked. He wanted to keep Katie as far away from the supernatural as possible.

Katie agreed and Suzanne volunteered to guard them both while we went searching.

Our next step settled, we went our separate ways. Adam veered off to his room and I followed.

He stopped in front of his closed door, his back to me. "I need to be alone."

"I'm so sorry, but no. I won't leave you."

He rolled his shoulders back, took a deep breath, and opened his bedroom door.

We had to be on set in less than an hour. Though exhausted, neither of us slept. My astute, confident, powerful boyfriend lay motionless. In a single night, his family had been stripped away. I was filled with terror. I had nearly been killed; I was in danger of being captured and tortured by Maggie and the Leviathan; Queen Cora had murdered my mother, and now she was dead. But I was given the grace to set aside how this awful turn of events frightened me.

Grace allowed me to set aside my fears and focus on Adam's great sorrow. I got to be his lover tonight in the way that mattered most. He allowed me to see him at his lowest, and I offered consolation, empathy, and silence.

The morning came too quickly. Echo's knock had me fumbling for my phone. My blurry eyes read the time.

"Shoot! I'm late. I was supposed to be downstairs almost 15 minutes ago." My voice sounded urgent, but my body was finding it hard to care.

"Adam. We gotta go, man," Echo called from the other side of the door.

"I'm supposed to be at the school," Adam said tonelessly.

"No one will blame you if you call in sick," I said." You're supposed to get one month, right?" The Families allowed a grieving period when a loved one died.

"Not this time. Not me," he said, rolling out of bed.

I was about to ask why, but he beat me to it. Pulling a fresh t-shirt over his head, he looked back at me and said, "There is no time, not now. Maybe later…" he trailed off, stuffing his grief all the way down, pulling on his well-worn mask of indifference.

He shoved on his boots, grabbed his jacket, and kissed the top of my head. "See you this afternoon."

I reluctantly got out of bed and hurried down to the basement, making my sincere apologies. I sat in the make-up chair next to Lucy, who was almost done.

"You look like hell," she said. "What happened?"

"Rough night."

"Looks like it. Wow," she said as she rose to leave. "Thank your lucky stars that what Carrie can't cover with make-up, they'll fix in post. Well, I'll see you soon."

Katie had been standing at the door, waiting for a chair to open.

"That was actually kind of nice, coming from Lucy," she said, taking a seat.

We were the only people being worked on now. The rest of the hair and make-up team were at the high school.

Carrie exhaled loudly. "I can't believe it. Anna, your foundation. It's in my kit at the school," she said, putting on her coat. "I'll be back in ten minutes, tops. Okay?"

Carrie stepped out, so it was just Katie and me.

"Andrew upstairs?" I asked.

"How did you know?" she asked, smiling.

"I can tell when he's around. He has a distinctive feel, different from anyone else."

"Yeah. Different," she agreed in a curious way.

"Care to elaborate?" I pushed.

She looked at me, thinking about whether to share what was on her mind. Whatever it was, it was really bothering her.

"You can trust me," I encouraged.

"You know I like him, right?"

That was a funny question. To look at them was to see they were in love.

"Everyone knows it," I replied.

"I'm not sure he does," she said, the pain in her voice obvious.

"Come again? Why in the world would you say that?" I asked, truly puzzled. "I mean, I see how he is with you."

And then I remembered their troubled past. I did not believe that Andrew as he was now was capable of hurting Katie in any way. But I also couldn't forget their story. "Has he done something?" I asked. "What's going on?"

She slumped back in her chair. "That's just it. Nothing's going on."

She wasn't making any sense. "Are you fighting?" I prompted.

"I wish."

"You wish?"

"At least that would be something," she said sadly. "Maybe...maybe we aren't a good match after all."

"I don't get it" I said, totally bemused. "The way he looks at you. And you at him. I'm part of my own starry-eyed couple, and it's even a lot for me!"

I was glad she laughed. She was also, though, on the verge of tears. She was so mixed up, she could easily go one way or the other.

"He treats me like I'm super fragile. Like I could break."

When I didn't immediately respond, she continued to muse, "But then, I guess I am fragile, compared to his brothers and sisters."

She looked up at me, surprised at herself, as if she'd let out a state secret.

"You forget," I assured her, "I've met some of his family."

"Oh, yeah. So many secrets to keep straight."

"Tell me about it," I agreed. "But his treating you as if you're fragile isn't what's bothering you. It isn't the secrets either. Do you want to talk about the real problem?"

Katie's intense blush gave me the first hint. "Oh," I said a little uncomfortably.

"It's not what you think," she said hurriedly. "At least, I think."

"What is it, then?"

"If he likes me so much, why won't he kiss me?"

Chapter Twenty-Four

I was shocked. They had never kissed? And I thought I had it rough.

"Have you done anything physical with him?"

"We hold hands, sometimes. But even that seems like it's...painful for him. Sometimes I touch his arm, or his back, and he winces. What's wrong with me?"

"Let's get two things straight. First and foremost, there is nothing wrong with you."

"And second?" I was glad to see a smile on her face, even if it was marred by tears.

"You have absolutely come to the right place!"

"I have?"

"Oh yes. Let me tell you. These supernatural folk are *weird* when it comes to dating."

"But you're supernatural," Katie pointed out.

"Yeah, but I didn't know it until last year. So, I wasn't raised that way." I turned to fully face her. "Do you know how people get married in the Families?"

She shook her head, riveted.

"When two people sleep together, somehow everyone knows, and that's it!" I exclaimed, still scandalized. "Seals the deal."

"Get out! That's crazy!" she snorted.

"Tell me about it. But it doesn't matter what I think. They've had these customs for generations. I might hate it, but I can't change it."

"So, do you think if Andrew kisses me, he's, like, saying he wants to marry me?"

"That's entirely possible," I said. "I know he's old. Like, as old as dirt. Way older than the Families. So, it stands to reason his ideas about dating and physical intimacy were developed long ago, not according to modern American hook-up culture."

"I think it might even be worse than that," Katie said, wide-eyed. "However many eons old he and his siblings are, I don't think *any* of them have dated until very, very recently."

"Then you just gotta do it."

"You think I should just kiss him? Make the first move?"

"No. You shouldn't kiss someone if they don't want to be kissed. What I meant is, you have to talk to him. You need to tell him what you're feeling and what you want."

"But he should know," she said stubbornly.

"It would be so nice if our partners always knew exactly what we wanted. But how could he? It sounds like, on this issue, he's lost."

"I…we…"

I saved her from explaining. "It's okay if it's hard. But, I mean, if you truly don't think you want to talk to him about this, then maybe you should listen to that. Maybe you feel that kind of effort wouldn't be worth it." I looked at her closely. "You don't owe him anything. You do know that, right?"

"Yes. It's just that…" she trailed off again.

The way she was fidgeting in the chair, coupled with her anxiety, I had to ask. "Are you afraid of him?"

She took a deep breath. "I'm afraid that he won't want me. The girl he used to be in love with, Lizzy, is perfect. I can never measure up to her."

I'd met Lizzy before. I was hanging out with Adam when he was on tour and a weird scary fight broke out where we were eating. Lizzy and Andrew were there and fought off the attackers.

Lizzy was kind of perfect, in a literal supernatural way. I knew she was something old, powerful, and unbelievably good, but Adam didn't know what kind of being she was, so neither did I. Being around Lizzy was like being bathed in light and love. I'd hate it if she'd been Adam's first love. Nonetheless, Katie didn't belong with Andrew if he made her feel bad about herself.

"If he makes you feel less than because you aren't her, then you shouldn't be with him. I can't believe I'm saying this, but maybe you should break up with him."

I heard the manor's front door open. Carrie was back.

"As long as you are safe, physically and emotionally, the real question is, what do you want? Do you love him?"

As I asked the question, the answer registered on her face and radiated out of her being. She loved him.

Carrie hurried in, hastily dropping her bag and taking off her jacket. "Sorry, ladies. Time for me to get to work."

"Thank you," Katie mouthed to me.

"Don't let me interrupt," Carrie grinned, catching the silent exchange. "But does it have to do with that strapping young hunk upstairs?"

"Carrie!" I exclaimed in mock astonishment.

Katie's smile grew wider, then faltered. "I hate to ask, but would you talk to him for me? I know it's asking a lot," she added hurriedly. "No, don't worry about it. I'll figure it out somehow."

Carrie caught my eye in the mirror. She gave me a look that said, "Why on earth would you not help this poor, lovesick girl out?"

"Sure," I said, swallowing. "I'll talk to him."

I would have sooner agreed to throw a party for Maggie than have a sex talk with Andrew, *about* Andrew. But Carrie's eyes were right.

Chapter Twenty-Five

The morning shooting schedule was interior scenes at the manor with Meg and Lucy. I was so preoccupied that shooting was difficult. Sylvia was frustrated, tension levels were high.

On top of that, Lucy could tell there was something going on with me and Meg, and it made her crazy. She hated being out of the loop. It wasn't a small miracle we'd kept all this supernatural intrigue from her. Lucy normally saw all. But she had no frame of reference for the paranormal, and she was utterly blind to it.

If her not-so-subtle social media posts about social climbers were any indication, Lucy also wasn't thrilled by Meg's new roommates. Besides her ramped-up bitchiness leveled at Katie, she couldn't seem to stand the sight of Andrew.

In the past, Lucy's theatrics bothered me. But my feelings about her had begun to change. I now saw it as my job to protect her, and her nonsense barely registered with me.

That's how Adam saw all who were non-Family. They were just the faceless masses to be protected from the viciousness of the Fourth Family. If you weren't from his world, or involved in the struggle, you barely registered in his vision.

I understood that now. Family members came to me vividly, in bright colors. Almost all others were dull and flat.

I could feel how badly Meg wanted to talk with me, but I was so over-scheduled I didn't know when I'd find the time. I'd already had a difficult conversation with Katie, and had promised to have what was sure to be an even worse conversation with her boyfriend. Mr. Seacrest would be invading my dreams as soon as my head hit the pillow tonight, and going into the caves on Friday was going to make me sick. I needed to check up on Jade, and Corey too! All the while my heart was bleeding for Adam. It was entirely too much to deal with, and I didn't have the option of taking a time-out.

I felt it coming, something beginning to flow through me. I could not stop it.

We were in between takes when Meg announced loudly, "I feel sick!"

All attention turned toward Meg, and Suzanne slammed into me. She grabbed me by the waist and dragged me into the bathroom off the foyer.

Lifting me up like I weighed nothing, she plopped me in the bathtub. Water was balling on the top of my arms, my face and neck, my legs. Water somehow coming from within me was pushing its way out.

"What the hell is happening?" she asked, trying to keep her voice low.

I knew what was going on because it wasn't the first time, though I was still shocked. I was being pulled apart. The energy inside was bubbling over, becoming water, trapping me.

I sank down in the tub. My fractured thoughts, impossible puzzles, swirled. The horrid messes my friends were in and the impending war threatened to overwhelm me. The ease of giving in, being swallowed whole, seduced me.

The water had pushed out, forming a bubble and encasing me, lapping over the side of the tub. Suzanne's face was a mask of sheer shock. Her instincts took over as she charged me, trying to burst the water bubble.

To my amazement, she fell through, trapping her inside with me.

"What the hell's going on?" she panted. Trying to put distance between us, she hit her head on the wall of water and was repelled. She pulled out her dagger and tried to puncture the bubble, but the blade bounced off. She looked to me in desperation.

Twice before, when I had been filled with anxiety, I had been engulfed by water. It had flowed through me, threatened to take me with it and break me apart. But this time was different. I was conscious, present. That's how I knew that, though this may have begun with my burdened thoughts, it wasn't me causing this now.

"Iris?" I called out.

Suzanne went instantly slack beside me. Lifting her head she whispered, "Will you come?" But they weren't her words. It was Iris, speaking through Suzanne.

"Yes! Where are you?"

"In the water."

"But where?" I cried in frustration. "What water?"

Iris, using Suzanne's hands, scooped up water from the tub and held it out to me. "In the water," she repeated.

Before I could ask another question, the bubble burst. Iris was gone and Suzanne was back, gasping to find her breath.

"I know where she is," Suzanne said, shaking.

"So do I," I replied, touching my wet clothes. "She's in the water. Our water."

I didn't see Adam all day. I couldn't wait until we were alone, and I could unload to him about my morning. But after dinner, Echo caught my arm and pulled me into the study.

"Suzanne filled me in. She is freaked out, and that's hard to do. Are you okay?"

"It's hard to explain, but I'm starting to understand what's been going on with me."

"I'm glad for it," Echo said firmly. "But may I offer you advice?"

He had never acted so paternally before. "Um, sure."

"This should be Adam's time to mourn, but we both know he won't get as much time as he needs. Unless you feel it's an absolute necessity, maybe you shouldn't tell him about what happened with Iris yet. You and I can protect him for as long as possible."

I went to my room to take off the day's pound of make-up, Echo's words bouncing around in my head. Adam and I had promised each other to be open. Wouldn't he want to know right away?

Adam's relationship with his mom was different than what I'd had. When my mom had died, I hadn't given a rat's ass about anything but my grief. I didn't even try to function.

What was Adam doing the day after his mother had died? He was at work, pretending. Could I really add to his load?

No. I'd follow Echo's lead. I'd spare Adam this burden until it was necessary.

Unfortunately, necessity reared its head way too soon.

Chapter Twenty-Six

The next day, after a long morning shoot, I was grateful for the lunchtime break. Filling my plate with the yummy spread craft services had out for lunch, my thoughts went to Iris, the unsettling feeling of being pulled apart, and puzzling through what she said. I was eyeing the pitcher of water when Suzanne walked by, looking over the spread, deciding against it.

"Not hungry?" I asked.

"I'm on my way out. Need anything at the market?"

My stash of honey roasted peanuts and tampons was dangerously low. "Mind if I come along? I can be ready in ten minutes."

Her expression clouded over. "I've got to go right now. Echo's got a headache, he needs me to get him some stuff," she said, already backing away. "Why don't you text me what you need," she offered as she went out the door.

That was weird. Something was going on she didn't want me to know about.

I sat down to eat and turned over Suzanne's strange behavior. Echo jarred me from my thoughts, taking the seat next to me.

"Sorry to hear you're not feeling well," I said.

He paused mid-bite. "What?" he asked, his voice muffled by his sandwich.

So, Suzanne *was* up to something.

"I thought you had a headache."

"Why did you think that?" He looked around, eyes scanning the room, then he bent his head towards me. "I'm fine," he said under his breath, "but in the future, know it's bad form to let others know when you're suffering. Gives them an advantage."

"What are you two gossiping about?" Lucy asked, joining us and ending our conversation.

I'd forgotten the incident with Suzanne until that evening. My attention was split between worrying about Adam and worrying about Mr. Seacrest's return on Friday. I felt deep in my soul, change was coming. I tried to block the ominous clouds that gathered whenever I thought of going into the tunnels on Friday.

It was Wednesday, so Adam *should've* had two more days to mourn before we were pulled back into the fray.

Echo and I had just returned from filming an exterior scene at the farm. Suzanne was waiting for us in the foyer. The color was gone from her face. She looked like she was about to throw up.

I didn't sense any danger, but Echo went into warrior mode.

"What is it?" he demanded.

Suzanne looked physically pained. "I need to tell you something."

"Out with it," Echo returned.

"Adam needs to hear. I can't keep this from him."

Now I was worried. They both believed in letting the grieving alone. For her to violate his peace, whatever had happened must be big and bad.

It was the longest walk to his bedroom, every step filled with foreboding.

Suzanne knocked on the door. Adam opened, ushering us in. She didn't waste any time. "This afternoon I met with Maggie."

I was shocked and terrified. I couldn't believe Maggie was in the same town as me. I wanted to run, to hide.

Adam, on the other hand, seemed flattened by the news. He sat on his bed, hanging his head. "What did she want?"

"She tried to recruit me."

Adam didn't move. He didn't seem surprised. He was taut as if poised for action, and yet he seemed completely resigned, defeated. "For what mission?"

"She wants her sister's, your sister's, bracelet," Suzanne answered, but it was clear there was more.

"And?" he prompted, finally facing Suzanne.

"She wants me to deliver Anna."

No anger, no fury. Nothing. "What did she promise you?"

"Finn. She knows about him. She saw me looking at him and figured it out. I made a really stupid slip a couple of years ago about having a Fourth boyfriend I left behind," she said, mentally kicking herself.

"How did you respond?"

"I said I had to think about it. That I wasn't going to betray you."

Adam nodded. The silence stretched my nerves thin. I flinched when Adam spoke again.

"And she said you'd be helping me, right? By getting rid of Anna?"

Suzanne glanced at me. "She thinks Anna's a witch."

"Witch," he repeated. "And our sister's bracelet. Why?"

"She didn't tell me, and I didn't ask," Suzanne answered. "She said it was a gold bangle, about an inch wide, with diamonds so small they look like dust."

"I remember it," he said in a hushed tone, nodding to himself.

I was bursting with questions, but deep silence had descended over the room again.

Adam looked over at me before lying back on his bed and closing his eyes. "Go ahead and ask, Anna."

I flipped through the questions in my mind and landed on an obvious one that he hadn't asked.

"Why you, Suzanne? She's the queen now. She can order anyone to do what she wants."

"We're friends," Suzanne said simply. "I don't make them easily and neither does she. But when Adam took me in, so did Maggie. We hit it off; I suppose we're sort of kindred spirits. From what I hear, after the incident last weekend at Crimson Hall, she doesn't have many, if any, allies left."

"Is she still in town?" Adam asked, eyes still closed.

"I don't think so. Our meeting was kind of rushed. I'm afraid she may be meeting with others as well."

I asked my next question. "Why does she think you'd be willing to betray Adam in exchange for Finn?" This seemed unlikely for anyone who really knew Suzanne.

"She was in a similar circumstance once. She was in love with someone, but Queen Cora separated them and had him killed. She knows how I feel," Suzanne explained. "She also offered protection. Since she believes she's the rightful ruler, once Adam is gone, I'll be left unprotected. She said she'd take me on."

"Maggie plans to kill Adam?" I asked incredulously. Even as deranged as she was, that didn't seem believable.

"No, she thinks he'll be collateral damage. She knows that once she hands you over to the Leviathan, Adam will do anything to free you."

"Enough," Adam's barely audible voice silenced her. "I've heard enough."

He turned on his side, facing the wall. He wanted us to leave.

I didn't see Adam until the next day. It was hard to give him space. I knew he wasn't intentionally trying to wound me, but it hurt that he wanted to grieve by himself. There was a small part of me that wondered if he resented me. If it weren't for me, he wouldn't be in pain now. His life would be less complicated. His family would be whole.

When he did appear Thursday morning, Adam kept to himself. Not one for small talk on a good day, his whole vibe was that he wanted to be left alone. The cast and crew got the message and stayed away.

It was hard to steer clear when all I wanted to do was make the pain go away. I didn't want him to hurt. But that was asking him to be inhuman. The only way forward was through. He was in the middle of it, engulfed in a thick haze of despair.

For all the backward and archaic ways of the Families, they were very advanced in their dealings with death and suffering. They were not embarrassed to cry or mourn. They also didn't try to mitigate others' sorrow for their own relief. They'd grown comfortable with letting others experience their full range of emotions.

This was not my nature. I wanted to fix him. Put bandages on his wounds. But that would have been for me. I tried to find the courage to stand by and let Adam feel what he needed to feel.

The weekend came soon enough, and with it Mr. Seacrest's return to Gold Manor. While I'd seen Mr. Seacrest every night, he'd left Adam out of it. When I'd told him of Maggie's offer to Suzanne, he had choked up. I'd never seen him at a loss for words before.

When Mr. Seacrest arrived at the Manor, he had taken Adam into his make-shift office. When they eventually emerged, Adam wore his normal face. He'd been given a week of mourning. More than he'd thought he'd get.

Maggie was on the move. We couldn't afford to waste any more time. Soon we'd take Mr. Seacrest to Samuel's cave. Since Maggie had killed the queen, I hadn't been able to shake the sense that something terrible lay just over the next hill. Or, should I say, in the tunnels we would soon be entering.

But now that the day was here, I felt oddly prepared and well rested.

Chapter Twenty-Seven

We met at the appointed time, deciding to enter the cave from the basement. I went through behind Jade, talking him up about his morning shoot to get his mind off his claustrophobia. On the other side of the narrow entrance to the cave he smiled back at me. I wasn't fooling him with my small talk.

We needed all the help we could get, which was the only reason I'd agreed to Jade's involvement. He had mended physically, but he was still shaken from his encounter with Iris.

We had a better idea of where to look for Iris now. Though we didn't know the exact location, Suzanne and I did know that she was in the well the house drew from. That meant that all this time, she'd been in the water that we had been drinking from, bathing in.

"Maybe this is your answer," Adam said to me as we headed to Samuel's cave.

"Which mystery are we clearing up?" I teased.

"Your preternatural relationship with water. Before you moved here, nothing like that had ever happened to you, right?"

"Yes, but you could say that for any number of the bizarre things that have happened since coming here."

Andrew chimed in. "It does make sense. These Immortals can send out psychic energy to those above ground. That's how they communicate with the Seers who serve them. It could be Iris has been attempting to make contact, sending out a type of SOS. I doubt Samuel Perry properly prepared Iris for what he was doing to her. If she is in the water we've consumed, her despair might be passing to you through a metaphysical connection."

"Why did Samuel Perry do this?" I asked, trying to distract myself.

Adam gave an involuntary sigh. "Why did he murder everyone in Gold Manor? All the men, women, and children? I know it's hard for you to understand such vicious and senseless killing. I couldn't venture a guess as to why he experimented on Iris or how he came in possession of the means necessary to make an Immortal. But it doesn't surprise me. He was a tricky and absolutely brutal original Third."

The closer we got to Samuel's hideaway, the tighter the knot in my stomach grew. So far, no ghosts, but that didn't mean a curious one wouldn't pop up at any moment. As soon as I entered Samuel's cave, a wave of nausea hit me.

"Sit down and rest," Jade urged, noting my pale, clammy face.

Adam helped me down and sat beside me.

"Does anyone see anything out of the ordinary, or feel anything?" Adam asked.

Echo and Suzanne made a meticulous sweep of the room, Finn standing in one corner, taking in the space.

"Andrew? Uncle?" Adam asked.

"I don't see anything. Let me think," Andrew said, going to the back wall of the cave. Mr. Seacrest stood quietly by the entrance, scanning the room.

"Adam? Do you sense anything?" I asked, trying to calm my churning stomach.

"Nothing but you," he said, gently rubbing my back.

"Same." As soon as I said those words, I knew I was going to lose my lunch. I made a beeline out of there, barely getting to the main cave corridor before heaving.

Adam was right behind me, holding my hair back.

Once the convulsions stopped, I used him as support to stand. I wished for a towel and a toothbrush but pushed on through. "I'm ready to go back in."

Adam didn't try to dissuade me. We needed to find Iris. But as soon as I walked back in, my stomach started twisting again.

We walked over to where Finn, Jade, and Andrew were gathered near the back wall of the cave.

"Do you see that?" Andrew asked, kneeling on the dirt floor to touch a small stone near the bottom of the rock wall. "That probably shouldn't be there."

"Why do you say that?" Finn asked.

"That's amber."

"I remember seeing those stones in my childhood. Relatively common in Poland," Mr. Seacrest confirmed.

While my rolling stomach made it hard to think about anything else, as soon as Andrew pointed out that stone, I had a flash of recognition. Bits of amber were embedded in the walls of Crimson Hall.

"What's on the other side of the wall?" I asked.

"Good question," Adam nodded. "Let's find out."

"Let's bring it down," Echo agreed, looking around for a tool.

"While you work on that, I'm going to step out for a while. Call me when you want me back," I said to the team.

"What are you going to do?" Adam asked.

"I'll take a walk, get some air. Maybe head out to the barn where they're shooting."

That caught Andrew's attention. "Mind if I walk with you? I think this project is going to take a while."

No one objected, so Adam kissed my forehead and we left. I looked back through the entrance as Echo returned with

Corey and tools, and Mr. Seacrest took off his sports coat and rolled up his sleeves.

Chapter Twenty-Eight

My stomach settled once we were clear of Samuel's cave, the autumn air cooling my flushed face. The breeze coupled with the late afternoon sun warming my back felt amazing. We walked in the woods in silence. Before we reached Heaven's Gate, I realized this was probably the best opportunity I'd get to talk to Andrew about Katie. But how to start?

"So, how long have you and Katie been together?" I asked lamely, ending the peaceful moment.

Andrew didn't answer for a beat. He didn't look at me when he replied, "That's an odd question, out of the blue. Do you have something on your mind?"

I wanted to yell, "No, you're the odd one!" and run away. I really didn't want to do this.

He slowed down. I could see he was tensing, preparing for bad news.

"It's nothing like that," I said, responding to his body language, trying to reassure him.

"Then it is something about her," he said definitively. "What is it?" he asked gruffly.

"I..." I could feel my face getting red. "It's really embarrassing," I said, turning from him.

"Lucky for you I don't get embarrassed, so you don't need to either. If you know something about Katie that I need to know, tell me."

"You say that now..." I tried to tease, but my attempt to lighten the mood didn't work.

Andrew had turned to stone. I needed to get this awful conversation over with. I was pretty sure that what I had agreed to talk to him about was not nearly as bad as whatever he was imagining now.

"Katie asked me to talk to you," I began.

"I've been waiting for this," he said, sounding defeated. "Does she want me to move out of Meg's? I will, but I'm not leaving town until this business with the Families and the Leviathan is resolved. She can't expect me to do that."

"What are you talking about?" I asked, completely confused.

"She doesn't want to be with me any longer," he replied. He was trying to keep his emotions in check.

"Uh, it's actually the opposite. I know this is ridiculous, but she wants to know why you won't kiss her."

Andrew didn't relax. He had prepared himself for the worst and didn't know what to do with what I'd just dropped on him.

"If you don't mind me asking," I said uncertainly, "why would you think she wanted to break up? She's clearly in love with you."

Andrew just stood there, still tense, his hands fisted. His energy was shifting, and while he was always hard for me to read, whatever was bubbling beneath the surface felt dangerous.

Then I understood. "You don't think she'll ever forgive you for what happened, when you scared her."

"She told you?" he said with a hard laugh. "Is that what I did? I *scared* her?" he scoffed, his voice quiet and harder than steel.

"She forgave you. You've gotta do the same."

"Not possible," he said flatly. "And she shouldn't forgive me either."

"What? You think she should hold a grudge?" I asked in disbelief. "That's what you want for her? You do know that will only hurt her in the end?"

"No, I don't want that for her," he agreed.

133

"And what's so special about you? You don't deserve forgiveness? No second chances for a god?"

"I am no god."

"Well, there you go, smart guy. Get over yourself and move on."

Andrew was silent a moment, then asked, "Did Katie tell you about Lizzy?"

"Well," I hedged uncomfortably. "She told me that Lizzy was your first love. That she was perfect, and she broke your heart. She seems to be the third member of your relationship."

"Why would you say that?"

"Katie feels she can never measure up to Lizzy. Maybe it's just jealousy and insecurity on her part, but…what have you done to help her *not* feel that way?" I took a breath before pushing a little more. "There's more to your story with Lizzy than just a simple break-up, am I right?"

Andrew stared mutely at me, not denying it while not supplying any details.

"Fine, keep your horrible break-up story to yourself. But if you're going to be with Katie, it's only fair you lay your cards on the table. Tell her what's up. If you aren't that into her, tell her."

"That's just it!" Andrew exclaimed. "I feel so much for Katherine. Too much sometimes." He composed himself and began again. "It was always Lizzy. It could only ever be Lizzy. No one else. You have no idea what I did for her, what I gave up. What I lost."

I was shocked. I'd thought he really was in love with Katie.

"So how can it be," he continued, "that, after losing her, after giving up everything for her, I could have found

134

Katie so quickly? How could I love her so completely?" His face was raw with anguish.

"Grace?" I offered.

The effect of that word was like a bucket of ice water dumped on his head. His eyes immediately cleared; his countenance returned to the wise old soul I knew.

"For me?" he whispered.

"Sure. I mean, aren't you always speaking of redemption, beauty, love? Why would there not be a measure of it for you?"

"Love and Beauty are two sides of reality. They refer to the same thing," he said quietly, thinking.

I had no idea what to say next. This conversation was giving me whiplash. Fortunately, Andrew started walking again, saving us from staring awkwardly at each other.

"So…what you actually wanted to talk to me about is why I haven't kissed Katie?" he asked calmly, as if I hadn't just witnessed him in the midst of a personal crisis.

Okay, back to this. "In hair and make-up this morning, Katie and I were alone for a little bit. She confided in me about your careful no-contact attitude towards her. She wanted advice. I told her to talk to you, so be prepared for that. But she also wanted me to talk to you."

"Why do you think this is?" Andrew asked.

"I think it has to do with Lizzy. She just doesn't know where she stands with you, and the fact that you won't kiss her confuses her more."

"We kissed. Once. She is the only person I've ever kissed. But it was *that* night," he said, trying to shake off a demon that wouldn't let him rest. "I won't make that mistake twice. I'm protecting her."

"From you," I added, filling in what he'd left unsaid.

"Yes."

"Sorry, doesn't work that way." This poor guy really needed to be clued in on how to function in a romantic relationship.

"She doesn't understand the intense passions I have," he protested.

"We all have intense passions," I scoffed. "You know how people in the Families marry?"

"Yes," he smiled.

"Well, Adam and I are not married for several very practical reasons. But we drive each other crazy. You have no idea how hard it is for me to keep my hands off him. What I'm getting at is, you are not alone. Everyone has to deal with reigning in their passions."

"It's new to me and it's much harder than I imagined. What really gets me is, half the time I don't want to keep them in check. And that sobers me right up. I will not ever hurt Katie again."

"But you are hurting her, by not telling her these things."

"I wish she had come to me with her worries."

"Me too!" I laughed, drawing a smile from him. "But really, it's not all on her. You should have been open with her about all this from the beginning. Also…you're intimidating."

"I'd hoped not to her," he said, his smile fading.

"Add that to the list of topics you guys need to discuss. But I will tell you what I told her." I lowered my voice as we emerged from the forest, the barn in sight. "You're not obligated to stick it out with her. If you don't want to be open and honest with Katie, then don't. Move on and leave her alone."

I waved to Meg, who was standing in front of the barn with Lucy. She looked relieved to see me, while my presence didn't register with Lucy. Katie was sitting in her chair. I was thinking of taking the seat next to her when my cell buzzed with a text from Adam. They had gotten through the wall.

"Guess we need to go back," I said to Andrew, whose eyes were boring a hole in the back of Katie's head. What was his problem? Why not just walk over and plant a giant kiss on her and be done with it?

"I'll be a moment," Andrew replied.

I watched as he walked up to Katie and took her hand. Whatever he said to her made her face light up. He reluctantly let go and we walked back to the cave.

Chapter Twenty-Nine

On the way to the cave, Adam called.

"Please tell me you found Iris," I said into the phone. "I don't want to go back down there." I hoped to never go in those caves again.

"Why don't you put me on speaker," Adam said darkly.

"Okay. What's the problem?" I asked.

"We've found her, but we can't get to her."

"Why not?" I asked.

Andrew replied, "The ritual performed to create Leviathan includes a defense mechanism that protects them and ensures their immortality. For those who look for the Leviathan, there is no return trip."

"This would've been helpful information before we began," Adam chided.

"I hoped this might be a different situation since Iris was entombed by force, against her will. It took a tremendous effort on her part to lead us to her. Unique as that was, I wondered if perhaps she had overcome the recovery problem as well."

"You want me to go down there," I said, cutting to the chase.

"We think you may be able to connect with her. But-"

"Yes?" I had already begun to feel something odd, and we were still a good distance from the cave entrance.

I could feel Adam's hesitation on the other side of the line. "I'm not going to lie. I'm having a hard time down here. Everyone is."

"What do you mean?" I asked, hoping they weren't all feeling as awful as I was.

"It's physically hard to be here. We've all come and gone at least once. You need to be prepared. In and out as soon as possible. Got it?"

"What do you have in mind?" I asked, trying to contain my fear.

Andrew and I listened to what I was supposed to do as we walked through the forest.

Several feet from the fixed ladder that the crew had installed to the entrance of the cave system, a wave of nausea hit.

Andrew took my arm for support. "Are you okay?"

"Something's down there. I can feel it. It's making me sick all the way up here." Beads of sweat were forming on my forehead.

"Do you want to go down? Can you make it?"

I had a feeling my reaction was only going to get stronger the closer I got to it. "Let's just get this over with," I replied, knowing my presence was inevitable. "Why don't you go down first, in case I fall. I've already done that and don't feel like a repeat."

Andrew wasted no time, knowing the longer I was there the harder it was.

By the time we got to Samuel's lair, I'd already thrown up and was sweating through my clothes.

Adam called through the hole they'd made in the back wall. "We're down here."

Andrew looked over at me where I sagged against Samuel Perry's old bed. "I think you're going to have to carry me," I said weakly.

He eyed the narrow hole in the wall skeptically and looked back at me. As if on cue, the a Gold Ghost appeared. Saying nothing, she scooped me up and carried me to the wall. She passed through the rock, carefully maneuvering me through the small passage to the other side.

I was too sick to be freaked out. The unnerving feel of her leathery arms barely registered given the warning sirens shooting through my nervous system, shouting at me to run as fast as I could away from this place.

Andrew followed us. "Thank you, sister. I will take her now."

The Gold Ghost looked at Andrew for the first time and gently rolled me into his arms. She said nothing and didn't move from her place by the cave entrance. She looked like a guardian standing watch.

These thoughts left as immediately as they came, for my sickness kicked up a notch. I shivered uncontrollably in the damp cool, and the toxic air made my skin itch.

Adam came up to us. Through my haze, I saw his face blanch when he took in my state in Andrew's arms.

"Does she really need to be here? This air is poisonous," Andrew said, ready to get me out.

Adam was struggling, clutching his stomach. "Believe me, I don't want her here either, but we have to give this a try."

The cave was riddled with glittering stalagmites. Or maybe I was hallucinating. I was having a hard time recalling my part. Andrew set me down next to a pool of water.

By my side, Adam spoke, telling me to clear my mind. He was telling me to do something else, but I couldn't make it out, couldn't focus on the words. My senses felt stripped away, overwhelmed and burned out. And then he dipped my hand in the fire.

It was my own screaming that brought me back around. I was in the glistening cave, lying on my side, my arm in the boiling water. I immediately yanked it out.

"It's a trick," Adam said, slumped beside me. I watched Jade run from the cave. "He's sick," Adam explained. "We all are. But is it real?" he asked me.

He was asking me to push back, push out of my emotions. I looked at my arm, covered with welts. My skin felt like it was peeling off.

I pulled free from Andrew, who was supporting me from behind, and threw up again. Holding my stomach, bile in my mouth, an errant thought blew through my mind. The toxic air, the boiling water, the fear. This was coming from Iris, was real to her, but didn't have to be real for us.

I crawled away from Adam to clear my mind and concentrated on my burned arm. *You're fine, you're okay. It's not real.* I repeated this to myself, trying to shake the horror gripping me. I clenched and unclenched my fist, turning it over, willing it to be whole again. But there was no change.

I turned to Adam. "Look!" I cried, showing him my injured arm. "I can't do this!"

Before Adam could answer, Corey collapsed, slamming into me as he went down, sending me into the water.

Chapter Thirty

I felt consumed by fire. And I was sinking at an alarming rate, my friends gathered at the shore too far away. I had to make it to the surface, needed to breathe.

I tried to fight my way up, but I was falling like a stone, picking up speed and at the end of my breath. Suddenly I slipped from water into the dry air and rammed into something hard.

I held my sides, working to right my breathing and gather my bearings.

I was in a half-domed bubble of air, surrounded by water, just big enough to hold me and a coffin. The air was putrid and thick, stinging my eyes, but breathable. The ground was bone dry, as was the nondescript pine coffin, pristine as the day it was made.

It must be Iris's. This is where she was entombed.

"Iris?" I whispered. My voice was rough, my throat sore from being sick and holding my breath as I descended into her tomb.

There was no reply.

I sat beside her coffin, thinking of what to do next. How could I communicate with her? I closed my eyes and tried to center. But the millions of questions constantly cluttering my mind descended. I didn't have time for this. This was not a time for conjecture, but action. I called out for them to *stop*…and they did. No questions, no worries or chatter. Quiet.

I let my mind center on my breathing, on what it felt like to be here. Clarity came as I counted my breaths. The only way to the other side was through. No sidestepping, no denial, only embracing the present. All of it.

I'd been holding my nose, closing out the sickening smell. I let that go. I let go of my many defenses and willed myself to be completely present.

Sitting, breathing, tuning into the rhythm of my breath, I heard her. At first, I thought it was a worry trying to worm its way back into my head. Instead of pushing it out, I allowed it to come. The fear was a piece of me that had a place, a function, but not something I had to give into. Turning it over, I realized it wasn't coming from me.

"Yes?" I asked, reaching my hand out to the coffin. Opening my eyes, I saw Iris outside of the dry bubble, holding hands with the sister ghosts.

I closed my eyes again to center my heart and breath, taking a minute. Opening them again, I repeated, "Yes?"

They hadn't moved. My natural desire was to fill up the empty space between us with questions, with plans, with something. Instead, I waited, my hand still on the coffin.

Looking at the ghosts flanking Iris, I let my mind wander. Fears came and went. Plans presented themselves and dissipated. And I sat still, breathing, letting my thoughts flow like the current around me.

Relaxed, letting the moment unfurl as it would, I watched as Iris slowly turned her head to her left, kissing the cheek of the Green Ghost. She let go of their hands and walked through the water and into her tomb.

Chapter Thirty-One

I slowly removed my hand from her coffin and put it back in my lap, waiting for Iris to direct me. This was her space, her world. She'd called to me, brought me here. I was washed with an overwhelming sense of gratitude that I could help to set her free, that I could be the instrument to end her suffering.

Iris slowly approached me. I noted in the back of my mind that though she appeared to be floating in water, she wasn't wet, or even really dry. She possessed that ethereal quality the Gold Ghosts had, yet she seemed more solid. Not as sheer.

Before she spoke, I was struck with fear that she was going to ask me to find her in her dreamscape, a place I didn't want to be. I felt so strongly that if I went there, I wouldn't return. Being in this place, I saw all too clearly the power of the Immortals. While I could do a lot in dreams, I would be like a baby compared to what they were capable of. I would be at Iris's mercy, and she didn't exactly seem stable.

But what if this was the only way to help her? I would have to go into her world, help her destroy the object the Immortals wanted, setting her free. Killing us both. Fulfilling my role as the Fifth and ending the plague of the Fourth.

So be it. *The only way is through.*

I took a deep breath and stood up. "I will come to you."

Iris shook her head. "You are here."

She waited for me to recognize that this fear was all my own, that what I feared was not what she needed from me. Her immortal tomb was like a mirror world where my intuitions were upside down.

"What can I do?" I asked, searching her eyes.

Iris looked over her shoulder to the sister ghosts and back to me. The Green Ghost was holding something glowing. She glided towards us and gave the object to Iris.

Iris turned to me, her arm outstretched, her palm closed. "This is now your burden. You will be its vessel. Can you suffer it?"

"I don't understand," I said, pleading for Iris to answer openly, plainly.

Her palm still closed, extended, she repeated, "Can you suffer it?"

"Will it free you?" I probed. Iris nodded, looking back again to the sister ghosts who were now floating half-in and half-out of the bubble.

"Will it set them free too?" I asked.

The twins moved again to Iris's side, the tight space barely holding us all. I didn't know if she couldn't tell me what would happen if I consented, or if she didn't know, but she didn't answer.

I was about to ask another, but Iris spoke, "It will break the Family curse."

"What?" I breathed. "How?"

"Will you take it? Serpent Star they call it," she responded, opening her hand to reveal a thin gold bracelet studded with small, iridescent stones. "Ouroboros. To doom us forever."

It took a moment for me to see the bangle was in the shape of a snake eating its own tail. I had to touch it. As if of its own volition, my hand reached out, but she was faster, pulling it from my reach.

Iris shook her head. "Some choices we make for ourselves. Other choices are made for us. If you accept Serpent Star, you will be making a choice not only for

145

yourself, but one that affects many others. Can you suffer the burden?"

I slowly dropped my hand, reminding myself to think before acting.

"What is it?"

"It is the object Samuel stole. It is the means to produce the Immortals. It tied me to this place for all eternity. A sleepless, eternal hell. But you can set me free."

"I want to set you all free," I replied. "I desperately want to end the curse. But I thought I had to die for that to happen. Is there another way? Are you offering me another way?"

Iris nodded.

"So, this will free you all and end the curse now? Like, right now?"

She nodded again.

I knew I had to do it, but I wanted to know the real price. "Can you tell me what else will happen if I take this?"

"No," she replied, opening her hand again.

My heart sank. So, this was it. I had to choose blindly. I could take what she offered and possibly fulfill my mission of ending the Family curse now, *and* set Iris and the twin ghosts free. But at what price? Could I do this without knowing the cost? And what if this was a trap? Could I trust that Iris and the Gold Ghosts were on my side?

"Anna Rose Ellington, no one knows the future. If you take the stones, you become the vessel. I will pass on, as will they," she said, the ghosts beside her laying a hand on each of her shoulders. "All tied to the curse will die. Can you suffer it?"

I finally understood. If I said yes, I'd be directly responsible for taking the lives of all the still-living original Family members. Mr. Seacrest's face flashed before my eyes.

I was crushed. All Adam had left was his uncle; could I really take that from him? Then my mind went to others, like Finn. Could I deprive him of his parents? Evil as I thought they were, could I be the cause of him losing them?

"You are the instrument of their deaths, either now or at the time of your own demise," Iris reasoned. "You choose how many more of the innocent will suffer before that day arrives. Even now, the killing continues, the torture continues."

"How do you know that?"

Iris went deathly still. The whites of her eyes filled with red, bulging veins. The skin on her arms began cracking, festering gashes on top of old scars.

"You will take this or come with me," she said in an awful voice, the ground beneath my feet shaking.

Her shift was so sudden. I had forgotten I was talking to an incredibly unstable, tortured, immortal being.

"Not immortal; everlasting," she corrected, eyes glowing. Done with words, she showed me her hell instead, communicating directly into my mind.

She showed me the horror of the Gold Manor massacre.

I saw glimpses of her long torture, bound as she was to the other Immortals, slowly falling apart. Tied to both worlds, as no one should be.

She showed me that the Seers coveted the immortal properties the stones had, which their medicine man had used to curse the Four Families. They wanted to use the stones to gain their own immortality, but the medicine man forbade their use. And so the Seers made him their first victim, and used him in their experiments in their quest for immortality.

147

Iris and the medicine man plotted together in their watery graves, seeking revenge and escape, until he lost all sense of reality and right from wrong. This is where she learned of the Fifth, and she began searching for me.

And then she showed me what I needed to see. The missing link.

Her vision shifted so that I was seeing through the eyes of the Gold Ghosts. They showed me Iris searching for the bracelet in their old bedroom and being caught by Samuel. He decided to punish Iris by using her as a guinea pig to test out his new plaything he'd stolen from the Seers.

He drugged Iris so that she would appear dead, staging her death, watching as she was buried. Digging her up, the perspective shifted from the Gold Ghosts to Iris's. What she saw, the terror she felt, as she was revived and bound, fully conscious as Samuel performed the Immortal ceremony on her.

"Once I was buried alive in this forever torment," Iris's voice sad and low, "he buried Serpent Star at my grave marker beneath the oak tree for safe keeping, to be retrieved when he had need. He thought he was so clever, but he didn't foresee my friends, whom he had murdered, were watching. They've kept watch so he couldn't find it. So no one would find it until it was time.

"The Serpent Star ties the fate of the Four Families with the fate of the Immortals. The same stones used to curse the Families, delivered immortal life to the Leviathan. Destroy the stones and end both curses. Both known, and unknown. The Leviathan don't think of themselves as cursed, but they are – and a plague to the land."

Iris sent me out of her mind, her words clear and ringing. "Can you suffer it? This is your fate," she repeated.

"Because I do it now, or it happens later anyway?"
What if I say no?

Iris was in my face, bearing down, having read my thoughts. "Even now they are searching for you. There may not be a later if they find what we've hidden. You were called and you answered. You uncovered what was stolen. They are coming!"

I looked again at the glistening bracelet in her palm. "Serpent Star," I whispered to myself, feeling it's draw, feeling my fear give way to what I knew was the right thing to do, no matter the cost. I nodded and breathed, "Yes."

Grabbing my arm, she pressed the bangle onto my wrist, clasping both of her hands around it. She pulled me to her, no space between. Her severe thin lips pulled into a sad, small smile. She whispered into my mind, "What's done cannot be undone."

Chapter Thirty-Two

Iris's firm grip on my wrist fell away. She stepped back, taking the hands of the twin ghosts. I tried to speak, wishing for a few more answers, but they quickly faded, leaving me utterly alone. The light in Iris's tomb was dim, and I looked around for what to do next. How was I going to get back to the surface.

My thinking was distracted by an ache in my wrist. I rubbed at the bracelet, turning it round. Serpent Star began to glow. There was no more slack in the bracelet. It was shrinking, digging into my skin. I tried to pull it off, but it was too tight. My wrist was burning. The gold was turning to jelly as the stones sank through the metal and burrowed into my skin like drops of lava.

I screamed and clawed at my wrist, trying to get the liquid metal off. It just sank deeper, searing, now imbedded in my bubbling flesh. I rammed my arm into the water, seeking relief.

But as soon as I touched the water, the small air bubble burst. I would have been crushed from the weight of tons of water, but I threw my arms open wide and commanded it to stop. Instantly the air hissed all around me as the water trying to engulf me turned to steam.

"Dry up!" I commanded, the water scurrying from me, repelled.

The distance between me and the water continued to widen. Soon the lake was gone, the water which hadn't evaporated finding an exit and new home in the labyrinth of caves, leaving the air thick with steam.

The air was so heavy, the darkness so complete, I was unable to see my hands in front of my face.

"Anna!" Adam called from somewhere above me. My mind spinning, my first thought was that he was flying.

Adam's and Corey's desperate calls mingled with others as they called out for me. Just as I was about to answer, I felt Andrew's approach.

"Here she is! I've got her!" he called to the others. "Anna, can you make it out?" he asked, rattled.

I was utterly confused. Taking one step towards Andrew, my knees buckled.

Catching me, he asked, "May I help you out?"

I just nodded, too exhausted to ask what he meant.

In his arms, I had the strangest sensation of rising. Going higher and higher. As he climbed, the air began to clear. I saw enough to realize that Andrew was navigating a steep climb and thick mud, all while holding me. I could still hear Adam and Corey yelling in fear, asking if I was okay.

"I see them," Suzanne's voice called out.

Reaching the top of the mud mountain, Andrew said, through labored breath, "Please take her."

The feel of Adam cleared my head. Was I dreaming?

"Love, are you okay?" he asked, setting me down on a large, damp rock.

I was spent. I didn't know if I was okay. "What happened?"

"You tell us." Corey bent down, brushing the hair from my face.

"Give her a sec," Adam chided gently.

"Yeah, yeah, of course," Corey agreed.

I closed my eyes and reached out in my mind. I couldn't feel much, I was just so tired. "Could you help me back to my room?" I asked Adam.

"Uh, not for a bit, I think. Yes?" he asked, glancing at the others for agreement.

This woke me up a little. I looked around to see why he was asking them, and why he wouldn't want to take me to my room.

The air up higher was reduced to a light cloud of mist, and my eyes were finally able to focus enough to see the state they were all in. The four of them were completely drenched. It looked like they'd gone swimming with their clothes on, shoes and all. But it wasn't just that. They were muddy too, brambles stuck in strange places, Suzanne's hair matted with muck.

I patted my own clothes and hair. Other than the damp spots from being pressed against Andrew and Adam, I was bone dry. I stood up and looked around the cave. The underground lake was gone, replaced with a giant muddy pit. The walls of the cave were covered in grime, the shininess of the stalagmites barely peeping through.

It was abnormally bright. Before I fell in the water, the only light had been from our phones and flashlights. Looking around now, I saw no phones or any other light sources. Where was it coming from?

The haze in my mind slowly clearing, I saw the source of light. It was me.

Chapter Thirty-Three

They watched as I turned my hands back to front again and again, inspecting my shining body.

"How are you feeling?" Adam asked, as I steadied myself against the cave wall.

I couldn't respond. I couldn't stop looking at my skin, light emanating from every pore.

"She's in shock, but she doesn't appear to be damaged," Andrew surmised.

"What should we do with her?" Corey asked. "She can't stay down here, right? I mean, it will be morning in a few hours. How are we going to explain her absence again?" His worry hung in the air as he voiced what everyone was thinking.

Everyone but me.

"Again?" I asked carefully. What was that supposed to mean?

Instead of answering me, Adam spoke to Suzanne. "Get my uncle. Tell him we need him now," he commanded.

She began to leave, then turned back to ask, "What if he won't come?"

"Tell him what's going on, he'll come. Go."

Suzanne hunched down to get through the hole connecting this cavern to Samuel's lair.

Adam called after her, "Get Echo, too."

She disappeared from view, yet I still felt her clearly. I sensed her pass through Samuel's room.

As she moved out into the tunnel, I was assailed by her sudden change in mood.

Why is he here? I'm so glad to see him. How did I leave? How is it possible I love him more? He's looking at me. Is he going to talk to me? Touch me? Suzanne's internal chatter rushed through my mind, my pulse taking off to match hers.

A weeks-old memory bloomed in her mind. She was on set, falling apart with worry on the inside, but stone-cold on the outside. Today the humiliation would be complete. Today she had to kiss Finn on set. Not just kiss. They would have to make out, on camera.

She was kicking herself for agreeing to this. More evidence she was a glutton for punishment. His words from the day before hung in her head. "I bet this is the first time for you. Not for me," he'd said matter-of-factly, as Suzanne reluctantly got out of her chair to block the scene. "We're professionals. Just pretend I'm someone else. That's what I usually do."

Just pretend I'm someone else. That's what I usually do reverberated in her skull. *He's over me. He doesn't want me. Maybe he never did.*

Suzanne's despair was thick. When they'd blocked the scene, they'd touched as little as possible. But today. Today they'd be all over each other.

Suzanne said her lines. The moment arrived. She took his hand, fire shooting up her arm as she gave up, committing to the moment.

Finn's touch was almost painful. She hated how much she wanted it. How hollow she'd been these past years. They held each other, his arms around her waist, his fingers curved at that familiar spot in her back, bringing to Suzanne's mind memories of intensely private moments between the two of them.

I felt it when she was jerked from these memories by Finn's voice in the cave now, dragging her to the present.

"What happened to you?" he asked.

His voice, his words, pierced her, set her heart on fire. I clutched my own heart. I had to get out of Suzanne's head. I wasn't seeing all this from the outside. I was *inside* her mind, feeling it all.

And then he touched her. I saw his unchecked reflex to reach out, pulling a twig from her hair. *Keep it together, keep it together, keep it together,* she chanted repeatedly.

I was pulled from the moment when Adam grabbed my hand. "What is it? Why are you crying?"

Why was I sobbing? My heart was breaking, squeezing painfully with hope, and breaking again at the impossibility of loving Finn. I felt it all, all the angst running through Suzanne. It was too much.

I clutched my head. "Make it stop!"

"What, what's happening?" Corey held my shoulders, searching my face.

"I can't take it. Please! It's so awful!"

I was in Suzanne's head. Her past and her present, I was living it. All her memories, all she'd done. What'd been done to her.

"No!" I screamed. So much pain. Losing her family. The assaults she'd suffered when she lived on the street. The people she'd hunted and killed – the looks on their faces. Every time, a piece of her soul gone. Her desperation and despair. The hope that bloomed in her when she met Finn. Imploding, as she decided to leave him and the Fourth.

"I don't know what's happening," Adam said helplessly, crouched down, arms encircling me.

And then his mind hit me. Two minds spewing forth, open to me, and I couldn't stop it. All of Suzanne's past was still pressing in when Adam's opened to me. His memories of death, malice, desire, murder, torture.

"Do something!" Corey yelled.

155

Now Corey's mind was bearing down on me too.

I was being buried. Crushed

I couldn't stop screaming. It seemed the only way to tune it out or slow it down.

Please, please, let me die. Please.

Barely conscious, I felt Adam loosen his grip. This was it. I was dying. Finally, finally. My mind had fractured.

"Peace to you," a new voice said, adding to the noise in my mind.

I could not take one more person in my head. *No more, please! No more.*

"Peace to you," she said again.

I could feel her hand on my back. Her words were worming into my head, finding the center of my thoughts, soaking up the other voices.

She said nothing else, but left her hand on my back. It felt like she was siphoning poison from my veins, clearing it out. I'd felt energy transfer before, taking from Adam or pushing it out of my system. This had a similar quality, but there were images in tandem with the clearing. The quiet solitude of an ancient forest, cut through by a softly bubbling wide stream came to my mind, helping me unclench my teeth. I felt a calm redirection, the knowledge that this place was not meant for me. Now I was on the beach at sunset. The waves crashing rhythmically, my heart finding their music and falling in line.

The screaming, the unending pain receded. I didn't move, afraid she'd take her hand away. Afraid the voices and memories would rush back. I couldn't withstand a second assault.

I held still. If I didn't move, maybe she'd stay. If I didn't move, didn't think, maybe they couldn't find me.

"Thank you," Andrew said from somewhere behind me.

No, no, not his thoughts too! I'd just been washed clean. I didn't want to see what he'd seen. What he'd done.

"Peace," she whispered one more time.

"Please don't go," I breathed to my angel.

"You are safe. It's okay. No one here will hurt you."

Silence descended on the party in the cave.

It was hard to push past the feeling from my rescuer, so I decided to rest in her. To trust her. As my muscles relaxed, I realized who was holding me. It was Lizzy.

Chapter Thirty-Four

My head was clearing, the pain dulled. Lizzy's arms were still encircling me, and I didn't want her to leave. She gave me the telltale sign of the extra squeeze before she let go.

"You're going to be okay. Peace," she murmured, stroking my hair.

I opened my eyes to see everyone staring at us. My mind scrambled to catch up. I had so many questions. Where to start?

"How...how are you here?" I slowly unfurled, hoping she wouldn't leave my side.

"Andrew," she answered unhelpfully.

I couldn't help but return her radiant smile. I wanted to thank her, but I was stuck on the impossibility of her being here. Didn't she live in California, some two thousand miles away?

"But how are you here?" I repeated.

She sighed, letting her hand drop from my back. Her smile faded, replaced with a pensive expression.

"Anna, no questions please," Andrew said firmly.

I looked around. I didn't want to feel out, afraid of what I might find.

Suzanne was back, sitting on the large rock just a few feet away. Andrew and Corey were gathered near me and Lizzy, looking strained. Adam sat beside me, ashen faced.

"I'm sorry," I mumbled, involuntarily stretching. I caught sight of my arms. They looked normal. No glow!

"Look!" I exclaimed, turning my hands over. "It's gone!"

"Let's get her to her room," Corey said as I tried to hide a yawn.

I was all kinds of tired. My body ached, my mind numb and as empty as my stomach. Looking at Adam, my stomach dropped.

"What's wrong?" I asked, responding to his taut muscles, not his mind. I didn't have the courage to test the room.

"I'm sorry, but I really must go," Lizzy said, gently placing her hand on my back again, sending a soothing sensation through my bones.

"Already?" The ache in Andrew's voice was palpable.

"I'll be missed. But I'll check back soon," she assured him. Then she turned to me. "You're going to be okay."

Was I?

"You're going to be okay," she repeated. "Peace to you."

Lizzy got to her feet and stretched. She looked different from the last time I had seen her. There were deep, dark rings under her eyes.

"Andrew, may I speak with you for a moment?" she asked.

They walked to the entrance of the secret cave. I had a strange sensation as I watched them. They shared something in common I'd never seen before, as if they were cut from the same cloth. His large frame and fair complexion were accentuated by her slender, petite build and olive skin. But their movements, their mannerisms, were mirrored. Not from some false mimicry, but what would naturally develop if you lived a lifetime with someone.

Their brief but solemn conversation ended with a laugh, Lizzy pulling him into a hug.

And then she was gone. So fast I couldn't believe my eyes.

Andrew walked back to our small group with a renewed confidence.

No one spoke for what seemed like an eternity. Of course, it was Corey who finally addressed the elephant in the room.

"What was *that*?"

I realized Corey and Suzanne had never met Lizzy before. I'd only met her once, and it had been an intense experience. I didn't know what she was, but she wasn't from the Families, and she definitely wasn't bad. She felt like sunshine. Goodness incarnate. Whatever they were, she and Andrew were the same.

"There are some things that must be accepted," Andrew replied.

"That was Lizzy," I added helpfully.

"That was Lizzy?" Corey repeated, shocked. "You mean, the one that dumped you?" Corey said, staring at Andrew.

Much to Andrew's credit, he didn't bark back or even glare at him.

"That's not accurate," he replied tightly.

"She's his sister," I added helpfully.

Andrew whipped his head around, "Enough," he commanded.

I was caught off guard by his sudden hostility. But before I could get my feathers ruffled, he apologized, hanging his head.

Sometimes Andrew shifted so quickly, it was hard to keep up. I didn't want his moods to scare me, but they did. He was unstable in a way that Lizzy categorically wasn't.

"This falls under the promise you made to me. Do you understand?" He said, staring us down.

Suzanne and Corey bobbed their heads in consent, but I could feel Adam's reluctance.

"We will do our best," Adam carefully responded.

I knew why he, we, couldn't absolutely agree to silence on what had just happened. Mr. Seacrest would demand a full account.

"Mr. Seacrest!" I yelled, my hands covering my mouth.

Chapter Thirty-Five

I jumped to my feet a little too quickly. Adam caught me before I toppled over.

"What is it?" Adam squinted, looking into the darkest corners of the cave.

"Where is he?" I asked, trying not to panic.

The images of Iris's watery grave came crashing back. Had it worked? Were the original Family members dead? They must be, or wouldn't he be here?

"He was here when I went in the water," I continued. "Where did he go? Why isn't he here?" Maybe his unnaturally old body had just…disintegrated? And what of the others, like Echo….

"Echo? Where is he?" My heart was pounding. What had I done? Had I killed him too?

"Stop it! Anna, calm down," Adam shouted.

"What's that on her cheek?" Suzanne gasped. "Her chest. It's happening again!"

The room was steadily growing brighter. I looked down to see I was the cause. The light was emanating from me.

Adam closed the space between us. I was mesmerized by the wild glow, growing in intensity, as were the thoughts and memories of those in the cave. I couldn't focus on him, and he knew it.

"Anna," he whispered, gently caressing my cheek. "Please look at me."

I looked into his eyes but was distracted by his face brightening as my increasing light bounced off his skin. What could he do to help me? Any minute now the floodgates would open, and I'd be on the floor writhing in unbearable pain.

The look of helplessness on his face tore open my heart. "You can do this, Anna. You are strong."

Shaking my head, I heard Iris's voice in my head. Soft, at first. Fuzzy. I saw her asking a question. I saw myself saying yes. But what was the question again? What had I said yes to?

The incessant noise of the others' minds was growing. I concentrated on Adam. I held on to the heat radiating from his body as an anchor. I closed my eyes and looked for space. Was there space in this tidal wave of memories? Could I find my own?

I tried to picture Iris. What did she look like again? I was distracted by the terror coming from all directions. I couldn't concentrate.

The minds in the cave were completely open to me, pouring forth all they'd done, seen, and felt. Through gritted teeth I cried, "Get out! As far away as possible!"

I got no resistance from Corey and Suzanne, only the sound of their retreat and the panic in their minds.

That was better. The further they went, the easier it was to tune them out. Now I only had to deal with two. But two was too much.

My mind was being battered with his terror and dark deeds. They were just memories for him, but it was fresh for me. As if they were happening right now.

"Adam, you too."

His anger hit me. His resistance was crushing. But he quickly retreated, fleeing as fast as he could. I didn't want him to go, so I followed him. The longer I watched him, the deeper his past deeds sank into my mind. Into my memory forever.

Stop, I said to myself, letting him leave.

Only Andrew remained. I felt my muscles loosen, most of the pain receding once I let go of Adam. But it was still there. Andrew was able to close off his mind like the others couldn't. But the closer he came, the more I felt a dam was about to break. When he touched my shoulder, I was flooded by his mind.

The images of his life rushed over me. At first it was like a toxin, but soon the noxious river of memories changed to clean, clear waters. A life-giving spring. I couldn't look away. To see what he had seen, what he'd done. Who he'd been.

"Peace," he breathed, pulling his arm away, stopping the flow of images.

"I...I don't understand. How is that even possible?" I asked, struggling to absorb the knowledge of what he really was, had been. And what Lizzy and the rest of his family still were.

"What did you see?" he asked gently, as if I hadn't completely invaded his privacy. His most inner self.

"Beauty. I saw beauty itself."

All the vile images and memories that had assaulted me were nothing next to the vision he'd shared.

"I am glad for you. Beauty will redeem the world," he replied with such assurance. I finally understood what he meant. How he could know this. And that he was right.

I sat down on the giant rock, and he joined me.

"You're not glowing anymore," he noted.

I looked down to confirm. Silence filled the cavern. I was glad for it. I'd had too much noise.

I focused on my breathing, keeping my senses tightly reined in. I didn't hear anything coming from Andrew, which was my normal around him. It was good to be back to my normal insane situation.

"Do you know about what's happening? What's happened to me?" I asked, breaking the silence.

"No." I thought he was done, but he added. "Would you like to tell me what happened?"

I wasn't sure which "happening" he was asking about, but I was sure I couldn't explain anything that had happened anyway.

Seeing my befuddled expression, he clarified. "Your wrist. What happened here?" he asked, lightly touching it.

His small touch sent memories shooting through me. Dark memories of bottomless loss. I doubled over, tears flowing for the depths of his despair. How could he function, living with such loss?

"I'm so, so sorry. I didn't know. I just can't believe it," I sobbed, rocking to cope with the pain.

Andrew sat stoically beside me. "I'm sorry for whatever you saw."

He was sorry for me? I would never look at him the same again. Compassion and admiration for his loss and progress filled me, helping me to right myself.

"I'm sorry. I didn't mean to see. Didn't mean to intrude." I couldn't bring myself to verbalize what I'd witnessed. His fall from grace. His banishment. His darkest moments afterwards.

"It's not your fault."

"But why did I see that and not all the good?" I wondered. When I'd first seen his memories, I'd been immersed in his awful encounter with Katie. But what had flowed from him after that blackness was pure light. The utter contentedness of his past life.

"I don't know." He looked pensive, struggling for answers. "It could be, as I have found, that the bad is drawn out first and then the good comes. Like sucking out the snake

165

venom to cleanse the blood or removing the vice to allow for the virtue."

I turned over his explanation. But what was I going to do if the mere touch of another sent me their darkest deeds and vilest thoughts?

Forget their touch. I didn't think I could even be in the presence of anyone whose mind wasn't as strong as Andrew's. No one else in my life fit that description.

Before I could rabbit hole down that avenue of despair, Andrew drew my attention back to his original question.

Pointing this time. Decidedly not touching, he asked again, "Your wrist. Will you tell me about it?"

The mention of my wrist recalled the fire of its burning. Where the bracelet had melted into my skin were surely fourth degree burns. The angry red tissue looked destroyed, but I felt nothing when I gingerly touched it. How had I, or anyone else, not noticed my mangled arm?

"I was in Iris's tomb. She had a bracelet. The Serpent Star?"

Andrew surprised me by nodding.

"Do you know it?" I gasped, completely incredulous.

"Yes. It should not have been used for evil," he replied. He continued, answering my unspoken question, "It was the artifact used in the turning ceremony."

And then he smiled at me. "Well done. You did it, Anna. You broke the curse."

"I did?" I asked, hope filling my heart. "I really did?"

"Nature always finds a way to restore balance. There is always a way to bring about justice. Soon after the curse, the cure was made. The old medicine man, with the help of his new tribe, made the object from the earth. All pure elements.

166

"The medicine man sought out ancestors from the Families to see if he could use the power of the past to set the future free. That's why he settled with them and they took on his name. He was the Seer in his tribe. And yet, as happens in this world as it is now, the instrument chosen for redemption was turned to one of annihilation. The Seers, at first protectors of it, were seduced by the possibility of using its power for themselves. Seer is an ironic moniker, since they really are blind to what they do. While it could bring an end to the immortality the Four Families were cursed with, the Seers turned the power around, twisting it.

"But what they could not see was their undoing. By linking the Leviathans with the stones, they set themselves up for death if the artifact were destroyed. In their hubris, they believed they could outwit nature. They never considered the possibility that they hadn't controlled the path nature had made as a means for redemption.

"And so, to destroy Serpent Star is to destroy the Leviathan Immortals and the Families. Which you have done."

His tone turned bright at the end. He sounded so bright as he told me I was a murderer.

Chapter Thirty-Six

"I killed all of those people?" I was trying not to hyperventilate.

"You cannot kill what is already dead," Andrew replied.

"Please. In plain English? I don't understand."

"Unnatural long life is stolen. All are called to account. You were the means by which nature meted out justice, nothing more."

I shook my head. "I was the means of their death."

"You did them all a great mercy. You set them free."

"I don't think they'd see it that way," I said skeptically. "Nor their loved ones." I was beginning to really see what I'd done.

"Does the sinner believe he has sinned? Does he think he deserves to be punished? Independent of his selfish definition of justice and what he is owed, truth will out. You simply were the instrument of grace to bring it about. For them and the rightly living."

"Rightly?"

"The Immortals are thieves. The Families were cursed. You chose justice. You were chosen for justice. Either with your natural death or with you destroying the Serpent Star."

While he had admiration in his voice, I felt awful. Used, even. "You mean, I was fated to bring about the death of Mr. Seacrest? Someone I love?"

"No, no," he said calmly, reacting to my shifting mood. "It doesn't work that way. You could have said no. There is always a choice for the living."

His words knocked loose the memory of Iris's repeated question to me, and I finally understood.

"Iris kept asking me, 'Can you suffer it.' I thought I could. I thought 'it' meant being the cause of death to the Families in exchange for setting her free and breaking the Family curse. But it's more than that. I...it doesn't look like I can be around anyone. Not without glowing and going mad."

My vision blurred as a new wave of pain began to swell, spreading steadily from my heart to all parts of my body. I couldn't think anymore. Couldn't hear what Andrew was saying. His past invaded my mind, slamming me hard. I had to get out of here.

I blinked.

I stood looking out into the starless night sky, the crash of the waves drowning out the noise in my head.

This stretch of beach was different. I turned around to get my bearings. I was in Oceanside, not too far south from Huntington, but a very different beach. Desolate.

Gazing at the emptiness in the horizon where water and sky met, I wondered if a void like that could ever be filled. Or was it like a black hole, a bottomless pit?

I felt bottomless, and empty. The choices I'd made had led to a life I wasn't sure I could handle. How could I cope with exile? I clearly couldn't be around people anymore. I was strong, but not strong enough to live through one more person's darkest memory. I would start screaming and never stop. It would break me.

I involuntarily flinched as I relived the images of Suzanne's past. My mind flicked to Adam killing an older man. I knew it had been self-defense, but I felt the savagery and adrenaline of the kill. How could I look at him again?

No. I would not see him, or any of them.

I was cheered with the thought that not seeing them meant not knowing what I'd done. Who was dead or dying

169

because of me? I wouldn't have to face Adam or Finn. I wouldn't have to face the loss of Echo and Mr. Seacrest, if I weren't around. I had no first-hand evidence they were even dead! So, as far as I knew, everyone was fine.

They'd miss me, but they would be grateful I was gone. No one, and I mean no one, would want me around, drawing out and witnessing their vile deeds. Devastatingly for us both, as I lived in those past moments, I drew it to the foreground of their minds as well. Misery might love company, but shame does not.

Sitting on the beach, not willing to take my eyes off the horizon, I made my plans for isolation. For once, I felt some gratitude for my power; I'd get along just fine. I'd find a place to live and food, I'd be safe from anyone who wanted to harm me. I could spend the rest of my life looking out to sea and reading.

Not such a bad fate.

I lay back on the cool sand, willing the overcast sky to clear so I could see the moon I loved so much.

Heavy with fatigue, I closed my eyes.

Lying on the beach, lulled by the crashing waves, I willed sleep.

Chapter Thirty-Seven

Sleep didn't come.

I lay there hoping to fall asleep until dawn was on the horizon. I gave up in frustration. Why was sleep eluding me? One of the first lessons from Mr. Seacrest was how to fall asleep on command. One of the only tricks I'd mastered. Or so I'd thought.

Sleep wouldn't have me. I'd been outside all night, but despite the dampness, I wasn't cold. The angry wounds on my wrist radiated heat. It was a testament to the pain in my head that I hadn't been bothered by the festering blisters ringing my wrist. I didn't mind the physical ache. It was a welcome reprieve from the psychic one.

About to give up and decide my next move, I felt her by my side.

"Would you like to talk?" my angel asked.

Lizzy was standing over me, looking out of place in a blue satin Georgian gown. She wore a giant wig with a bird cage set in the middle.

"You look..."

"Crazy?" she finished with a smile.

"Surreal," I breathed, sitting up, brushing some of the sand from my arms. "How did you find me?"

She cocked her head to the side. "Andrew's worried about you, and so am I."

"Thank you. Because of you, I'm alive. I would've certainly, literally, lost my mind if you hadn't helped me."

"I'm thankful I could help."

It was easier to think clearly with her sitting next to me, lifting the haze from my brain. But I knew it was temporary. She'd leave soon. "You did help. Now, I think, it's up to me. I just have to find it in myself to bear the consequences of what I've done."

She smiled, nodding. "Yes, you do. But not as you think."

"What do you mean?"

"We are made for community. Real community, Anna. I think you are plotting a self-imposed exile. Yes?"

"It's not like I want to leave, but I know I can't stay," I said. "Not only for them, but for me. If reliving their memories didn't drive me insane, the overload of all of it would kill me. I mean it. It would physically kill me."

"I'm so sorry you went through that. I've seen much heartache in my time, but I don't think many could withstand what you've been through. And no one should have to."

I shook my head, trying to keep the images at bay. No one would ever know what this was like. Yet another form of isolation and alienation.

Lizzy hung her head. "I may not know what it was like for you, but I know what it was like for me. That was one of the hardest things I've ever done."

I could hear the tears in her voice.

She raised her head, so our eyes met. And that's when I saw it. What I'd done to her. The harm I'd caused her. In the cave, when she'd touched me, it had felt like she was pulling out the venom from my system. Cleaning me out. I hadn't thought about where it was going. I guess I imagined it was being dumped into the earth, like when I get rid of excess energy. But it hadn't. It had passed right into Lizzy. She had seen and felt what I'd seen and felt.

"I'm so sorry!" The tears flowed. From both of us.

It took her a moment to gain her composure. "You have absolutely nothing to apologize for. I freely decided to help you."

172

But I was too angry with myself to be consoled by her words. There was no one I would not hurt. There was no good left in the world that would be spared when it met me. Now I was the curse!

"Anna, I can help you. Will you let me?"

I instinctively recoiled. I knew what she would say. She would tell me I wasn't a bad person. She would tell me that I was not a murderer, a torturer. That I deserved to show myself the same kindness and generosity I extended to others. I did not want to hear it. But before I answered, I looked out to the sea. Out to the horizon, which last night had been a black void of nothingness. But this morning, it was bright, beautiful, and limitless. Full of possibilities. Even for me.

"I will try."

"Thank you. Close your eyes," she said, taking my hand.

I yanked it back. It seemed she needed to touch me to help me, but I wouldn't harm her anymore.

"Shhh," she said, taking my hand again. Reluctantly, I let her hold it.

I breathed out and relaxed my shoulders. I trusted Lizzy. I would listen as best I could.

"I have lived a long life," she began calmly. "My relationship with time is different than yours, so I experience all things within a different frame of reference. Do you remember when you were a child, waiting on your parents to take you to the store or to go to a friend's house? Do you remember how frustratingly long it took them to get ready? You wanted it now. Why were they so slow?

"Yet when you're in the midst of an awful event, like what happened yesterday, it feels like that's all there is. It will never end and what's happened will define everything forever. But I don't experience time that way. For me, each moment is both fleeting and eternal."

"You mean, you forget?" I asked.

"I forget nothing. I hold all that's happened in my life. The things that I have to face work to shape my character and refine my understanding. Though they may be beyond my control, they do not decide who or what I am, or how I respond. Only I can do that. I make the choice. Every day. I'm blessed to see the moment for what it is. Just a moment. This makes the sweet things sweeter and the horrific tolerable. The events come and go, yet I remain."

A glimmer of hope appeared. "Are you telling me to let go of what happened?" I asked. "I certainly would if I could. But even if it were possible, it doesn't solve my problem. As soon as I'm around anyone other than you, it'll start all over again. And even if I could learn to tolerate the pain," I shuddered at the thought, "I'd still be inflicting it on others. Making them relive the worst moments of their lives."

Lizzy listened, not dismissing what I was saying. "I know what caused that," she said, eyeing my wrist. "I also know how to help you. That's why I'm here. Will you let me?"

"Please," I whispered, wondering if there really was a way.

"First, I want to relieve you of any guilt you feel towards me. I am well acquainted with pain, but it passes, see?" she said, pushing up her long satin and lace sleeve, revealing faint traces of weeks-old bruises.

I didn't know what that meant, but I understood that she was telling me I hadn't damaged her as much as I'd imagined.

She continued. "Long ago, Andrew and I, along with a few of my brothers and sisters, were working on the

174

Continent. We knew of the slaughter. We saw the price of the curse. We learned of the cure, the Fifth, which was a great relief to me."

Lizzy paused, lightly touching the blisters on my wrist. "This was not supposed to happen. The pure fulfillment of your purpose, the reconciliation of the Families, shouldn't have done this to you. But this artifact, the Serpent Star, was made, linking you to it. It is inevitable the consequences would be grave, as it is for all who deal in evil artifacts."

The memory of Mr. Seacrest's library popped into my head. The crystal-clear call of the hexed silver comb and my desire to use it, even now had I the chance, sent a shiver down my spine. He had it because people needed to be protected from it. And there was no way to destroy it.

I was like a living version of his library. I would house the bracelet. It wouldn't hurt anyone anymore. But I could, its power radiating through me.

"Did the Leviathan know about the link between me and the bracelet?" I asked.

"I doubt it. Evil deceives evil in countless ways," Lizzy explained. "Even self-deception through denial or willful ignorance. But all know that justice will be served, that there is no workaround. Their greed for immortality may have blinded them to the risks of what they did, the link between the cure and the artifact."

"So, Dom and Emma weren't looking for me specifically?" I asked in bewilderment. "And, let me get this straight, it's just a coincidence that I, the cure, linked to Serpent Star, happened to end up where it was buried?"

"Any explanation I tried to give you would be conjecture. Who can pretend to understand how the future unfolds, how it is nudged by our choices and actions? Yet now that it is behind us, I see it clearly. Don't you? The honor bestowed on you to be the end of so much suffering and grief? In one act, you ended the Family curse and freed Iris, Helen, Marie, and the Leviathan Immortals!"

I had to know, even though I didn't want to. "Can you tell me what happened? What I caused? Who's dead?"

"I would if I knew. I'm sorry. I'm in the middle of something I've been working on for a long time," she indicated her costume, "and haven't had the chance to check in with Andrew."

Maybe it was for the best. A sign I should stick with my original plan of ignorant bliss. It didn't really matter; I wasn't going back.

"Thank you for checking in on me." Her presence had been a reprieve, a breath of fresh, clean air. "Please tell Andrew I'm fine. Also, will you ask him to tell Adam that I'll get in touch when I can?" Could I call him? Would the sound of his voice bring back the agony?

"You misunderstand why I'm here," Lizzy said sympathetically. "You need to go back."

I stared at her in confusion. Go back? Had she not listened to a word I'd said? Of course I didn't want to be here alone, without my friends, without Adam. But what other practical choice did I have? They couldn't be around me either, it was harmful to all of us.

"Anna, will you let me do something for you?"

"What do you have in mind?" I eyed her skeptically.

"First, I think it's really important for you to go back," she urged gently. "There is still more for you to do."

"Can you see the future?" I asked.

"No. I've never met a person who can. The future is not a set, unchangeable thing."

"Oh," I said lamely, mulling over one more piece of evidence that I was a freak.

"Oh," she replied, surprised in turn. "Can you?"

"Only in small bits. Unhelpful stuff when I do."

"Curious," she paused, thinking that over. "Well, no, I can't see the future, but Andrew says you need to go back, and I trust him. He knows more about your situation than I. And I can help you do it, but it won't be without pain."

"Pain for who?"

"Mostly you, I'm afraid."

"Tell me," I said desperately. The thought of being back with my people, my new family, was overwhelming.

"I'm going to heal your wrist, partly, by taking the inflammation away. Before you protest, I'm going to put this on it."

From her sequined clutch she produced a gold and black enameled compact. Opening it, she swiped her thumb over the clear gel ointment inside and spread it over my wrist.

The smell of charred flesh wafted through the air, overpowering the saltwater tang I'd grown used to. I watched as the dull fire in my wrist began to recede, the oozing flesh drying.

She looked up at me as I marveled at her miracle cure. "My sister made this for you. It's organic. That's all. I told you nature finds balance."

My wrist held no trace of the burn. But the bracelet was still there, embedded like a white tattoo, noticeable only if you were paying attention. And if you really looked, you could see the band was a snake. The tiny, embedded gemstones looked like scales. When the sun caught my arm at just the right angle, you could see the refraction.

I rubbed my wrist. I would never be free of this bracelet I now wore. It felt more like it wore me. The power pulsing through me was palpable.

The unmistakable scent of roses flooded my already overwhelmed senses, replacing the sour stench of char from a moment before. There were no rosebushes on the beach. I idly wondered if I were having a stroke. "Do you smell roses?" I asked hesitantly.

"I believe it's coming from you," Lizzy answered. "It's lovely, isn't it?"

"No," I shook my head incredulously, raising my arm to smell. "It is! How wonderfully strange." I was having a hard time accepting this latest development…until I asked myself if a supernatural smell was really any stranger than anything else that had happened to me over the last year. Besides, I loved roses.

"It is permanent, yes? All of it?" I asked.

"Serpent Star? I believe so," Lizzy answered, "though I don't know if it will fade with time. I'm sure the aroma is tied to it. Does it bother you?"

"If I were going to get something like a tattoo, I would've preferred to be asked first and then chosen what and where to place it," I said, unable to take my eyes off the permanent adornment. But then, maybe I had said yes. When I'd told Iris I could handle it.

I turned back to Lizzy. She was here, helping me, from sheer goodness. "Thank you for this. I feel much better."

"Do you?" she said happily. "I was hoping it would settle you."

She pulled her phone out of her clutch and answered it. "Hello? Yes. I think so. Okay, okay," she said, pensively. "I can start it, but you'll need to help. I know you can."

I knew she was talking to Andrew, but I couldn't grasp his part of the conversation. Which felt weird. I could usually gather what was being said if I but heard the outlines of someone's voice, even one step removed, like through a phone.

She hung up and took both of my hands. "I'm sorry I can't be fully present for you right now. But I'm going to help you begin, and then you'll need to go back."

I shook my head. I wasn't going back, I couldn't.

"Please trust me. I don't know everything that is troubling you, but I think I can relieve you of at least one major source of stress. I believe your current condition, being assaulted by the memories and thoughts of others, is temporary. A side effect. I suspect that it will drain out of your system, that you can even move the process along faster by intentionally touching someone."

My exile gone as quickly as it came. I couldn't believe what she was saying! So why wasn't she happier?

"But," I guessed, "it might happen again."

"I wouldn't rule out the possibility, but I think not. I really believe that part's just about over," she said, her eyes full of compassion. "I wish this burden wasn't yours to bear, but it is."

She was telling me I didn't have to leave my friends and family and live in isolation. So, whatever was making her look so sad for me must be really bad. "What?" I whispered, my stomach churning with acid. I knew whatever she was about to tell me would change my life forever.

"They should've never been mined," Lizzy said cryptically. "They should've been left. But just like Pandora's Box, once opened, it cannot be closed."

"What is it?" I began to tremble. I was just so tired; it was hard to think.

"The truth is hard. There's no easy way to tell you. But you are not alone. We will help you. Andrew, amazingly, has had experience with this before. He'll help you. I know you'll survive it."

I went absolutely still. Her words hung in the air between us. *Survive what?*

Chapter Thirty-Eight

Lizzy decided I should have Andrew and Adam with me for support. She called ahead to ask them to meet us, then took my hand.

The landscape shifted and we were in my room in Gold Manor.

My bed called to me. I wanted almost nothing more than to hit my pillow and let sweet sleep wash over me. The one thing I wanted more than that was to throw my arms around Adam. But I was afraid of what would happen if I touched him. He made no move towards me. His feet were glued to the floor, as far away from me as possible in my tiny room, his fists clenched.

"Nice to see you again," Lizzy greeted Adam. "I wish it was under happier circumstances."

"I am forever in your debt," he bowed.

He hadn't looked at me. He'd glanced in my direction but had not yet really looked at me.

Lizzy and I sat on my bed, Adam leaning uneasily against the door. Andrew sat in the desk chair to my right.

"There are a few, who…" Lizzy paused, looking into the distance, trying to be careful with her words, "who don't sleep."

"Vampires," I whispered.

"No." Her smile lit her eyes. But it didn't last. "No, nothing like that. Once these people reach a certain age, the sleeplessness kicks in. If they can't work through it and find a way to cope with their inability to sleep, they die. Do you know much about the biology of sleep and the effects of sleep deprivation?"

I shook my head. "Am I one of these people, too?" How many parts supernatural could I be?

"No, you're not. But you have been caught up in their story. If the Leviathan had not used the stones to make them what they are, you would not share in the sleepless ones plight. But stories are constantly being woven together. You are truly blessed," she smiled at me, taking my hand as a happy memory trickled out of her and into my mind.

"Those stones," she continued, pointing at my wrist, "have many powerful properties, which is why they were chosen and used by the Leviathan. One of their best uses is to help these ones who can't sleep adjust to their new reality. Unfortunately, whoever, regardless of who they are, ingests one of these stones, becomes incapable of sleep. Anna, you will never sleep again."

"What?" Adam shook his head, incredulous. "That's not possible. If you don't sleep, you die."

"The stones have a quality such that they help those who can make the transition," Lizzy explained calmly. "Anna's artifact, the Serpent Star, has dozens of the stones."

"Dozens!" Andrew exclaimed. "I can't believe it didn't kill her."

Lizzy and Andrew looked at each other, some memory passing between them.

"Anna," she returned her attention to me, "you are making the shift. Since you've already absorbed the gems without harm, I have little doubt you'll make it. But you still have a difficult process to go through."

Lizzy laid it out, as best she knew. I would never sleep again. If I couldn't adapt to sleeplessness, if my body couldn't adjust, my brain and organs would break down, little by little. It would eventually be fatal. I'd already been awake for more than twenty-four hours. Around the seventy-two-hour mark, I would either be out of danger, or showing the first signs of brain degeneration as hallucinations began. If I couldn't find a way to deal with what the stones did to me, not even my Fifth abilities could save me.

Grabbing my attention with her intense stare, she emphasized the necessity to stay awake. "Remember, if you fall asleep, you won't wake. It's crucial you don't succumb to your desire to sleep. You must fight it. If you don't, your body will shut down." Lizzy stopped for a moment, slightly relaxing. "I wish you had a different fate. It is hard."

"I will help you," Andrew promised.

But what I heard above all was Adam's silence.

"You are in the best of hands," Lizzy said, hugging me. "If you need me, let me know," she said to Andrew.

The somber mood in the room dimmed further when she departed. It felt like a lightbulb had burned out, and we were left in the dark and cold, even though the bright morning sun streamed through the window.

"If you'll excuse me," Adam said out loud, but to no one in particular.

I watched him make his quick escape without so much as a glance at me. I didn't know what to say or think. I felt completely stripped, shredded from the inside.

Andrew approached. "This is my choice, Anna. My gift to you," he said, placing his hand on my wrist.

Immediately his mind was ripped open. I felt not only intense physical pain, like being stabbed repeatedly with a sharp knife, but any distance between us as two separate people was completely obliterated, his mind laid bare to me.

Light shot from every pore in my body, throwing Andrew across the room, the plaster cracking as he hit the wall.

And then it was over. At least, the light coming from my body and the physical pain ceased.

"Why did you do that?" I screamed, holding my head, needing to purge the memory I'd just lived through with Andrew. But I couldn't. It had been a gut-wrenching scene of the day he'd been severed from his family, Lizzy at the center of it all.

I had to get out of there. I couldn't take anymore.

"Stop!" Andrew commanded, halting me in my tracks. "That was the last of it. Lizzy thought you had a bit left. It's gone now. This won't happen to you again."

I gripped my sides, willing myself to stay together. Feeling what he'd done and suffered, the utter despair of rejection...how could a person survive it?

"Why?" I looked up through my blurry eyes.

"I wanted you to know there is nothing you can't come back from."

Adam burst through the door, Suzanne on his heels.

Chapter Thirty-Nine

Quickly appraising the room, he cut into Andrew, "What did you do to her?" Adam was livid, ready to fight. And though I would've never thought so before, I wondered if maybe Adam could take Andrew once the fists were flying.

"Stand down!" Andrew spat back, caught off guard by Adam's fury and struggling to reign in his own usually tightly controlled feelings.

Suzanne stood shoulder to shoulder with Adam, ready for his command.

"No. Stop it," I rasped, still trying to catch my breath after living through Andrew's nightmare.

"Tell me what's going on," Adam seethed through gritted teeth.

But before I could explain, Echo appeared in the doorway.

I melted to the floor, sobbing. I couldn't believe he was here. Alive. It was too much. I was fracturing.

Adam crossed the space and dropped to my side, his rage at Andrew forgotten. He nearly put his arms around me, but let them fall to his side instead.

I threw my hands over my face. My brain fought to process all that was happening. Adam wouldn't touch me. Echo was alive. Andrew's shared trauma. And my new fate. A sleepless existence, *if* I made it through the change.

I wanted to run, scream, fall into oblivion; but there was no going anywhere. What was left for me, of me, was here, in this moment, in this room.

Suzanne broke her warrior stance. I could feel her relaxing, her breathing returning to normal. Then Echo calmed, followed by Andrew.

Adam was beside himself, arms twisted tightly across his chest. "Echo, you stay with her," he said, rushing off as quickly as he had come, taking Suzanne with him.

I couldn't believe he'd left me, a puddle on the floor.

"I'll be in the lounge. Don't let her sleep, no matter what," Andrew said to Echo. "If you have any trouble, or if anything happens, don't hesitate to get me. Understand?"

Now it was just Echo and me.

Echo. I hadn't realized just how integral he had become to my life. Until I'd thought he was gone, I hadn't realized how much I loved him. "I thought I killed you," I said through my tears.

"Nah, nothing can take me out. I'm as tough as nails and older than the dirt in this house," he joked, helping me up from the floor, seating me on the bed.

I hugged him tightly. It took a beat for him to reciprocate. When he did, I immediately relaxed into his arms. It was like being hugged by my dad.

All cried out for the moment, I gave him space, drawing my legs into a pretzel on the bed. "Are you really okay? I thought when the curse was broken, age would catch up to the Families."

He grinned at me, patting down his body. "Same-old, same-old. No getting rid of me that quickly."

I wanted to know more. Curiosity raged in me about what had happened to the original Family, but I couldn't go there. Not yet. What was pressing on me, making my chest so tight I was gasping for air, was Adam's response to me.

"Why is he… what did I…" I broke off, finding it impossible to ask.

"Anna, we've got your back. Whatever you need, ask," Echo encouraged me.

"Adam…" I didn't need to say more.

"Oh," he said lamely, clearly uncomfortable.

"Does he hate me?" My voice broke and my mind splintered on the word.

"I'm sorry, what? Hate you?"

There was a ringing, a pressure in my ears that made it hard to concentrate.

"I don't feel so good," I said, taking hold of his arm to steady myself. Somewhere in the back of my mind it registered that I was touching Echo and nothing abnormal was happening. No painful fireworks, no vicious assault from his memories. Just a solid mass of a person keeping me from falling over.

"Adam," he called softly, as if Adam were in the room with us.

Quicker than I would've thought possible, Adam appeared in the doorway, ashen faced.

"I'm going to leave you two," Echo said. Neither of us protested.

The click of the door set my tears rolling, my hands trembling in my lap.

Adam stood against the door, his face dark with emotions I couldn't read.

I tried desperately to understand what was going on, but my mind was littered with chaotic thoughts. "Are you angry with me?" I asked.

Images of his violent and brutal past, which I had witnessed without his consent, came to my mind unbidden. I had violated his most private, inner self, uncovering secrets he had kept even from himself. "I can never tell you how sorry I am," I said shakily.

The disgust in his eyes deepened. "No!" he bit out, closing his eyes. "You cannot do this to me. Please, have pity on me." Tears streamed down his face.

187

Slowly opening his eyes, he approached the bed. "I have no right, Anna. I cannot tell you how sick I am, how I hate myself," his voice dropped to a whisper, "for what I did to you. There is no path forward, I see that. I know you can't, shouldn't, be with me. All ends in death."

What the hell was going on? The ringing in my head was growing. Adam was falling apart in front of me, but I couldn't understand why. My brain was so foggy. So sleepy. If I took a beat, a moment to collect my thoughts, maybe I could figure it all out.

My eyes sliding shut, I let myself fall back, hoping to find my pillow. Quick as lightning, Adam caught me, holding me up right. He took my hands in his, rubbing them vigorously.

"No, no, no. No sleep for you. I'll get someone to sit with you," he said, looking over his shoulder, letting go of my hands.

"Stop it!" I screamed, grabbing him, burying my head in his chest. "Please," I whimpered. "Please hold me. I need you. I know you're angry with me, but I'm falling apart."

He didn't resist, but he also made no move to hold me. "This is too much," he whispered.

My head pressed against his chest, I tried to find his heartbeat, focusing only on that. In between sobs, I caught hold of it, steadily humming.

I studied its pattern behind my closed eyes, listening to its melody. Finding its song, I began to relax. My wayward, anxious thoughts - *Why isn't he stroking my hair? How could someone not sleep? My mom would help me. I'm glad she doesn't have to see me this way. Am I supposed to be on set?* - grew fewer and less intense.

My heart settling and my breathing controlled, I let go of him.

I took a deep breath. "Please tell me what's going on with us."

"Why are you pretending with me?" he choked out.

My heart began speeding up again, another emotional tidal wave on its way. "I'm trying to keep my head above water," I explained slowly. "It's harder when you say things like that. Since I don't know what you mean, just tell me. Plainly."

"I cannot look at you without remembering what you saw in me," he began, his voice filled with pain. "I felt you there, in all the evil I've done. The things I worked hard to forget, the stuff I've kept hidden because I can't bear to face it. It was carefully buried, but you pulled it out. I can't stop seeing it all, an endless loop, with you in the middle. How can you stand to look at me, much less touch me?" he finished, full of self-loathing.

"I love you," I said simply.

"You shouldn't," he barked.

We sat a moment in silence, each of us processing the mess in front of us. "Adam, I don't want to minimize your pain," I said hesitantly, "but aren't you being a bit...dramatic?"

"Don't you see?" He clenched his teeth, furious. "We will never be able to touch each other without those black memories coming between us. Don't try to tell me you don't see them when you look at me."

"We've been through too much for this," I managed to say through total exhaustion, fighting to keep my eyes open. "Can we talk about this later?" I heard myself slurring, losing the battle to stay conscious.

"Open your eyes!" he commanded.

I wanted to open them, to see him, but it was getting harder to swim to the surface. I heard him call frantically for Echo, who rushed back into the room.

"Let's take her for a walk," Adam said.

He stood by as Echo swung my arm over his shoulder, helping me stand. I made it to the bedroom door before wobbling.

Echo steadied me. "Can you make it?"

Surely I could walk myself down the stairs, I thought. But I was finding it hard to answer. And then I was sailing through the air, swaying, descending. Down the stairs we went, Echo carrying me, Adam and my friends following us to the ground floor.

I was jolted by their worry.

"How is she?" Corey asked worriedly, putting his hand on my head to check my temperature. "She's cold," he reported to the group.

"When's the last time she ate?" someone asked. I thought it was Finn, but I couldn't make out his face through my blurred vision.

Echo set me down at the long wooden table, drawing me to the memories of when I'd first come to Gold Manor, of when I'd first met Adam. Everyone watched me nervously, dotted around the dining room, unsure of what to do.

"Maybe some water?" I asked, looking up at Adam.

He hurried away to get it for me, but the instant he was gone, what little energy I had bottomed out. I felt them rushing anxiously around me, telling me to do something, but I couldn't make out what they wanted? *Leave me alone*, I begged in my mind.

And then I felt another slight jolt, just enough to bring me around.

"It's you, Adam. She's reacting to you," Corey surmised. "Touch her."

Everything, every word and person came to me through a thick fog. Even Adam's face, until I felt the warmth of his hand on my knee.

Another jolt.

"Drink this," he said roughly, pulling up a chair but not lifting his hand from my knee.

The throbbing in my head calmed, my vision began to clear.

"Thank you," I said to everyone, as they also took seats around the table.

Their faces made my heart ache. Corey, Suzanne, Finn, Echo, Andrew, and Adam. My little band of warriors. My protectors.

"Do you all know what's happening?" I asked the room.

"I filled them in," Andrew replied.

"What time is it?" I asked. "How much longer do I have to go?"

Lizzy had said that undergoing this change would take about three days. Surely then this unbearable heaviness from want of sleep would fall away. I wouldn't live with perpetually drooping eyelids, desperate for sleep.

"You've been awake for about sixty-four hours," Andrew informed me.

That didn't make sense. I thought I had been awake only through one night. But the sequence of events from when we'd entered the cave until now were tangled up in my mind, and I couldn't concentrate on sorting it out.

"I'm so tired." My words hung in the air.

No one said anything, no one moved. The moment seemed to extend infinitely.

Chapter Forty

"Anna," Adam called to me, squeezing my knee. "You must keep your eyes open."

I pulled them wide, blinking, trying my best to focus.

"She should know what happened," Corey said from just behind me.

"Not now," Adam bit out.

This sparked a debate between everyone at the table as to what I should know and when I should know it. Their conversation grew in intensity, erupting into a shouting match. It was just the slap I needed to make me sit up and pay attention.

Adam noticed. "Feeling better?" he asked, looking me over, trying to figure out what had roused me.

"You guys are a good distraction," I said. "I need distraction. It feels like my bones are melting and someone is rewiring my brain with a jig saw."

The sadness returned to their eyes. I was sorry I'd said anything about the pain running rampantly through my body, turning my insides to goo.

"Don't worry," I tried to comfort them. "It will be over soon, one way or the other." Based on their reactions, that was definitely the wrong thing to say. I might've been a little off my game.

"Don't talk like that," Adam said harshly, his eyes fierce. The love for me he was working to hide ripped through his façade, jolting my veins.

A bright flash of green light burst from me, filling the room and soaking up the dry ache from my bones. I straightened in my chair, renewed energy surging through me.

I shook my head at their bewilderment. "I have no idea what's happening to me," I said, as confused as the rest of the room.

"You are approaching the final stage of the shift," Andrew explained. "The closer you get, well, we should all expect some unusual occurrences. It's your body adjusting. It must find a way to replenish and renew itself since it won't get it through sleep. Anna, you can find your way," he encouraged.

The moments ticked by, uncertainty in the air.

"I think it would help me to know what's happened. Where is Uncle Seacrest?" I asked, looking around at their downturned eyes.

"He's dead, isn't he." It wasn't a question. I could feel the truth of it.

"All of the original Family are," Adam answered.

"How many?" I whispered.

Silence.

"How many did I kill?" I repeated, feeling Finn's eyes on me.

"There were seven from the Fourth, my parents among them," he said. "You did not kill them," he stated firmly, looking me dead on.

"That's too gracious," I said, looking up at him. "I'm just so sorry."

"You set my parents free," Finn answered, some complex emotion constricting his words. "They have suffered every night of their unnatural lives. Then each day they woke and made the world suffer. All are better off now they are dead," he said with conviction. "It feels wrong to say, but I am better off. I cut them out of my life years ago. I'd never been anything more to them than a piece of property, a weapon. By the time I was born, they were... hard."

193

Finn's words swirled around the room, each of us trying to understand how it would feel to be the child of ruthless murderers.

Adam spoke next, trying to absolve me. "Uncle gave his entire life for this cause. Gladly. He said fortune had smiled on him because he fulfilled his mission. He always thought his death would be by assassination. He never dreamt he'd actually get to see the end of the curse. You gave that to him," Adam said, absently rubbing my knee.

"You were with him when he died?" I asked.

"Yes. When it happened, we all felt it."

Heads bobbed in agreement around the room.

"Like a shockwave," Corey explained. "It felt like when I was shocked changing the light bulb in your room, remember? Zap!"

"Yes," I smiled.

"But this lasted a little longer, and it left me with an ache like after a super long workout. Yeah?" he glanced around the room for confirmation.

"That's kind of like what it was for me, too," Suzanne agreed.

Finn and Adam were noticeably silent. They were direct descendants of the cursed. Their silence told me it hadn't been like that for them. I suspected their experience had been much more intense.

"So, what does this all mean?" I asked. "Is the war off?"

This brought a round of chuckles.

"You have a way with words, A," Corey laughed.

Adam actually smiled. "We don't know. Too soon to tell. But this did buy us time."

"My Family has no idea how this happened," Finn said, his grin belied by the bitterness in his voice. "All they know is the curse is broken, the leaders are dead, and they will die someday too. But in the meantime, with no one leading, you can bet they'll be busy fighting each other for power for the foreseeable future."

"And the First and Second?" I prompted.

"They've guessed what happened, given your performance at the inquest," Adam replied.

"How many died, besides Uncle Seacrest?"

He averted his eyes, not willing to say.

"Echo," I asked instead. "How many?"

"Fifty-two."

I gasped. I'd had no idea there were so many original Family members left. I hadn't even known there'd been that many to begin with. In my mind, I'd pictured a little remote village of maybe a dozen or so families.

"All but three were Second," Echo added.

"That's enough," Adam barked.

"Why didn't you tell me?" I pleaded with no one in particular.

"What was there to tell?" Echo answered, despite the dagger eyes Adam was shooting him. "Every single one of them would've given all to do what you did. Everyone. Suzanne and Adam included."

The conviction behind his words was comforting. But there was a world of difference between those who had lived with the curse for centuries knowing the stakes and choosing the consequences, and me, the ultimate outsider, being responsible for what had happened to so many of their loved ones.

Honing in on Echo opened me to the feelings of everyone present. I realized, as my attention spread outward past the dining room walls, that no one else was here. "Wait. Where is everyone?"

"After the cave-in, the studio shut us down," Corey explained.

"Cave-in?" I said in alarm.

"Yeah. Apparently, when you took off in a blaze of glory, the cave started crumbling. Andrew barely made it out alive."

"It's gone?" I asked, alarm giving way to shock.

"Buried," Corey confirmed. "The entire underground cave system collapsed."

"They're calling it an earthquake," Suzanne added. "That's what they think happened to Mr. Seacrest."

"So, how…why have they let us stay in this house?"

A smile played on Adam's face, but no one spoke.

"What is it?" I urged.

"They can't kick me out of my own home."

Chapter Forty-One

"Your house?" How was it he'd never told me about this? I'd assumed money wasn't a problem for him since his parents were royalty, but I was shocked to learn he owned Gold Manor. "How?"

"Uncle left everything to me," Adam explained a little sheepishly. "He put just about all his assets in my name last spring. He bought Gold Manor when I decided to take the gig on the show. I had no idea," he said, lifting his hand off my knee to stretch.

The moment he broke contact, I crashed.

I'd lost control of my body. I couldn't move, couldn't respond to questions. It didn't seem to matter that Adam was touching me again. I tried to listen to them, to anchor myself with their conversation. But it was just so much easier to drift. And so I floated on the tide of their voices, dangerously close to being swept out to sea.

"Is she supposed to be like this?" I heard Adam ask, felt him hovering over me. "Is this normal?"

"I doubt this transition will be usual for her," Andrew answered. "But, yes, this means we're at the last stages of the change."

I was vaguely aware as they moved me to Meg's old bedroom, the largest in the house. Everyone crowded in, keeping vigil. Someone was always talking to me, Adam never leaving my side, lying next to me on the large bed.

When Katie arrived, I felt a shimmer in the air. She stood by Andrew's side, watching me. Walking to the side of my bed, she gently laid her hand on my forehead. "Do you really think she'll be okay?" she asked, looking back at Andrew.

I could feel him towering over me as he moved beside her. "I believe she will."

"And she won't ever sleep again? What will that do to her?"

"I don't know. Those who have gone through this change don't usually have long lives," he responded with brutal honesty.

"Why?" Adam murmured, stroking my cheek, his panic tightly tamped down.

"As you can well imagine, it's incredibly hard on the body. Unless they find a source of regeneration and take great care to manage their condition, the body shuts down," Andrew explained. "But she's come to this in a different way. I don't think we should assume the side effects will be the same for her."

I was glad for their chatter. Hearing them discuss what was in store for me made it easier to concentrate and fight the desire to fall under.

"What are the possible side effects, what else might happen to her?" Adam asked. His question hung unanswered in the air. Time was loose and seemed to be unraveling for me, so I couldn't gauge how much was really passing, but the silence seemed to stretch endlessly.

"Time brings all things to pass, as Aeschylus aptly noted," Andrew eventually replied, his non-answer as maddening as ever.

"Have any of you ever heard of this supernatural sleeplessness before?" Adam asked, looking around the room. He seemed to forget his anger and self-recrimination in this new compulsion to figure out what was happening to me. "Echo, what about you?"

"No. The only people I've ever heard of who don't sleep were the Leviathan Immortals. Immortals no more," he added.

"But you have known one of the sleepless," Andrew corrected Echo.

"If I did, I had no idea," Echo said, baffled. "So, they hide it?"

"Not exactly. There's no need," Andrew answered in his cryptic way.

Katie swatted his arm. "Just tell us. Don't make him pull it out of you."

Watching this interaction, I finally understood that Andrew's whole existence had centered around keeping secrets. He was withholding as a matter of course, not out of a desire to be difficult.

"The sleeplessness changes the chemistry of a person," he said now, obliging Katie. "It makes them out of step with the world. When they interact with the rest of us, those who aren't sleepless, it interferes with our normal synapses, causing a kind of amnesia when we're no longer in their presence."

"Plain English," Katie sighed.

"He's saying I don't remember because I physically, biologically can't. Strange," Echo said, shifting through his past, trying to remember something that his brain had never properly recorded.

"If you came across her right now," Andrew continued, "she'd be a stranger. They are wiped from the memory of the world, no matter the attachment. I wonder how long my memories of them will last, now that I am like you."

"That's no problem," Adam said, tracing the side of my face. "I'm never letting her out of my sight."

The new hatred he felt for himself being in my presence wasted further away faced with the possibility of me being wiped from his mind. His doubt and bitterness were no match for the depths of our connection. His determination to find a way for us sent a refreshing breeze of energy through my body.

"Yes," he said, kissing my cheek, reacting to my minuscule movement. "We will figure it out, whatever the cost."

Corey and Andrew continued musing about what would happen next. The words rolled over me like gentle waves, swirling in the numb chaos of my mind. Occasionally some new and deeper pain would hit. I was isolated in my suffering, with no way of knowing what it looked like to the outside world.

My people were in various states of agitation, exhaustion, and hunger. It vaguely registered with me when Jade came into the room. As he talked with the others, I was caught up in his presence. Why was he here? I had absolutely no idea what they were discussing, but the fact that he was here called to me. I became consumed by his presence.

An itch started in the back of my mind, and it grew. When Jade stopped speaking, desperation gutted me.

The room erupted into commotion. Voices and emotions blared from all sides. Jade's voice returned. I followed it.

I knew I needed to stay awake to stay alive. The more I struggled to stay awake, the more energy I burned. Jade's disembodied voice came from above me, muffled and distorted as though filtered through a poor speaker system.

I grappled with the words, trying to pull them into focus. Slowly, his voice began to clear.

"There's no going back. It was my fault," I heard him say.

Suddenly my vision cleared, too. Looking around, I saw that I was sitting in my pew at church. Jade was at the pulpit giving a eulogy. As he continued his speech, I slid out of my seat to peek in the casket.

I stared down at myself, dressed in white eyelet, lying on a bed of fully bloomed red roses.

I stumbled back. Not at the sight of my corpse, but because it hit me just how bad this was. I was dreaming.

Chapter Forty-Two

I'd lost.

They'd said if I slept my body would shut down. If I was dreaming, I would be asleep.

I fell into a pew, defeated.

I realized Jade had stopped talking. He smiled, taking the empty seat next to me.

"My mom is worried," he said.

"Why?"

"I'm moving to L.A., she's afraid I'll never come back. Dad is sick, and I'm going to break her heart by leaving. I'm an awful son."

"I'm certain that isn't true," I tried to comfort him.

Jade was silent. The nave was empty now. Why was no one at my funeral?

I heard the unmistakable roar of rushing water and looked back at Jade in time to see the panic on his face. "It's coming!" he cried, as a tsunami broke the large wooden doors of the church, the windows exploding. We frantically grabbed at each other to brace for impact, but the instant we made contact, the water broke over us, and he was gone.

The impact of the water was excruiating. It felt like being hit with bats from all sides. I was seeing stars, literally. No longer the lone attendee at my own bleak funeral, I was back in the black void, surrounded by darkness and pinhole lights in the sky.

I fought to think clearly, to hold on to reality, but there was just so much noise in my ears, in my mind. I was splitting apart into all the tiny atoms that composed me. The pain turned me inside out, pushing me into the void, making it impossible to stay in my own body.

I was being made and remade, stuck in the grasp of the eternal recurrence. Over and over and over, endlessly, my body was torn to bits and reformed. Each time I got a handle on the pain, just as it became bearable, another wave would hit me, the fragmentation beginning all over again. Each wave was agonizing at its crest, yet with each release, the pain became a distant memory, leaving only a dull ache. Pulled and pushed through infinity, time was lost to me.

Suspended at the end of a wave, I felt a feather-touch. Instinctively, I knew it was Adam, his fingers tracing shapes on my back. I focused, straining to see the meaning in the nonsensical figures he drew. I studied the lines until I understood. He was writing song lyrics. Falling through space, I crashed back into my body. It wasn't the same, but familiar. Remade for a new era.

I heard Jade's voice, cutting through the noise, right into my brain. "I just had the strangest dream about Anna."

I was back in Meg's room, lying on a bed, Adam beside me, his heat warming me.

I had been in Jade's dream without falling asleep, the only reasonable conclusion if I was still alive. But was that a good sign?

I wanted to talk to Adam about it but didn't want to interrupt the conversation he was having with Andrew. I tried to be patient, but my muscles were sore and stiff. I just wanted to stretch and fall asleep in his arms.

That would be nice, but a hot bath would be even better. I was cold from head to toe. But I couldn't seem to get out of bed.

It was the burning itch of my wrist that made me consider the gemstones. I wanted to scratch my wrist, but couldn't move my arms. *Not with your body, use your mind.*

I touched one in my imagination. Its texture was rubbery instead of cold rock. Gathering my courage, I tried again. A fleck broke off and jolted through my system. I braced myself for an explosion. The pressure built and swelled until it overflowed, cascading through my veins with the sweetest release.

My senses flooded. I inhaled, the faint scent of rose in the air strangely comforting. This wasn't the artificial second wind of a caffeine high; I was completely renewed.

Adam's conversation with Andrew finally ended. I squeezed his hand and rolled out of bed.

Chapter Forty-Three

"Anna?" Adam sprang up behind me as I stood stretching.

Corey rushed me, crushing me in a giant hug. When he let go of me, I stretched from side to side.

"How do you feel?" he asked.

"Like a boulder landed on me. Sore, but the good kind, like after a workout."

"Andrew? What does this mean?" Echo asked.

"I believe she has successfully made the transition."

The collective sigh of exhausted relief made me laugh.

"Can I get you something?" Suzanne offered happily.

"I think I could use a run," I said, twisting my upper body, rolling my neck. I noticed Adam had backed away as the others drew closer. "Anyone want to go with me?" I scanned the room. "Oh. I guess not," I said, a little deflated.

"We're all exhausted," Corey explained. "It's been a long couple of days."

They had been treading water for me, with me, expending every ounce of energy with worry and talk of possible solutions. And now they were zombies on their feet. They needed their rest. Their beautiful sleep.

"But if you need to go out, I'll come, love," Adam offered, betraying himself with a yawn.

"No, it's my turn to wait on you," I said, wrapping my arms around him.

I don't know what came over me, but when he finally pulled back from my enthusiastic kiss, I flushed at my loss of composure.

An awkward silence filled the room for a beat, broken by Corey. "Yeah, okay," he coughed. "I'll see you guys later."

Dead on their feet, they each found a place to crash.

I stayed with Adam in Meg's old room. He was too tired to protest. I ran my fingers through his hair as he fell asleep, surprised by how quickly he was out. I was dying to talk, but it was my time to wait.

After a while, I gingerly disentangled myself from his floppy arm and tip-toed downstairs to find something to eat. The house, full of the sleeping, was still.

Eating a sandwich, I idly wondered if one of the Gold Ghosts would show up. For their sakes, I hoped they were really gone, freed with Iris.

How wonderful I felt. I was alive, my body feeling better than it ever had before. My life had been shrouded in mystery and confusion, but I was finally in the know. On top.

I was awash in strange new sensations. I wasn't happy, so much as contented. My heart ached for what had been lost. I never got to say goodbye to Mr. Seacrest. Then there were the scores of Family deaths I'd brought about. Their loved ones also hadn't had the opportunity to say goodbye, hadn't realized they were sharing their final moments, saying their last words.

And yet, a deep sense of pride swept through me at the thought that I had ended a war, and a supernatural one at that. How many people would ever play a part in something so much bigger than themselves?

I had no idea what would happen next. What had my friends planned while I wrestled death? I watched as the sun went down, waiting for the dawn and my answers.

Chapter Forty-Four

After a sweet morning reunion of kisses and light talk of nothing but us, we were brought back into the hustle of the house by a tap on the door.

Adam shot upright, on full alert, closing off his feelings from me.

Shocked, I scrambled to my feet. I could feel it was Echo and Andrew on the other side of the door. I knew it was them and I didn't sense any danger, which ratcheted up my heartbeat, matching Adam's fierceness.

"Breakfast for two," Echo said, handing us his homemade orange berry smoothie.

"You brought two," Adam relaxed, relief flooding through him and into me. "Thank you," Adam nodded at Echo, who retreated.

"I asked everyone here. No one has forgotten." Andrew replied.

"I don't understand." The smoothie stung my hand with its frost. "Adam?" My heartrate was climbing again.

"Andrew said…." Adam stopped, setting his smoothie on the nightstand and putting mine with it.

Andrew took over. "The usual effect of ingesting the kind of stones in the Serpent Star, the kind that robs someone of sleep, has a particular effect on anyone you encounter."

"You mean, knowing and reliving their deepest, darkest moments?" Yeah. I'd done that. But I thought that was just a passing side effect.

Adam shook his head, looking at me with the saddest expression, as if what Andrew was saying was physically painful to him.

"Out with it," anxiety rising through me. If it was worse than that, what could it be?

"Once someone transitions, as you have, everyone else forgets about them when not physically present. Though, as you can imagine, it's vastly more complicated than that. Sufficed to say, whatever you do to maintain the ability to replenish yourself and not sleep disrupts the magnetic field in others."

"You've got to be kidding me," I gasped, hands over my mouth.

This could not be happening. Not after everything we've gone through. Now I was going to lose them anyway.

"Peace, Anna. Adam. I asked everyone in the house. Echo contacted your father and others. There is no loss."

"For now," Adam quietly added.

"It is my experience, and I confirmed with some of my family, that the amnesia of others happens right away, within a few hours. Anna has transitioned magnificently. This fate for her, it seems, has been spared.

After restarting my heart with the mild assurances I wouldn't fade from the memory of my friends and family, we went to work, preparing to attend the funerals for Mr. Seacrest. There would be the massive, televised one in Los Angeles, followed by the small, clandestine funeral at Crimson Hall.

By the time I'd shifted, Mr. Seacrest had been dead three days. The time leading up to his first memorial service passed in a flurry of activity.

By day we packed, planned, and said our goodbyes to the town and the friends we'd made. By night, I attempted to reign in my abundant energy, and chatted Adam to sleep. He wasn't yet ready to face our encounter in the cave. But we'd have to deal with it, I hoped sooner rather than later.

Once he was asleep, I read, wandered the house, and meditated. No one knew what this shift meant for me. Given what I could do before, it was highly probable this change came with new abilities for me. But we all agreed it would be best for me to lay low and not explore those new boundaries, for now. Andrew said it was typical for those with my new condition to take months, or even a year, to settle into sleeplessness. The body and mind needed to acclimate. Disruptions might be damaging.

I'd had enough pain to last a lifetime. No way I'd go looking for more.

Chapter Forty-Five

Adam was spared making most of the funeral arrangements because Mr. Seacrest had made his requests known. This was Family custom, but especially important for someone like Mr. Seacrest, who had publicly interacted with the outside world. There would be only a few Family members attending the public event. They would be there to make sure it went off without a hitch, guarding against an attack from the Fourth.

Now that Adam was in control of Mr. Seacrest's assets, we used the private jet to fly to L.A. We had made plans to meet Sylvia, Meg, and the rest of the cast and crew for dinner the evening before the funeral at Mr. Seacrest's California estate.

In the air, surrounded by Corey, Suzanne, Echo, Andrew, Katie, Jade, and Adam, I allowed myself to hope that the worst was behind us, though I couldn't shake a sense of foreboding as we touched down on the tarmac.

There was a limo waiting for us, and I was surprised to see the driver was none other than Ewin. I shouldn't have been. He was Second, in Adam's band, and had known Mr. Seacrest for over a century.

"I'll be your driver today, as well as house sitter. Jack of all trades," he laughed as we pulled out of the airport.

Mr. Seacrest's Los Angeles estate was a historic mission-style mansion in Brentwood. I wasn't surprised by its grandeur and impeccably manicured grounds.

"What is it with old houses?" I whistled, as the limo drove through the wrought iron gates.

"It wasn't old for him. He commissioned the building of this house," Adam said, relaxing now that he was on familiar ground.

I was always caught off guard at the casual mention of their unnaturally long lives.

We were all staying at the mansion since it boasted an impressive sixteen bedrooms. I would have liked to have Meg stay with us too, but she had volunteered to run interference on the Lucy issue. Lucy had finally begun to suspect that all was not as it seemed, and we hoped Meg could help nip any questions in the bud.

Before directing people to their bedrooms, Adam gave us a quick tour and a few directions. "Mr. Seacrest loved cats," he said, pointing to one sunning itself in a patch of sunlight. He scooped up the toothy, tiger-striped beauty. "This one's Ronin. He thinks he owns the house. He runs hot and cold with the petting. He'll let you know when he's had enough. The gray one, Cosmos, doesn't want to be picked up. She loved Mr. Seacrest only and hides from everyone else. You probably won't see her."

"I didn't peg him for a cat guy," Corey said, petting Ronin on the head.

"They love cats," Finn responded, as if it were a well-known fact that everyone knew about the First and Second Families.

Corey made an intrigued-yet-skeptical huffing sound, eyebrows raised.

"It's true, of course," Adam concurred.

"There are lots of cats at Crimson Hall," Echo added. "I miss Nacho."

I assumed he was talking about his cat. Adam answered my unasked question. "Cats help with the stress and horror of constant war."

"No pooches?" Corey asked. He was more of a dog guy.

"We are gone too much. Cats are independent," Adam said, putting Ronin down and resuming the tour.

"Mr. Seacrest left these poor guys alone all the time?" I asked. This didn't sound like a nice way to care for animals that cared for you.

"Of course not. There's always someone here to oversee the property when he's gone. Ewin is more of a cat-sitter than house-sitter whenever he's on caretaker duty," Adam explained. "There!" He pointed, and we turned in time to see the end of a gray tail disappear under the door of the room Andrew was staying in.

Tour over, we settled into our rooms. I was in a corner room on the second floor. It was painted in a deep turquoise, which could've made for a dark room, but it was flooded with light from the diamond-shaped windows that extended from the middle of the wall to the ceiling. Under the gorgeous, old, leaded window was a window seat, perfect for reading a good book. The floor was wide plank hardwood, peeking out from the enormous Persian rug.

In the middle of the room was a four-poster canopy bed, velvet drapes tied to each post which could be pulled for complete privacy.

On the edge of the bed was a box with a silver bow.

"Go on. It's for you," Adam coaxed. "It's from my uncle."

Inside the white cardboard box was another, much smaller box, which bore Mr. Seacrest's family emblem in gold enamel. Opening it, I found Werden lying on a bed of black velvet. Werden was Mr. Seacrest's most prized possession. He always wore the ruby stone on a gold chain, concealed beneath his clothes. Werden has a way of protecting and bending the world to the will of the wearer. I'd worn it twice. It affected me by helping me focus the energy flowing through me as if I'd found the outer corner of a ley line.

"For me?" I breathed.

"He said no one could wear it like you. He told me that after you returned it to him, it never felt the same again. It was then he began to feel he was on borrowed time."

"That's awful."

"No, love," Adam said gently. "That's a gift. He was able to set his affairs in order as he saw fit."

"Should I wear it?" I asked, reaching out to touch it.

"Maybe let's wait," he suggested, drawing my hand back, kissing it.

"Yes. Think before touching." I smiled up at him.

Chapter Forty-Six

Adam went for a run with me and Echo, showing us the property. I felt like I could run into eternity. My endurance was vastly increased from what it had been before, nearly endless. I only stopped for my running partners, which was usually Echo. Ever since the curse was broken, his stamina was in decline. It wasn't super noticeable, and it remained unsaid between us.

Our agenda for the next couple of days included dinner with most of the cast and crew of Ghost House, the funeral, and then on to Crimson Hall.

I was disappointed Katie wasn't coming. Andrew didn't want her anywhere near Mr. Seacrest's funeral. I felt like his fear had more to do with his past than the likelihood of a bloodbath at the service.

Katie texted me her condolences to pass on to Adam. I wasn't totally comfortable with Andrew forbidding Katie to do something, nor with her acquiescence. But I'd been given first-hand knowledge of his past; I'd seen, through his eyes, how quickly things can get out of hand when dealing with strange people. So I understood. And yet, he'd have to get over it. He'd have to trust that the future would be different from his past, and Katie would need to learn not to give in to his fears. And I'd have to learn to mind my own business, which was difficult given what I knew about others.

Sylvia was the first to arrive for dinner, half an hour early. Adam greeted her at the door and ushered her into the living room. Corey snapped off the TV.

After she'd taken a turn about the room, saying her hellos, she returned to Adam. "I need to speak with you. Can we go somewhere to talk?" I heard her ask as I walked up to them.

"How are you, Anna?" She asked.

"Fine," I said politely, though none of us were.

"Let's go into my uncle's office," Adam said to Sylvia.

Sylvia rocked back on her heels, inhaling deeply. Scanning the room, her eyes landed on me. "Do you smell that?" she asked, with the most curious look on her face.

I sniffed the air but didn't smell anything out of the ordinary.

"What is it?" I asked, wondering if she smelled something burning.

"Roses. I smell roses," she said, looking for where the scent was coming from.

There were no cut flowers in the house; it was me. She had picked up on the scent that few others had, and even then, only when very close.

Her eyes were on me again, unfocused, as if trying to look through me. "Anna, why don't you come with us," she suggested. Adam's eyebrow shot up.

Whatever she'd originally wanted to speak to Adam about suddenly included me.

Once in Mr. Seacrest's office, she dug through her purse. Not finding what she was looking for, she started to take items out one by one until there was nothing left. "I know they're here somewhere," she said to herself, putting all her things back in her bag. Looking around the room she suddenly stuck her hand in her front pocket and pulled out her keys. "Of course," she said, frowning at being uncharacteristically forgetful.

"Why don't you take a seat," Adam suggested.

"I don't know what's come over me. I feel off," she said, rubbing her forehead.

215

"Can I get you something? A glass of water?" I offered.

"Yes. And do you have any Advil?"

"Sure. I'll be right back."

I turned to leave but was stopped when she nearly shouted, "No! Don't go."

There was desperation in her voice.

"Okay," I said, returning to her side. "Adam, will you go get Sylvia the water? Is that okay with you, Sylvia?" I asked gently.

She nodded, staring at me.

Adam left without a word. I felt Echo's presence on the other side of the door, no doubt sent by an alarmed Adam.

I took a seat, trying to figure out what was going on with her.

Adam was back shortly with the medicine and water. Sylvia drank the entire glass in a series of gulps.

Shaking her head, she apologized. "I don't know what's wrong with me. Excuse me. It must be...well, I don't know if I can pick just one out of the many awful things. I still can't believe Mr. Seacrest is gone."

I could see Sylvia fishing to explain her bizarre behavior to herself. She seemed to be coming out of her fog, and I tentatively moved from her side. The further away I got, the clearer her eyes became.

"Mr. Seacrest made me swear to give this package to you in this home. He even made it legally binding," she said, almost to herself.

She worked to remove a key from the ring, presenting it to Adam. Before she laid it on his palm, she drew it back. Digging back through her purse, she produced a sealed envelope. "You need to read this to yourself in my presence and sign it on the back. I'll notarize it and then give you the key. He gave this to me two Sundays ago. Incredible." She cleared her throat, handing the envelope to Adam.

As Adam broke the seal, the rafters groaned. He walked over to me and we silently read it.

My dear nephew,
You are now the steward of the past. If you are reading this, it is time to dispose of what I've collected. Ask Andrew for Sophia's assistance. Remember, always think before you touch.

Yours faithfully,
Alastair Seacrest

In addition to most of his vast fortune and property, Mr. Seacrest had left Adam the Family library. Adam turned the letter over and signed.

Short as it was, it was a binding Family contract and transfer of power. Sylvia had her notary seal and official ledger ready. Once she finished, she placed the tarnished skeleton key on the desk beside the letter. Adam's hand hovered over the key as he thought through the ramifications of taking on this charge.

Decided, he swiftly pocketed the key. The Family library was now in his care.

The cast and crew trickled in with a few minutes to visit before dinner. Sylvia was back to herself. Mostly. Occasionally she sniffed the air and her eyes glazed over. I had no idea what this meant, but I suspected my new status as someone who doesn't sleep was responsible for her mental haze. Adam was just as baffled, though he immediately concluded it wasn't good. That was his usual assessment of anything out of the ordinary.

Just before dessert was served, Sylvia announced that TeenTV had put the show officially on suspended hiatus. This was unfortunate because we hadn't yet finished shooting the two-part season finale.

One would think this latest "mishap" would've been the deathblow for *Ghost House*. But people love a mystery. The constant tragedy behind the scenes had developed a cult following. Podcasts, YouTube channels, TikToks, all the kinds of social media accounts were devoted to the mayhem and drama.

This organic attention made it all but impossible for the studio to cancel the show. Sylvia refused to speculate when we'd be back at work, but she did say all future filming would be on studio property. It would take a bit to recreate the sets, so I was betting a few months.

"You are unusually perky tonight," Lucy observed, pushing the food she wasn't going to eat around on her plate.

"I feel good," I said, with no trace of fatigue or exhaustion, even though it'd been six days since I'd slept. I was exercising more and eating like a horse.

"New diet?" She eyed the developing muscle tone in my arms.

"Not really. It's hard to explain. It's like a weight lifted from my shoulders, you know? I feel kinda free."

Lucy wasn't interested, as per usual. But I understood the change she was seeing in me. Last night, as the rest of the house slept and I didn't, I'd had an epiphany.

I'd always felt my life was shrouded in mystery. *No one understands me* was my mantra, on continuous loop in my head. I believed no one else could understand the trauma I had experienced and having to hide so much of myself from the world. I wrestled with coming to terms with what was true about me because I didn't understand it. How could they?

And then I realized: it didn't matter. The not knowing was as true for everyone else as it was for me. What am I? I am the same as everyone in the world, a work in progress. A mystery. Each of us has our own story, our own pain. I look at people's lives, their problems, and the solutions are so clear and obvious to me. But when it comes to myself, I'm at a loss. For the first time, I realized that my troubles connected me to others, rather than keeping me separate from them.

At the end of the meal, Sylvia addressed us again. "I feel I need to say this. If I had known, if I'd had any inkling of the suffering this show would cause, none of us would be here. I would have never signed up for this," she said, directing her attention to me. "I am sorrier than you'll ever know, Anna. Adam, my condolences."

"Thank you," I choked. It was still difficult to talk about my mom in public.

Adam put his arm around me.

Sylvia shook her head. "They," she said, pointing behind her, to the paparazzi at the gate and all the viewers they represented, "they think this is a joke. Something to consume, to feed their insatiable desire for scintillating news. Never a thought for the suffering, for those whom they hurt. No compassion for the incalculable loss. It's a game to them. I try not to think about it. I'm in this business to entertain, and maybe to add something to the conversation about real friendship and need."

Sylvia paused, collecting herself. "All this to say, Mr. Seacrest was a friend of mine. I knew him my entire professional life. He cannot be replaced. And… I wish I could torch every single media outlet that wants to profit off his death and our loss. But that would throw lighter fluid on their circus, which they'd love."

She scooted her chair out and raised her glass. "I say, give them nothing. No comment. No pausing for pictures nor ducking. We'll ignore them. I want you to ignore them. Tomorrow is for us, for those who knew and loved Mr. Seacrest, not for them. Got it? To Mr. Seacrest. May you rest in eternal peace."

"Hear, hear," Adam said, standing, glass extended.

Chapter Forty-Seven

After the toast, we went our separate ways. Sylvia told us to watch our email for updates. This was such a mess, but the studio had a team dedicated to messes. I had a feeling we'd be back to work sooner than I wanted. I was looking forward to an extended detox. How strange it would be to return to work, but not Martin. It would not be the same, which, I suppose, was the point.

The morning of Mr. Seacrest's funeral, Adam startled me when he sat next to me on the window seat in my bedroom.

"Caught in a fit of abstraction?" he asked, pleased he'd caught me off guard. I was hard to sneak up on.

I tried to turn to look at him, but I couldn't.

"What's wrong?" he asked, scooting closer.

"I don't think I can move." And I couldn't, not easily at least. He helped me onto the bed, gently propping my head up.

"When did this start?" he asked, smoothing my hair.

"I hadn't noticed anything until I tried to move just now."

Adam put his warm fingers to my neck, taking my pulse. "Much too low." He slipped off the bed. "I'll be right back. You'll be okay for a beat?"

He returned quickly, Andrew behind him. Andrew also took my pulse and felt my head. "Do you feel cold?"

"No," I said. "Should I be worried?"

"Adam, do you have a thermometer?" Andrew asked, ignoring my question.

Adam disappeared again, racing back with a digital one.

Andrew scanned my head. He repeated this two more times.

"What is it?" Adam's anxiety was making me nervous.

"95.9."

"You're certain?"

"Quite."

"How long has it been, Anna, since you've recharged?"

"I haven't yet. You told me to when I felt like I needed it. I've felt fine, until now."

Disapproval colored his voice. "What? No, no, no. You don't plug in a computer once the battery is completely depleted, do you?"

"Guess not?"

"It's the same with your kind. You must watch yourself, really pay attention. What you did to transition, you will need to do a modified version of that periodically. But take care. Do not overcharge yourself. There are dangers on either side of the extreme. Your life is contingent on finding that balance. But it's not as if you can count on the calendar. Suppose you average 8 days between being depleted. You might assume you should replenish on day 7. This is not the case. It all depends on what has taken place in the intermediate time. You may find, when you have less excitement, you could last a lot longer. And of course, the opposite is true.

"I apologize for not being thorough. Before I fly out tonight, let's talk about this more. I'll tell you all I can."

Andrew coached me, helping me relax into finding what I'd done before. Adam stood by, arms crossed, watching the process. It was hard to focus seeing the scowl on his face.

Since I was spent, my body resting like the dead, jump-starting my energy supply wasn't easy. I closed my eyes and reached for the calming waves. Retracing my steps, I found what had worked for me before. This time, however, my mind gently nudged a gemstone.

Instead of a blast of energy, I felt a trickle. It was going to take a while to completely recharge.

"Good," Andrew responded to my ability to sit up without assistance. "How do you feel?"

"Different. I still feel drained, but I can feel my energy rising. It's hard to explain."

Pleased with my condition, Andrew was about to leave the room when I stopped him with a question. "Who's Sophia?"

Adam answered instead. "We can deal with this later, love. We don't have time right now."

But Andrew cut in. "I suppose you're referring to my sister." I could hear the loss in his voice, taking me back to what I'd witnessed in his past. "If you're in need of Sophia's services, that settles it. Katie and I won't be going to Crimson Hall."

The funeral was in an hour, and I rushed to get ready. Skipping the shower, I pulled my funeral dress over my head. The thought that I *had* a funeral dress brought me up short. It took all the energy I'd regained to dress and pull my hair up in a tight ponytail.

I was sorting through my makeup dumped out on the bed when Adam came in to check on me.

"Guess I'm going like this," I frowned, bare faced.

"You mean breathtakingly beautiful?" he smiled. "You don't need any of that stuff. No one does."

"Yeah, yeah. But I like makeup. I'd rather not be photographed looking like the dead." I had giant purple rings under my eyes, my inability to sleep written all over my face.

"Need some help?" he offered, brushing the cosmetics to the side and sitting in front of me. He looked me over. "Right. Where do I start?"

I smiled doubtfully. Was he really going to put makeup on me? I preferred going bare faced to looking like a clown. "No, I'll be fine."

"You don't trust me? Give me a try," he said, tracing my jaw with his fingers. I started to warm up to the idea.

"Use this," I instructed, handing him a small jar. This was going to be interesting.

"Sponge or brush?"

I handed him the right brush. He methodically applied the cream, gently tilting my face as he worked. Finished with the base, he picked out a blush.

"Apples of the cheeks, right?" he asked, his face serious as he swirled on the rouge.

Bronzer, highlighter, concealer, eyeshadow, and brows. Not in the order I would've done it, but he was enjoying rooting around for this or that, occasionally asking a question.

He finished with my lips, pulling gloss across them with his thumb, and my heart began pumping. He pulled back a little, eying me skeptically. "Are you feeling better?"

"Much," I said, feeling electric pulses running throughout my body.

The light that passed between the two of us when we were in sync began to hum. I couldn't look away, nor would he.

I leaned in to kiss him, but Corey knocked on the open doorframe, breaking the rhythm.

"You two ready?" he asked, stepping into the room. "We need to be on the road in five."

He turned to go but looked back. "You do something different, A? Looks good."

"Thanks, I think," I said, amused at the sideways compliment.

"I'm heading to the car. See you there."

"What did you do to me?" I smirked at Adam.

"See for yourself."

He held up a mirror so I could inspect my reflection. It was the most understated makeup job I'd ever had.

"I like you the way you are. The natural look looks good on you," he said, gingerly pulling his hand through my ponytail, twirling the ends.

"Wow. If the acting or music doesn't work out, you've got other career options," I said, admiring his work in the mirror. "Okay. Let's get this over with," I sighed.

Adam looked down at my wrist. "You'll need to cover the Serpent Star."

Great. Another part of myself that I'd have to hide. At least I had practice.

I rummaged through my jewelry, but I didn't have anything that would cover it. Unzipping my makeup bag, I pulled out my heavy-duty concealer.

I smeared and blended and applied. The more I added, the brighter the Serpent Star appeared, melting the foundation so it outlined the tattooed bracelet, acting as a highlighter.

"Guess that's not going to work." I had to use my waterproof makeup remover to get rid of the congealed concealer.

"Oh, wait. I did bring a cool carved-wood bracelet a fan sent me." I rummaged through my suitcase to find it. "It

225

doesn't match my dress, but beggars can't be choosers," I said, putting it on.

As soon as it was directly over the Serpent Star, it burst into flames.

My bracelet was in ashes, the bedspread sported a large, charred hole, but I was unscathed. The smell of smoke gave way to the light scent of roses, emanating from me. I just looked at Adam, unable to believe what'd happened.

"Ideas?" I asked.

Adam seemed remarkably, annoyingly unperturbed. I watched as something clicked in his mind, the epiphany bright on his face. "Just one moment."

He slid out the door and was back in a moment with his brown leather toiletry bag. I wondered what he could have in there for this situation.

He took out his round jar of hair goop and untwisted the lid. He showed me the contents of his half-used hair paste. "Just wait," he said, playing the magician. He held the sides of the jar and twisted the rim of the container counterclockwise until it clicked. He tugged the false bottom off, revealing the hidden compartment.

"This was my sister's bracelet. It's been in our family for a very long time."

It was beautiful, and just as described by Suzanne. It had an ethereal quality that made you want to stare and look away in equal measure.

"It's lovely," I said, my fingers hovering over the bangle, hoping I wouldn't melt it too.

"Take it. It's yours," he urged gently. "I'm not saying *it is* magical, but I know it will work."

I carefully lifted the bangle, sliding it over the embedded Serpent Star. There was a faint hissing sound as the bracelet locked into place on my wrist with only the outline of the Serpent Star visible, leaving a cooling sensation.

Chapter Forty-Eight

Andrew would be going home after the L.A. funeral. Wherever 'home' was for him. It was hard to plan with so much up in the air. None of us knew what the end of the curse meant for the Families. Was the war over? Finn and Adam, some of the few full-blooded Family members left, hadn't changed. Finn felt no different to me, still radiating that Fourth hate. There was one change: Adam could dream. In fact, ever since I'd been severed from sleep, his normal dreaming abilities returned.

Finn said things at home were crazy. He knew this through his contacts, not directly. No one had notified him of his parents' death. When I suggested it was an oversight due to shock, he rolled his eyes.

"I've been written off. They don't care about me. I've been protected up 'til now only because of my parents' vanity."

"When's their funeral?" My voice sounded small, even to me. We were on our way to Mr. Seacrest's funeral. I was already tearing up, smudging Adam's makeup job.

"We don't have funerals," he said flatly. "We don't waste emotion on the dead."

It sounded like he meant it, but it was hard to believe. Could he truly not care that both of his parents had just died? That was so far out of the realm of my experience.

"I'm sorry you had such a bad relationship with them. I wish I could do something," I said, feeling lame at the gross understatement.

"Thanks. It's been a long time since I wanted anything from them. Do you know the real reason Suzanne left me all those years ago?"

I looked over at Suzanne, who was staring too intently into her phone. "She told me she left because she didn't want to get you in trouble," I recalled.

"It was my father. He'd heard I was with someone. He showed up at the compound we'd been assigned to and told me to call it off or he'd kill the both of us."

"That's so extreme!" I gasped. "Why?"

Suzanne and Finn laughed at the same time, intimating I didn't get it. I didn't.

"Oh, you're serious," Finn said, surprised. "It's all about power and manipulation. He had someone in mind for me."

"And you said no," I filled in.

"Uh, this girl was young."

"That's sick."

"It is. In many ways. But the point was control. Control and power. Control me and make a powerful allegiance through my marriage."

"That's seriously old school," I scoffed.

"They were. And old, as you know. To them, children were a means to an end. I had three full sisters, two half-brothers on my mother's side, and who knows how many half-siblings from my father's side. What about you, Suzanne?"

She looked up from her phone. "No way to know. My father was… active."

"Yes," Finn agreed in disgust. "Anyway, my sisters are dead. I only ever met one of them. One half-brother on my mom's side is around. A few that I know of from my dad's. Their children were just a kind of capital to them. It's hard, but it's true. You see why I find it hard to care?" There was only the faintest hint of regret in his voice.

I thought of my father who was going to Mr. Seacrest's funeral. I wasn't sure if it was a good idea, but it would've looked odd if he didn't show. Adam assured me the risk was low. This event was too public to turn bloody.

"Suzanne, the only person I've ever loved who loved me back, was taken from me because of him," he said, pulling me from thoughts of my dad.

I wanted to reassure him that they would be together now, but I didn't know that. I didn't know if they could be together, or even if they wanted to. That was yet to be determined.

Chapter Forty-Nine

There was a long line of cars entering the cemetery. Mr. Seacrest had arranged for a graveside service only, with his family and a considerably long list of friends and business acquaintances in attendance. Those watching would see a cannister of ashes being buried, as though he'd been cremated. His actual body was lying in state at Crimson Hall.

The service was well attended. Security was tight due to the numerous high-profile celebrities who had come to pay their last respects. I was seated in the front row next to Adam. On the other side of him were two of Mr. Seacrest's cousins. I recognized one of them from the meeting at Crimson Hall, when Maggie had killed the queen.

Adam greeted them both with a hug and formally introduced me. Few words were exchanged. This was consistent with what I'd noted before; Family members are habitually silent in the presence of regular people.

I had to be content with reading their body language. This was harder than usual because I was fatigued. Throughout the service, I fought to keep my mind from wandering into other people's private feelings. I also kept myself tightly wrapped up, protected from prying Family minds. My exhaustion was mounting.

Millicent Seacrest gave the eulogy. I realized I didn't know as much about Mr. Seacrest as I had thought. This part of his life, carefully reconstructed by Millicent, was fascinating. I'd had no idea Mr. Seacrest had started in the show business industry on the technology side, the bulk of his money generated by the technological advancements he'd had a hand in. His list of awards and achievements was enviable. This had me looking forward to the real funeral, where I'd hear the actual story of his well-lived life.

But I wondered if he would be remembered as a hero in the Family story. He had willingly given it all. And through his work, he'd also brought about the end of the Leviathan. It wasn't a coincidence that our show was filmed on location at Gold Manor. Mr. Seacrest had set it up, discovering it as a place of importance through his decades of research.

He had been the keeper of records, the one who remembered. Who would remember him?

Adam squeezed my hand, gently alerting me that my spiraling thoughts might be getting a little...*loud*.

I caught two interesting minds as I snapped back to myself. First, I felt Sylvia calling my name. She wanted to talk to me privately after the service. Secondly, as Millicent spoke, her eyes and attention kept falling on Suzanne.

I was proud of myself for keeping it together. I didn't like crying in public. But as Millicent picked up a handful of dirt and sprinkled it over Mr. Seacrest's coffin, I couldn't keep my tears back.

My eyes began to sting, making my contacts uncomfortable. I discreetly removed them, rooting around in my purse for sunglasses on this sunless day.

Thankfully, I'd brought a pair. Sunglasses securely in place, I opened my eyes. And immediately wished I hadn't.

It looked like I'd stepped into an alternate reality. The trees, grass, and headstones were unchanged. But the people emitted light. They shimmered with apparent bioluminescence, periodic electrical currents discharging from their bodies.

Forgetting myself in total astonishment, I whipped around to see what was going on behind me. The scene was insane.

Adam squeezed my hand again, recalling to me the fact that I was in public. As I reluctantly turned back around, I caught sight of a gray clawed creature attached to a man standing in the cemetery, some yards away from the official attendees. The man was clearly a Fourth. But whatever was whispering in his ear was not.

This was new. I had the feeling that I was not meant to see this, and I wanted no part of it. My tears dried up and eyes closed tight, and I shrank into my seat, trying to make myself invisible, trying to stay calm and breathe evenly. All this caused me to fixate on my breathing, and I could not control it. I began to hyperventilate.

"What is it?" Adam asked, his body completely rigid and ready to fight.

I shook as I pulled out my phone and texted him. "There's a Fourth behind us. Something on him. Not human."

I pressed send and waited for his reaction.

He was good. If anyone had been watching, they wouldn't have perceived the change.

"Did it see you?" he texted back.

"I don't think so. What is it?"

Adam sent out a text to our group. "Fourth in the northwest corner. Something is on it. Keep it away from Anna."

It was easier to calm down if I kept my eyes closed. Luckily, the service was over, and people were now milling around. I stood with Adam, holding his arm to guide me.

"My contacts are out, and you won't believe what I'm seeing," I whispered to him. "I just need to keep my eyes closed for a minute."

Andrew, who'd been standing in the back, found us. He wasn't alone.

233

"This is Cain," he said, introducing me and Adam in turn.

This person felt so odd, I had to open my eyes to see who it was. He was glowing, just around the edges. Cain was even taller than Andrew, but thin and extremely pale. Almost powdery. I could see how he might be intimidating to some, but not to me, since he was engulfed in soothing warm light.

I almost blurted out that he was like Lizzy, but I managed to gulp down my surprise.

Cain addressed me. "Did it see you?"

His voice lacked both Lizzy's gentle tenor and Andrew's authoritative edge. It was deep and raspy, as if he didn't use it much.

"I don't think so," I whispered. "What is it?"

"Wraith," he answered darkly. He wrapped his arms around me in an awkward hug so he could whisper into my ear. "I am sorry this burden has come to you. They are evil creatures. Do your best to not react to their presence. This is unfortunate," he added, pulling back.

"Will you come to the house for dinner?" I asked Cain, hoping he'd say yes.

Nodding, he looked at my arm. "I am truly sorry for your burden." I knew he wasn't only talking about the wraith.

As soon as we left the cemetery, I put in a fresh pair of contacts and dared to look around. The relief that flowed through me was intense. Everyone looked completely normal. No one asked me any questions, so I kept my mouth shut the entire ride back to the estate.

Chapter Fifty

After a morning of public scrutiny, it would've been nice to have a quiet, private lunch at Mr. Seacrest's home. I regretted the invitation we'd extended to Meg, Lucy, Sylvia, and the Ghost House crew who'd attended the funeral. But that was nothing compared to the fight that broke out when Millicent and August Seacrest, who showed up unannounced and expecting to stay the night at the estate, realized Finn was at the house.

Echo was able to take his aunts out to the garden while we figured out what to do.

"This is really bad. They think we're dining with the enemy!" Adam said as he paced the hall. "We need all the allies we can get!"

"It's just not right!" I insisted. "If they've got a problem with Finn, they can leave."

"Don't be so naive, Anna," he chided. "You think if my aunts see that Finn's not a threat, that we can actually work with a full-blooded Fourth, then, what? That's a game changer, right? It doesn't work that way."

It was hard for me to listen to him when he was condescending.

I don't know exactly what he said – or promised – but Adam was able to convince them not to declare war on our guest. At least for the night. There was clearly tension in the air, which our non-Family guests tried their best to ignore. They probably assumed it was family – with a little 'f' - issues. They had no idea how right they were!

While everyone sat around rather uncomfortable waiting for the catering to arrive, Sylvia asked if I'd take a walk with her.

I wanted to say no. I really needed to rest for a while, and I thought I should keep an eye on the aunts versus Finn situation. But it was clearly important to her.

As we walked in the manicured garden, I realized Sylvia was avoiding looking me in the face. She'd decided to bring up what had happened yesterday in Mr. Seacrest's office.

As our silent walk stretched on, I ran through various scenarios in my mind. It was clear she'd probably discovered one of our many secrets, based on her obvious unease and anxiety. But exactly what she wanted to talk about, I didn't know. If I guessed wrongly and accidentally told her more than she knew, I could be putting her in danger. So, I held my silence and waited for her to speak first.

We leaned over the railing of a little bridge and watched the giant koi in the pond. My arm brushed hers lightly, but it was enough for her to receive a sharp electrostatic shock.

"Oh my gosh! I'm sorry! Are you okay?" I was so embarrassed. "It's been extremely dry. I've been zapping myself all day when I open doors," I added, trying to cover up the energy I'd sent shooting through her.

She graciously shook it off, but apparently this was the jolt she'd needed to come out with what was on her mind.

"I don't know how to start… because I don't even know what I'm asking," she began, finally looking at me.

"Just go ahead, no worries," I tried to put her at ease. "Mind if we sit?"

Sylvia was wringing her hands, unable to stand still. I, on the other hand, was bleeding energy. I took a seat on the stone steps.

A frosty spring breeze ruffled my hair, and Sylvia deeply inhaled. "Do you smell that?" she asked.

"The cool air?" I guessed uncertainly.

"No. Roses. But there aren't any roses here." She gestured around us. "Do you see any?"

Uh-oh. So, my new smell was the issue. She had picked up on the scent, and it had triggered something in her.

I didn't know what to do or say. I was a curious cocktail of three mysterious groups: the Families, the Leviathans, and the ones who don't sleep. Though there was no way to know which of these groups I had to thank for my fun new supernatural fragrance, I was pretty sure it wasn't from the Family connection. I had smelled the aroma of roses after Emma, who'd been a lackey for the Seers, had invaded my dreams. And yet, my intuition told me this new aspect of myself, my own floral scent, had to do with being one who doesn't sleep, the part I knew least about.

Sometimes the best course of action is inaction. I sat and waited.

"Do you know why I let things carry on at *Ghost House*?" She sat down next to me. "That was only partially a rhetorical question," she laughed.

Her face changed as she caught the scent again, and she continued in an odd voice. "I know that smell, but I can't place it. It means something to me, but I can't explain what. All I can say is, all my life I've felt alone. Cut off from the world. As if I've shut out everyone, shut out love."

Gazing at her hands, she went on haltingly. "I feel like something was taken from me, something important, integral to my life. But when I try to think what it might've been, there's nothing." She looked at me helplessly. "And now you're...changed. That smell. It means something. Do you smell it?" She was practically pleading with me.

She was trying so hard to solve a riddle, so in pain, I couldn't stop myself from agreeing. "Yes."

She slightly relaxed. "I thought so."

I mentally kicked myself. Why had I said yes?

"Can you help me?" she asked plaintively. "Help me figure it out?"

I exhaled, my energy running dangerously low. "I don't know what I can do. I'm in the dark."

"If you figure it out, will you help me? Tell me?"

"If I can," I said, which was all I could promise.

She understood the double meaning of my words.

I tried my best to join in the luncheon conversation, but my body started to feel like lead. I was finding it difficult to even lift the fork.

Meg noticed. "It's been a rough day. I can't believe he's gone. What an immense loss."

I could tell she was trying to help me, thinking my lethargy was due to grief and the stress of the funeral. I wanted to stay and support Meg and be supported by her, but I was afraid of the consequences if I didn't do something soon to stop the cascade of leaking energy.

"I'm sorry, Meg, but I'm gonna have to lay down. I'm just really feeling out of it. Mind if I call you later so we can chat?" I asked, getting up from the table.

"Sure," she said, standing to hug me. Just before she let go, she whispered in my ear. "I really need to talk to you. It's...important. Just act normal."

I pulled back without acknowledging what she'd said, since she'd taken pains to make sure no one could overhear. I gave my apologies to everyone else for leaving and excused myself.

As soon as I was in my room, I sprawled out on the bed, trying to catch my breath. I tried to marshal my thoughts and my breathing. Just as I was about to fall into meditation, I felt Adam walk in.

"Can I help?" he asked, brushing the hair out of my face.

I always felt better when he was near.

"Will you meditate with me?" I asked between deep breaths.

"Certainly," he responded, preparing to join.

I didn't want to disrupt the state of calm I was easing into, but I needed to address the aunts and Meg issues.

"How do you think it's going with your aunts?"

"It's lucky Ewin is here. Millicent basically raised him. They also respect Echo. It's going much better than I'd expected."

Good. That eased some of my tension. "I need Meg to stay the night here."

Adam responded immediately, leaving to attend to my request.

It was the wrong decision.

Chapter Fifty-One

The house was asleep and I was recharging. The energy was mounting, slowly, like the second hand of a clock. Tick, tick, tick, the seconds stretched on. And with each minute I felt more and more like myself.

Around the witching hour, I padded down to the kitchen for a cup of coffee, with no need to worry about the caffeine keeping me up all night. I took my steaming cup and decided to explore more of the old mission-era house. Adam had mentioned a rooftop terrace. A perfect perch to watch the sky on this cloudless night.

I grabbed a light blanket on the way up. I had to put my shoulder against the door to work it open. No one had been here in a long time, evidenced by the cobwebs. But it was worth it.

The view was breathtaking. Since there were no close neighbors, the light pollution was minimal, making the night sky come alive.

From the rooftop I spied a long, narrow pool I hadn't explored. Seemed like the perfect time for a night dip in the crystal-clear water. There were perks to staying up all night. I loved the alone time.

Investigating the pool house, I found swimsuits, caps, goggles, and just about anything a person could desire for a fun day poolside.

Even though it was cool, and the water was chilly, it felt amazing. I wondered how many laps I could do before I'd tire. I couldn't run enough to feel that release I loved, but maybe swimming would do it for me.

I soon found a rhythm, clearing my head. I lost track of how many laps I'd done, when I started to flag, feeling weird. As I struggled to push through the water, negative thoughts flooded my mind. I suddenly recalled in vivid color the horrific things Suzanne had been party to. The terrible things Adam had done. *How could I remain friends with her? How could I love him? They were far from pure. Far from good, even. Adam was right: if I was a good person with a shred of self-respect, I would leave him.* The dark thoughts kept growing, spewing from deep within.

I climbed out of the pool, torn between marching into Adam's room to break up with him, and trying to get a handle on the intrusive thoughts tormenting me. But as I tied a terrycloth robe around my waist, I felt them. There were Fourth nearby. They were turning my thoughts dark.

I crouched down, uncertain where they were or what to do. I listened, trying to figure out where the vile vibes were coming from. I had all but decided to grab a pair of binoculars and return to the rooftop when I heard several loud popping sounds coming from the house.

Sprinting through the yard, as I flew through the kitchen, the pops turned to bangs. I raced up the side stairs, but the house was filling with noxious smoke, making it hard to breathe. I dropped to my hands and knees, crawling towards Adam's room. I didn't get that far. Ewin, Millicent, Suzanne, and Meg were a tangle of bodies, out cold. I pulled past them, my eyes stinging with the biting fumes.

I could feel them creeping up the stairs. I didn't need the use of my vision to know the house was crawling with Fourth.

I didn't know what to do. I had no idea where the rest of my friends were, or if they were even alive. I couldn't feel past the pulsing hate radiating from the intruders.

"Search them," a familiar voice said. It took me a moment to place it, but then I realized it was Finn's latest bodyguard. Finn claimed Ned had been recalled. But now I wondered.

Beyond Ned and the other nameless Fourth, there was something different. It wasn't Fourth, but I was under too much stress and sensory overload to pinpoint what it was.

"She's not here," another voice said.

"You can do what you'd like with those," said a new, imperious voice, "but leave Suzanne to me. Tie them and take them out with the others."

A-ha. Now *that* voice I knew. It was Maggie.

I'd crawled into the nearest room. The air wasn't as thick in here, but it was bad enough that Echo had passed out cold on the ground.

I managed to duck out of sight just as the door was kicked in.

"That one..." Maggie said, deliberating. "That one, take outside and shoot."

Two Fourth hoisted him up, the bigger one throwing Echo none too gently over his shoulder.

I thought I'd escaped notice, but then I felt the pinprick of her gaze, even through the gas mask.

Chapter Fifty-Two

"Well, well, well," Maggie said with suppressed glee, standing over me. "You got away once, witch. Not this time."

Calling over her shoulder, she said, "Take this one out too."

I played dead, hoping that would buy me enough time to figure something out.

"He's heavy." The Fourth who'd slung Echo over his shoulder was propping himself up in the doorway.

"Just throw him over the balcony," his partner suggested coldly.

"Good idea!" the large one laughed. Grunting to the second story railing, he hoisted Echo over the edge.

The sound of impact was sickening, but Maggie wasn't fazed.

"Much better. Should've thought of that myself," he said as he walked over and bent down to pick me up. "I'll throw her over too!"

"No!" Maggie commanded. "You can play with her later. Just take her downstairs with the others for now."

The house was still filled with a light haze of smoke, but it was beginning to dissipate. The way he held me over his shoulder made it difficult to breathe, but I couldn't adjust myself.

In the entry way at the bottom of the stairs was a mass of bodies. I counted. Everyone except for Echo was piled by each other, unconscious, hands and feet bound.

Hearing Maggie come up behind me, I clamped my eyes tight.

"Wake her up!" she commanded.

I hoped she didn't mean me, but of course she did.

The Fourth who carried me flung me off his back, my body slamming into a couch. Immediately, someone else grabbed me, propping me up right. I felt a rush of air before a hand connected hard with my cheek.

"What should I do with these?" Finn's ex-bodyguard asked, preventing me from being hit again, at least for the moment.

"Start the bonfire," Maggie instructed. "Except for those two. We're taking them with us."

I risked a peak as I saw Adam and Suzanne separated from the pile of bodies.

"Shove this in her mouth," she commanded a nearby Fourth. He took the rag from her hand and stuffed it into my mouth.

My eyes flung open as I gagged.

"This is your fault, witch," Maggie said with deadly calm. "You've taken everything from me. My mother, my sister, my brother, my very life, all lost to me, because of you!" she ended with a scream. "Since the day I first laid eyes on you, I've been planning your demise. You managed to escape the Immortal fate I'd orchestrated for you, but that was a mistake on your part. Because plan B is much more painful. The Fourth are experts in this sort of thing," she promised venomously.

I knew better than to plead with her. She was insane and out for blood. Mine, specifically. The others were just collateral damage in her war against me and for power.

Maggie had been overly influenced by how her mother, Queen Cora, acted in the last few years of her rule. Fear, intimidation, threats, and unpredictability became her hallmarks. Maggie seemed to think those same tactics would make her a legitimate ruler. The Families would fall in line behind her because they wouldn't dare otherwise.

She was playing like a Fourth.

But she didn't know she'd already lost. While there were a few dozen followers here, only a small fraction were Second. Most were Fourth. Maggie was being used by the other side, but she couldn't see it. She thought the Fourth were her minions. But Ned was really in charge, and they were following his lead. They were probably even planning to kill her or take her hostage before the night was through.

But I knew who in this room *actually* held power. It was me. The air was clearing, the open doors letting the brisk night breeze in, and I planned.

I had resented the power surging through me this morning, but it would be our rescue. I kept my gaze low, waiting for my opportunity to act.

A Second walked in, grabbing Maggie's attention. "The winds keep putting out the fire. What do you want to do?"

Maggie thought for a moment. "Just pile them in the van."

"Got it. We'll light it up on the way out," her lackey agreed.

"Put those two in my car. Put the witch in the Jeep. And give me my sister's bracelet!" Maggie commanded, pointing at my wrist.

For me, it all happened in slow motion. As the lackey approached, I felt my contacts burn away, showing me the unseen reality. Energy surged from deep within me, unbidden and uncontrollable, like the backdraft of a fire behind a closed door.

The moment the Second's fingers skimmed the Serpent Star hidden under the bracelet, pain shot through my body, like I was being liquified from the inside. But it didn't stop there. The energy shot out in a wave, instantly incinerating her, blowing out the glass windows, and rendering everyone inside the house and out unconscious.

Chapter Fifty-Three

Curled into a tight ball on the floor, I rocked back and forth in pain. I couldn't get on top of it. Eventually, the waves of pain ebbed, leaving me shaking.

I finally pulled myself up, digging Adam's sister's bracelet from the ashes and clasping it over Serpent Star.

I ran to Adam, over the shards of glass. I reached out to touch him, my hand hovering above his head, but thought better of it. I could feel untamed energy surging through me, looking for an outlet.

I sat on the cold stone ground beside him, my arms around my knees, my mind perfectly numb.

As I sat and rocked, waiting for someone else to wake up, my thoughts ran wild. *Millicent and August are going to exile me now that they know what a freak I am. Corey should stay away from me. What's going to happen to him? Are there more Second and Fourth on the way? Will I ever be safe? Is Echo alive? Will Adam ever forgive me for invading his most private thoughts? Will I ever be able to touch him again? Will I ever be able to touch anyone again? I'm poison. No, I'm not. If it weren't for me, we'd all be dead.*

When I couldn't bear to sit with my own thoughts anymore, I opened my mind, bit by bit, until I'd reached out as far as I dared, searching for a conscious soul.

Nothing.

I had to act while I still could. There were zip ties poking out of a Fourth's pocket. My first thought was to tie them all up, hands and feet. But if I touched them, would they go up in smoke too? My energy was leveling out, but I was still sparking. At the very least, I could figure out exactly how many of them there were and their location.

I ran outside and found three lying on the driveway, one passed out in the Jeep. I ran back in. There still wasn't anyone awake.

I frantically searched room by room, finding six more intruders, including one in the wine cellar and another in the bathroom near the kitchen.

I returned to the foyer, my brain in overdrive. I could not think of what to do next.

Untie your friends, stupid, my thoughts chided me, finally deciding on the next step.

I ran to the kitchen and grabbed a knife. Ewin was the first person I saw, and I crouched beside him. I had to take a moment to still myself before I began. I had to take my time and do this carefully. I would have to cut his hands and feet free without touching them. Breathing deeply and handling the knife with care, I started cutting. I only slightly singed the hair on the back of his hands.

When I got to Echo, I was seized with fear, his violent fall ringing in my ears. I tried to convince myself he was alive, but the pool of blood surrounding his head told me that might not be the case.

I cut him free before I forced myself to feel for a pulse.

A crackle of sparks shot up his arm. I yanked my hand back. Staring at him, I saw his chest move. He was breathing, at least.

The blood was from a gash on his forehead, which had already stopped bleeding. Looking him over, I suspected he had a broken leg and probably internal injuries. I wanted to call 911, but how could I with a house full of comatose people?

Still, I had to do something.

I sat on the ground next to Echo. I'd healed myself before, and Jade with Adam's help. And now, it seemed I was a weapon, not a healer.

I closed my eyes and tuned into my body. I tried to gauge how much energy I had, whether it would be enough to help Echo. And then I had a strange thought. What *kind* of energy did I have to work with? I'd never thought about the quality of energy before. It was either there or not.

But maybe there was more to it than that, other possibilities and types of energy. Without my contacts, my sight was different. I even saw myself differently, in a more holistic way.

Though I didn't yet know what it was, I could see there was something new in me. I turned my hands over, concentrating. Catching a flicker of movement to my right, I scampered up, back in defense mode.

I pushed my back against the wall, watching and waiting. Two long minutes passed, and when I saw nothing else, my thoughts returned to Echo.

If I touched him again, there was a slight possibility I could help. But given my track record, the chances were not in his favor. I was going to have to call for help. Echo's safety was more important than worrying about how I would explain the dozens of senseless bodies.

Chapter Fifty-Four

There it was again, a flicker of movement in my peripheral vision. I scanned the room and jumped out of my skin to find Cain looking back at me.

He put his fingers to his lips, as I gulped down a scream, shaking with nerves.

Cain bent down, checking Echo's pulse and ran the back of his hand across his forehead. "His pulse is steady. He feels fine, but he needs medical attention."

Feels fine? What does that mean. My mind was still spinning. "I was about to call 911, but...." I trailed off, the room filled with passed out bodies speaking for itself.

He took in the complete scene. "Did you do this?"

"Yes." I suddenly felt self-conscious. "But I don't really know what I did."

"Very impressive," Cain said approvingly. "You'll be a welcomed addition to the hunt."

"The what?"

"For another time," he said, surveying the scene again. "They won't stay immobile for long."

"What do we do with them?" I asked, relieved I was no longer on my own. "I counted twenty-one, including Maggie."

Cain rolled his neck back and forth, rubbing his temples. I followed as he walked through the house, looking for himself.

I started to worry that he didn't seem to know what to do any more than I did. "What do the Families normally do with their captured enemies? Do you know?"

"They are waging a war of attrition," he said flatly. "They take no prisoners, there are no survivors."

My relief from mere moments before faded. "Can't you just, I don't know, take them somewhere far away? Don't you have prisons or something?"

"We are not police, we do not hold anyone against his or her will," he answered. "That is not our business."

"But you do help, right? I mean, you're on the side of good, right?"

"We are not with the Families and their war. We don't act as they do. We are on the side of the individual," he said, leaving me feeling slightly chastised.

He was just like Andrew. Vague, cryptic, and exasperating. "Well, then, what do you suggest?" I asked a little huffily.

"Let them go."

"What?" I stared at him in shock. "Do you know what they planned to do? Shoot and burn us. The lucky ones, that is. A few of us were going to be tortured first. If we let them go, they'll just come back!"

"What are the alternatives?" Cain asked, crossing his arms.

"Like you said, it's kill or be killed."

"Anna, are you going to murder these people?"

That brought me up short. What was I advocating? Of course we couldn't kill them. Apparently, there was no way to detain them, and calling the cops wasn't going to happen either.

Cain finally took pity on me. "I'll call for help and we'll take them into the country," he said. "We'll find some place to leave them. We might consider calling the local authorities."

He pulled out his phone and called for help to transport them. "They're two hours away," he informed me after hanging up.

"They aren't just, you know, pop in like you and Lizzy can, and teleport them away?" I puzzled.

Cain smiled at me and shook his head. "Not this time. You've got much to learn."

"Yeah. Understatement of the year!"

My head was clearing from both the ringing and my poisonous thoughts. Cain was having a similar positive effect on my mental state, just like Lizzy. Huh.

Cain wanted to scan the entire property before moving the intruders to the front entry. The long wait wore on my nerves. How long did we have before they would begin waking up? And how were we supposed to move them all?

I went over to Adam. My momentary envy at how peaceful he looked soon switched to worry. "Are they okay?" I asked Cain. "Did I hurt them too?"

I hadn't allowed myself to really think about it. I'd tried to forget what had happened to the Second who had touched me, tried to ignore the possibility that maybe I'd also harmed my friends, but it had been in the back of my mind the whole time.

"They are just temporarily knocked out," Cain assured me. "Some might suffer a concussion."

My eyes fell on Meg, who had just recovered from a concussion. Not good.

"They should come around sometime today," he added.

I'm not sure what Cain saw on my face, but he sensed my disappointment at his words.

He stopped and looked at me. "It bothers you that they might sleep away the day?"

"I don't know. It's just... I don't like them like this." Here I was walking around on my own, and they were helpless. Just like at night. Every night they stepped out of time. They got a reprieve from the chaos. But not me. I was always here. Always awake. Time had my number. I felt a little…trapped.

He looked at me thoughtfully. "Well, let's get started," he said, glancing around.

I stifled a scream when a woman suddenly appeared in the hallway.

"I should've told you Sophia was on her way," Cain said apologetically. "She'll see to Echo."

I clutched at my heart, trying to get it to calm down. It was clear Sophia was part of Cain's circle because she was glowing. Their pure auras were steady and had the same bright white hue. They looked categorically different from any other human, their lights an unbroken line encircling them. Everyone else was in a slight fog, with licks of color flickering out based on emotion, thought, and action.

Perhaps Cain, Sophia, Andrew, and Lizzy weren't human. But if not, what were they?

Chapter Fifty-Five

Cain made quick introductions. Sophia winked at me, and then vanished, taking Echo. It was so sudden, my heart stuttered all over again.

"I've heard you've spontaneously appeared in rooms before," Cain observed with some amusement.

"Yeah," I said, shaking off the fright, "but it's a lot different when you're the one dropped in on. I'll have to keep that in mind."

"There are more reasons not to travel in that way," he said, dragging Fourth and traitor Second bodies around. I followed as he hauled the bodies to the front of the house, listening all the while. He was in a talkative mood, which I suspected was rare. But he was full of interesting and helpful information.

He explained the possible dangers of traveling the way Sophia just had and I sometimes did. There were hazards in general, and some specific to me, with my energy fluctuations. He especially warned me against taking anyone else with me, if I chose to travel like that.

"I haven't done it often, and most of the time it wasn't a conscious choice," I told him.

"You'll need to work on that," he assessed.

"You sound like Mr. Seacrest," I smiled. "He was always trying to get me in shape. So disciplined."

"That's good to hear," he chuckled. "When I met Alastair, he was a mess. Completely lost. I can't imagine what it was like for him, night after night, reliving his worst deed. I'm glad he's at peace."

"I miss him," I said, feeling useless as I watched Cain work, afraid to touch anyone out of fear of hurting them.

It took almost an hour to go through the house, moving the bodies around. I had missed two that Cain found.

As he hefted a Fourth over his shoulder, carrying him inside to gently lay him next to the others, I asked about his peculiar hunt comment.

"The hunt? Well, I suppose they're like any group of treasure seekers. They are relentless and driven. Highly motivated because what they seek helps them survive."

"Are these hunters like me?"

"No one is like you," he smiled. "But, if you're asking if they also don't sleep, the answer is yes. You know you must find balance. A way to revive your body and mind, since you are denied sleep. It was exposure to specific minerals from deep within the earth that made them – you – sleepless. It is these same minerals that will sustain you."

"Diamonds and such?"

"No. Those are on the surface of the earth. What they are looking for is much further down. Hard to find, harder to extract, and difficult to keep. Thieves will pursue you. You will become both hunter and hunted."

"What else is new?" I said dryly, looking around us at the large group of bad people who wanted me dead. Tortured first, for good measure. Maybe even used for ransom, then tortured, and *then* dead. Just another day in the life. I was dangerously close to feeling sorry for myself.

"Come on," Cain said, pulling me from my gloomy thoughts. "We should check the gardens."

"Is it safe to leave them alone here? What if they wake up?"

"It's possible they will. But it's also possible there are more of them on the grounds. It would be counterproductive to go to all this trouble of rounding them up and depositing them elsewhere, only to find we'd missed a nest."

Looking at my defenseless friends, I was hit by a wave of utter helplessness.

"Don't lose heart," Cain encouraged me gently. "This too will pass. Let's get going."

Now that the intense crackling energy was fading, my stamina also began to ebb. Soon I'd need to rest.

We swept the gardens, pool house, and the massively oversized garage that looked like a warehouse. I felt nothing and we found no one.

Walking up the long path from the outbuilding, we heard the faint sound of a motor idling.

Cain looked at his watch. "That can't be them. They couldn't have gotten here so quickly."

We picked up the pace, then started running when we heard yelling. Flying through the kitchen, I jumped over a dead Fourth in the hallway, a knife sticking out of her heart.

Cain ran past me, through the entry way, and out onto the front lawn, where an all-out battle was on. I stopped at the sight of Meg lying crumpled at the base of the staircase. A large knot was swelling on her forehead.

Her eyes fluttered open. "What's happening, Anna? Please don't leave me," she pleaded weakly.

I wanted to scoop her up and move her to safety, but the uncontrollable energy was back, and I felt like a simmering volcano. I could not decide if I should leave Meg, hurt and vulnerable, to join the fight, or if I should stay with her and leave everyone else to battle it out.

Wavering between staying and leaving, the cries, curses, and general mayhem of combat filled my ears. I had to go. Had to help.

"Anna..." Meg breathed, looking up at me in shock.

To my intense surprise, I found I was floating a good two feet off the ground. My fingertips were sparking. My body was working itself up. A blast was on its way, and I feared it would be even bigger than the last.

I concentrated on the entryway door and the blur of confusion beyond. *Calm down, calm down,* I chanted internally, clenching and unclenching my fists.

Corey ran inside, stopping in his tracks when he saw me. "She's in here," he yelled over his shoulder. "She's...all right," he finished uncertainly.

He turned back to me and urged, "Get down from there. We need you. Quick!"

His no-nonsense attitude shook me, and I dropped to the floor. The trance that had washed over me dissipated.

I ran outside to join them.

One of the enemy's vans was almost out of sight, followed by a car and a Jeep turning out of the driveway. The last of their fleet had just taken off.

"Stop them!" Corey shouted at me.

"What do you expect me to do?"

"Anything!" he cried. "They're getting away!"

The only thing I could think to do was another blast of energy. But that would knock everyone out again, not just the fleeing Fourth and Second.

"No!" Andrew shouted at me from across the bloodstained lawn. "It's not worth it."

I dropped my arms, glad to be spared turning my guts into jelly again.

Suzanne and Adam were running after the Jeep. Suzanne stumbled, colliding into Adam as the taillights left them in the dust.

Chapter Fifty-Six

Cain organized the clean-up process. He wasn't suffering the same ill effects of headache and nausea as the others. Meg had a concussion. This one was milder, but I worried that two in such a short time could have long term effects. August Seacrest had fractured her wrist and Ewin came away relatively unscathed. Echo was being cared for at Crimson Hall for the time being, since Maggie was MIA ever since she killed the queen.

Cain ordered us to rest up before Adam started the debriefing process. Everyone complied, except for Adam's aunts. They kept their scheduled afternoon flight.

I lay splayed out on my bed. I didn't have it in me to think about everything that had happened. I couldn't process it, or anything else. Adam came in to check on me.

"All right, love?" he asked, his voice colored with worry.

"No. You?"

I longed for a long, deep, cleansing sleep. I wanted to close my eyes and fall into the oblivion of my dreams, if only for a bit.

That was not possible. Instead, I reluctantly pulled myself up to meditate. Sitting, back straight but not rigid, I looked for peace.

Adam and I sat cross-legged, side by side on the bed, facing the windows as we meditated. I found my breathing, centering on it. The rhythm of my breath always reminded me of the tides, steady and erratic at once. And just like the waves came and went, bringing bramble and creatures with them, so did my thoughts.

I had been taught not to empty my mind, but simply to observe it without judgment. I allowed my thoughts to come and go. Some lingered, like my anxiety about my dangerous new energy and our upcoming visit to Crimson Hall, and some receded almost without notice.

Even as I tried not to control the free flow of thoughts, I was looking for the key to renewal. As I searched, I turned my attention outward, to my body, probing my aching bones and head for hints. As I scanned my arms, I felt a tiny pulse from my wrist. I knew the energy I needed was there, but the power – the power to easily incinerate a person with their mere touch – terrified me.

I was frightened of what I had done today, frightened of this new power. I was hiding from it, shielding myself as if trying not to look into the sun. Others were starting to fear me too.

"Don't be so hard on yourself, love," Adam said quietly, completely in tune with my fractured emotions. "You will figure this out. You don't have to be perfect."

I opened my eyes and our gazes locked. "You can find the balance," he continued. "If you get a bit too much or not quite enough, you'll work it out."

He looked down at my wrist. "May I?" he asked.

I was drained. The pendulum had swung from excess energy floating through me, to running on fumes. I nodded and he gently took my hand in his, kissing my palm. Turning my hand over, eyes lifted to mine, he kissed my ringed wrist. I flooded with anxiety as I worried I would hurt him.

A jolt of energy released through my body. The shockwave that had passed through me when the Second touched my bracelet had been intense and uncontrollable. But this was a smooth and manageable shock. The weariness was gone, and I felt wide awake.

259

My eyes refocused on Adam, who was trying to conceal a pained wince. I watched in alarm as his lips blistered from the contact with my wrist.

I raised my hand to touch his burned lips, but he flinched. "Give me a sec," he said, his voice jagged.

My heart racing, I sat and waited. It took a minute, an eternity, for his breathing to calm. He took a deep breath and visibly relaxed, the pain finally easing.

"Is it that bad?" he asked drily, reacting to my horrified face.

It was.

He lightly touched his mouth. "Ow." Going into the ensuite bathroom to check out his reflection, he poked at his lips. "Yeah."

I followed on his heels, appalled. I didn't know what to say. I silently pulled out the mini first aid kit my dad had sent. There wasn't much to do but pat his lips with antibacterial ointment.

I handed him the tube, unwilling to risk touching him again.

"No. You do it," he said, sympathy on his face. "Will you?"

I took a deep breath, scanning my body from head to toe. I felt entirely normal. Well, my new normal. I didn't feel like a human lightning bolt. The zap of energy from Adam's kiss had renewed me.

He sat patiently on the edge of the bathtub as I carefully dabbed the cream on his lips, my hands slightly shaking at the thought I might hurt him again.

"I've had much worse," he said, reaching for my waist.

Immediately my mind flooded with one of his memories. He'd been cornered in an alleyway by a group of Fourths. He'd held his own for a while, but he'd simply been outnumbered. They had beat him until his face was a bloodied mess, his ribs broken. I felt his fear and resignation as he accepted he was going to die, beaten to death.

But somehow, he hadn't given up. He'd kept on fighting long enough for Echo, Suzanne, and a couple of others I didn't recognize to take those Fourth out.

It was an awful memory. "I know."

I instantly regretted my slip as he stiffened. He hated that I knew all of his past.

"I'm sorry," I breathed, gently tugging on the hair at the base of his neck.

"Don't apologize," his words cutting.

Though his anger was entirely self-directed, it was a bitter pill to swallow. I also didn't want to know all the things I now knew about him. For many reasons. But there was no unknowing.

Looking into his eyes, I saw he was hiding something. Given that I'd just reminded him that I unintentionally, but grossly invaded his privacy, I didn't ask what it was. How could I? I wondered if we could ever be as we had been before.

A knock on my bedroom door drew our attention.

It was Ewin. I called for him to come in.

"There may be a problem," he started, then stopped when he saw the state of Adam's face. "What happened?" His body tensed.

"I'm fine," Adam said calmly. "Continue."

He didn't believe Adam, but relaxed. "Have you been watching the news? Their news." He pointed at me.

"What's going on?" Adam asked, all business.

"There's a contagious virus that's spreading rapidly around the world."

"And this affects us how?"

"There's talk of closing American airports to international travel. If we want to get out of the country, we should do so now," Ewin urged.

Now? I couldn't go now. There were still two and a half weeks until Mr. Seacrest's Family funeral at Crimson Hall. I had plans to spend my dad's spring break with him. We really needed quality time together.

"This can't wait a week or so?" I asked.

"It's up to you," Ewin said skeptically," but we've been through plagues before. These things are unpredictable. The WHO is considering declaring it a global pandemic."

Chapter Fifty-Seven

Ewin's world news struck me like a slap in the face. Where had I been? I mean, of course I'd known China was having problems with an outbreak of some kind, and my dad was concerned, but I'd assumed it was contained. I really hadn't paid much attention to the news. There was just too much craziness in my own little world.

"Let's get going, then," Adam decided. "Make the arrangements," he said to Suzanne, who was standing behind Ewin.

"Do you know who's traveling with us?" she asked for clarification.

"Is Finn? We never decided if it was a good idea to bring him along," I reminded them.

"Corey and Finn should not attend the funeral," Adam replied. "However, it's up to them if they want to go to Crimson Hall with us. What do you think, Anna?"

"After today, I think we should stick together," I answered. "A show of solidarity. If we want to start a new way for all the remaining Families to act towards each other, then we must model it. We have to show them."

Adam turned to Suzanne. "Tell everyone in the house to meet in the living room. Meg as well," he added as she left the room.

Once we were all gathered, Adam extended an invitation to Crimson Hall. Cain wouldn't be coming. He needed to get back to the project he was working on. Before he left, he gave me his cell number in case I needed him.

Andrew warned the rest of us, "Weigh your decision. If you leave this country, it's uncertain when you'll be able to return."

It seemed unreal that we wouldn't be able to travel freely, but since I started paying attention, all the news pointed to a long-term worldwide crisis.

Should I stay with my dad, or go with Adam and the rest to Crimson Hall? Whatever I chose might cut me off from loved ones for an indefinite time. The thought that airports would close, and remain closed for any length of time, seemed absurd. But Ewin and Andrew assured us it was a very real possibility. Risking my dad's safety by taking him with us to Crimson Hall was not an option. The fear that my dad might need me and I couldn't get to him was unbearable…but I already knew what I was going to choose.

Having no useful knowledge of the future was beyond frustrating, and at this moment was what I missed most about being able to sleep and dream. Now the only hints of the future I got came in daydreams, when my mind wandered. They were just flashes, images of a person or a place, but nothing helpful.

By the end of the day it was settled. We would all go to Crimson Hall together.

Meg came to my bedroom as I packed. She hadn't explained her surprising decision to come with us, but she was welcomed. I had noticed that immediately after Corey said he was going, Meg said she wanted too as well.

Gingerly sitting on the bed, she asked, "Did I shock you?"

"Yes," I admitted with a smile. "I'm glad you're coming with us, but I don't know why. Is it because of what you wanted to talk to me about earlier?"

The merriment in her voice was replaced with caution. "Yes. Is that okay?"

"Of course it is. I'm glad you're coming. But how are you going to explain it to your family?"

"They're used to me doing my own thing. And besides, it'll be better for them if I'm not around."

"Why is that?"

"Well, for one, wherever I go, a media circus follows," she explained with a shrug. "My family is private. Don't get me wrong. They're proud of me, for sure. But it's hard for them. The press camps out around the corner wherever I stay, going through the trash. I'm used to it. I've trained myself how to pretend and act. My mom and dad, not so much. They have a hard enough time getting my sister to her therapies, but when I and the press are around, it makes hard tasks even harder."

"But that's not the real reason," I said, zipping up my bag. I sat next to her on the bed to give her my full attention.

"It's just...." She stopped, rubbing her temples. I waited, determined not to push. "I don't want to go home. I can't explain it. It's like...when I think of going home, I start to feel anxious. Like I'm about to have a panic attack. I don't want to do it. I can't go back by myself."

I was drawn in by her fright. Her fear tingled on my skin. Meg was rarely so open. She did a good job of keeping her real self private, even from me.

She continued. "I don't think I could really explain it to my folks if I went somewhere that I couldn't pass off as studio-related, especially given this virus. And, anyway, I would be more harm to my family than the virus," she said, lowering her voice to a whisper, "because *they* follow me."

Chapter Fifty-Eight

About to tell me about the "they," Adam interrupted, disappointed at our lack of packing progress.

As Adam left to check on the rest, I said, "On the plane, then?" Rarely open about hard stuff, I hoped she wouldn't change her mind to share with me.

"Sure," she said, slipping off the bed, catching her reflection in the mirror. She turned back to me, with a question in her eyes. "Do you know my secret?"

"I don't read minds," I reassured her, again.

"But?" She pushed, waiting for confirmation.

"You already told me you've seen them before. Ghosts."

She nodded. "That's what I would've called them, before, you know," she said, waving at me.

"Before you met me?"

"Yeah," Meg sighed, a bit cheered by my knowing the issue was not of the usual drama variety. Drama, yes, but of the supernatural kind.

"Guys," Adam laughed, catching us still off task. "I don't want to break up this bonding session, but can you pick it back up later?"

Meg smirked at Adam in her playful way and padded down the hall to get ready to leave. We packed in a blur of activity and made our way to the airport. It had been a few days since the incident. Echo was stable, and we hadn't had any more unwanted, hostile visitors.

Nothing had changed regarding our immediate plans. And yet, everything had shifted. Since Millicent and August had been present at the invasion, they returned to Crimson Hall and testified to the remaining First and Second that Maggie was unfit to rule. Considering that Maggie had brutally killed Queen Cora, there hadn't been much doubt about that. But there was a significant minority that was committed to the old ways and structures. They reasoned it'd worked for hundreds of years, why change now?

But news from these impartial, powerful, and trustworthy Family members of what Maggie had done – and who she had done it with – had successfully changed the minds of the old guard.

The Seacrest cousins had flown to Crimson Hall hours after the fight. They'd called an immediate emergency meeting. It had been a unanimous vote. Maggie was out, and Adam, next in the line of succession, now ruled the First and Second Families.

As soon as we arrived at Crimson Hall, there would be a ceremony where Adam would be officially crowned. Or sworn in. Or whatever.

But for now, we were stuck in traffic less than twenty miles from the airport. I gazed out the window, wondering what it would mean for Adam to oversee the Families, especially in this new era.

Apparently, Adam had been thinking along the same track. "The old Families are dead," he said suddenly. "I don't want to hold to old prejudices. Neither does Finn. We have a new, common goal."

Finn nodded in consent. "Adam and I are going to hold a meeting with all the remaining Family members."

"All?" Suzanne asked warily.

"All," Adam confirmed. "Full and half-blooded alike."

"I don't think that's such a good idea," she said slowly. She wasn't used to speaking her mind on Family matters, especially in front of others.

I felt Adam's knee-jerk reaction to having his decision questioned. But as he opened his mouth to speak, he

267

reconsidered whatever he'd been about to say. "Explain," he said calmly.

"I know there are many Second who will not agree to a truce with the Fourth."

"And I know many more will oppose such a meeting," Ewin added. "You're asking a lot. Too much, too soon. I'm sorry, but we're not going to just suddenly start trusting the Fourth. I mean, even you, Suzanne. You know how others feel about you. Even with Adam's protection, I am surprised you're still here."

"Me too," Suzanne agreed.

I felt Finn deflating, as if Suzanne's words were really about the impossibility of a truce with him, and not the Fourth in general.

"Well then, what do you propose we do?" Corey exclaimed, frustrated.

"There is no easy way to change hundreds of years of deep-seated, well-earned animosity," I said. "But we need to start somewhere."

"Animosity?" Adam scoffed. "That's a massive understatement, Anna. Each faction's goal is nothing less than the total annihilation of the other." He gestured to Finn. "We, the people in this car, have had this experience of working together, but no one else has. If I hadn't personally experienced working with a Fourth like Finn, instead of against him, I wouldn't believe it. It will sound completely insane to the rest of the Families. And yet, I refuse to continue down the same path. We must do something different."

"But many know that Suzanne has fought by your side for years," I insisted. "So, there is precedent for working with Fourth, we know that they're not *all* evil. And now Millicent and August have witnessed Finn, the son of Lilian and Dane Varga, fighting beside us."

"That won't be enough," Ewin predicted.

"None of the Fourth really know what's been going on, all that happened at Gold Manor, and with Anna," Finn said. "They may have learned some of what's passed from Maggie, but they have no reason to trust a truce. And honestly, they don't want one. They are fine with how things are, obviously." Finn paused, caught in his own contradiction. There was no way to bring the Families together... but they had to try.

"Constant war?" I asked, incredulous.

"It's what they know," Finn said, his shrug speaking volumes. "It's simple. Kill or be killed. All energy is channeled into making alliances, amassing power, wealth, and status. When someone gets tired of the game, they die."

"So how do you explain yourself?" I asked. "Maybe there are more like you in the Fourth. People like Suzanne who would choose differently if they were given other options."

Finn crossed his arms over his chest and leaned back in his seat, nodding his head. "Possibly. And this is why Adam and I, against the odds, are going to try."

Chapter Fifty-Nine

Fighting standstill traffic, it took us two hours to get to the airport. Just long enough to have missed the rapidly closing window for international flights. There would be no more flights into or out of the U.S.

We walked back to the limo, dumfounded.

"This is crazy. Crazy!" Corey shouted, his voice echoing through the hangar.

Adam and Ewin argued with the tower, but there was nothing they could do. The order had been handed down by the federal government. We were stuck.

Naturally, traffic was clear on the way back to Adam's newly inherited home.

Adam seemed distant on the return trip. He didn't engage in the speculation as to when we'd be able to leave the country, or whether we'd make the funeral scheduled for the end of the month. His official coronation would have to wait too.

The rest of us vented our emotions, ranging from fear to frustration to resolve. But nothing from Adam.

When we arrived at Mr. Seacrest's house, we grabbed our luggage and went back to our previously assigned rooms. The house cleaning crew arrived minutes after we got back.

"Please pretend we're not here," Adam directed. Their presence had a calming effect. We couldn't speak freely with all the extra ears about. It was a large house, so they would be there for a while.

"Hey, anyone up for a swim?" I asked.

They all looked at me like I was crazy. No one was exactly in the mood for fun.

"Come on! It's cold but refreshing," I promised. "There's also a hot tub. And besides, the cleaners aren't out there."

Adam's face fell as the rest gave in to my coaxing. I wished I knew what was going on with him.

"Sitting in a hot tub sounds good right about now," Corey said, getting excited about the prospect.

"Great!" I said, clapping, inexplicably giddy. "If you don't have a swimsuit, there are extras in the pool house. Towels and goggles too. See you out back!"

"Let's leave cell phones in the house," Adam added, without explanation.

I showed Meg where the suits were. She was a little withdrawn, which I understood. Her initiation into Family affairs had included an attack by the Fourth, a real baptism by fire.

When Adam walked into the pool house, my eyes were immediately drawn to the gold ring on his right hand. It had belonged to Mr. Seacrest. "The hot tub's on, ladies," he said, holding the door open for us.

We walked out just as Corey made a running leap, bellowing, "Cannonball!" He sunk into the pool, a massive splash rising in his wake.

He was laughing as he surfaced, seeing my not too pleased face. He'd drenched the towels. And my hair.

"Get over it, A," he teased, sending a few splashes our way. "Come in! The water feels good!"

Meg tilted her head and raised an eyebrow. "Nice try, Corey. Your teeth are *chattering*." He grinned up at her unrepentantly.

Meg was right. Even in perpetually sunny Southern California, mid-spring was far too chilly for swimming.

Adam was already in the hot tub, which was nestled into the side of a hill. The knoll was an anomaly in Mr. Seacrest's otherwise level, beautifully manicured grounds. A sleek wall of marbled quartz was fitted into the hill, water streaming down its surface into the hot tub.

Meg and I settled into the tub with Adam, Ewin, Suzanne, and Finn. We lounged in the warm water, languidly chatting, until Corey tired of swimming laps and he joined us.

Adam roused himself now that we were all gathered. "Sometimes the way over is through," he began. "There are ways of traveling that aren't subject to government approval."

"Needs must," agreed Ewin.

"Anna is able to move thousands of miles with her mind," Adam continued, though he was quickly interrupted by Meg's shocked gasp.

"What?" She stared at me. "You do what?"

I threw Adam a look and waded over to her. "There are a lot of things we haven't had a chance to talk about yet. While Corey and I only recently got involved in...the Family craziness...I've always had some stuff of my own going on. I'll explain it all later," I promised.

Meg shivered, despite being immersed in the heated water.

"As I was saying," Adam went on, "there are other ways of traveling. I am loath to do this, but..." He trailed off, looking around. "Not here."

He moved to one of the jets beside the quartz wall. From my vantage point, it looked like he stuck his forearm in the jet and pulled on something. I felt a whooshing sensation around my feet and legs. The water level began to dip but then rebounded.

"Follow me," he said, taking a deep breath and plunging under the water.

Suzanne and Ewin followed immediately. Finn gave me a quick glance, his face an open book when it came to Suzanne. He was going wherever she was.

Only Meg, Corey, and I were left.

Corey swam over to Meg. "You coming?"

"I guess there's no turning back now. Right?" she asked uncertainly.

"It's a lot to take in, I know," he assured her gently. "It's been a few years for me and my head's still reeling."

He filled his lungs and was gone. Meg rolled her eyes but followed suit. I was the last to go.

Chapter Sixty

The reason for the odd-shaped hill in the rather angular yard was now clear. It housed a completely enclosed, secret hot tub.

I emerged to hear Corey exclaim, "Wicked. Like something out of a Bond movie."

"As you know, my uncle left everything to me. Including the library," Adam said, his voice echoing in the chamber.

"Which is full of dark artifacts that we need to destroy," I added, moving to his side.

He kissed my cheek and slid his arm around my waist. It felt like ages since he had touched me like this. I only wished I didn't have an audience for my flaming red cheeks.

"That is on our to-do list," he concurred. "But first we must attend to the dead."

"We have obligations," Ewin agreed. "We need to return to Crimson Hall."

"Is Anna going to take us?" Corey asked. "She's only moved me once, and it gave me the willies. Not something I'd like to repeat, if possible."

"I'm sorry. I can't," I said, looking around, hoping I hadn't dashed any hopes. I wanted to get to Crimson Hall too, but certainly Adam wouldn't ask me to do it. Andrew and Cain had been clear that such travel might have dire consequences, given my fluctuating energy.

"I would never ask Anna to do anything that could harm her, or others," Adam said, plainly offended.

Corey raised his hands in a conciliatory gesture. "Hey man, my bad."

Adam took a beat and continued, "I have the means to take us to Crimson Hall."

We waited for Adam's explanation, which he seemed reluctant to give. I had no idea what he was talking about.

"Before I can explain, I must bind each of you to your word that you will never reveal what you're about to learn," Adam said grimly. "I don't want to do that, but there is no other way. This is information that must be protected."

"What is he talking about?" I heard Meg whisper to Corey. Corey shook his head, just as puzzled as she was.

"Adam, they don't know about Family binding agreements," I interjected.

"A binding agreement is a covenant that must be kept throughout your life, or until the terms of the covenant are fulfilled," he explained. "To break the covenant will call down a curse upon you."

"No one enters a binding promise without dire need," Finn added.

"Sounds intense," Meg replied, trying to process this new knowledge.

"It is," Adam said flatly. "I must bind you to a secret of the library. I can't tell you more than that."

"You haven't told us anything," Finn scoffed.

"Finn, I'm asking you to trust me," Adam said. "The binding agreement will be about keeping a secret of the library, that's all."

"Nothing else will be involved in the covenant?" Finn asked, trying to suss out a hidden agenda.

Adam extended his arm to Finn, offering to bind himself in promise before asking Finn to do the same. "I promise to only bind you in secrecy about the library."

"No need," Finn said with a shake of his head, apparently deciding to trust Adam.

"What is the curse if we break the promise?" Meg asked.

"The consequences may differ, depending on the promise breaker and the kind of breech. The agreement is legally binding, but not a trick. No one loses their mind because of an accident."

"Loses their mind?" Corey scoffed. "That could happen?"

"Yes. I've also heard of death," Finn said.

"The penalty is tied to the breech of the covenant."

Ewin explained the details of the covenant. More questions came up and were answered. Finally, amazingly, everyone agreed.

Adam approached each person in turn. "Do you vow not to reveal any information about the Family library?"

We each responded with the words, "I do," and a simple bow.

"You are now bound," Adam cautioned. "If your vow is broken, I cannot undo the curse awaiting you, even if I wanted to."

There was a silence while we absorbed that. Then, the ceremony over, it was time for the reveal.

"Did you ever wonder how my uncle moved so seamlessly between Crimson Hall and L.A.?" he asked.

Immediately I understood. An entrance to the library was here, somewhere. And now Adam had the key and means of taking us to the other side of the world.

"He found a portal a long time ago," Adam continued. "Here. This is why he built this house. It was easy to explain why someone as private as my uncle would choose to live in seclusion. The real reason was to protect this weapon."

Everyone started scanning the space for a portal, while I idly wondered if we'd be going to Crimson Hall with nothing but borrowed swimming suits.

"Portals are weapons?" Corey asked absently, still looking for the entrance to one. "Don't they just link places?"

Adam looked at him like he was daft. All Corey and I knew about portals came from watching science fiction movies.

Clearing his expression with a little shake of his head, Adam went on. "This portal is directed at Crimson Hall. As far as I'm aware, my uncle shared this only with my sister Diane, and then with me."

He paused, taking a deep breath. "A part of this feels wrong, but there isn't another way to get us home. Once the cleaning crew leaves, so will we."

Adam wasn't giving the location of the portal just yet. We had some time to prepare.

With a few hours to spare, I called my dad. I told him we'd only have a little time together, but he came right over, as anxious to see me as I was to see him.

When he walked into the house and wrapped me in a hug, I relaxed in a way I hadn't for weeks. Maybe longer. His presence, his normality, was a breath of fresh air. He reminded me of who I really was.

Chapter Sixty-One

The cleaners' vacuum pushed us out to the back gardens so we could talk without shouting.

I could see something was on his mind. "What is it, Dad?"

He watched me for a moment before speaking. "You've...changed. You look different. And I know this is an odd thing to say, but you *smell* different."

It was somehow a relief that he saw the change in me. When I looked in the mirror, I couldn't tell. I couldn't see it. But I felt the radical alteration.

I shifted the conversation to him, his semester and department politics. He knew what I was doing but let me do it. We were operating on a 'need to know' basis. If there was something important for him to know, and it was possible to tell him, I would. And I knew he would always be there to listen and give advice. He was good at reminding me of basic truths. People were still people. Loving your neighbor and treating them with kindness, mercy, and justice still applied, even in my brutal new world.

"I have some news," he said near the end of our visit. "I'm selling the house."

I wasn't expecting this. "Why?"

"It's too big for me. With your mother gone, and you out on your own, it's too much."

"But you love that house," I protested. He did. And so did I. It was also a tangible connection to my mom. When I was there, I felt her in every corner.

"I didn't want to burden you," he said hesitantly, his face flushing slightly.

"What is it? What's going on?"

"I can't afford it," he admitted quietly. "The university is making changes. There's talk they are going to eliminate my department. We're not a 'money maker'. We're not supposed to be," he said emphatically. "Philosophy is the cornerstone of every university. Plato founded the first university!"

He embarked on one of his favorite lectures about what comprised a university education. I had heard it many times before. It was on his greatest hits playlist, along with his distaste for compatibilist fence-sitters and the intellectual untenability of moral relativism. We had interesting dinner conversations.

"And so, we are living in an anti-intellectual age," he said, winding down. "I don't know how much longer I can stay at the university, with their obsession for quantifying meaning and increasingly stifling intellectual curiosity."

"What will you do?"

"I'll finish out this year, which looks like it's going to be online due to this virus. I'm thinking about writing full-time, like your mother. Or, maybe… well, I have many options," he said optimistically. "No need to worry about me. But, when I make this career transition, it will help to have a lower mortgage. I need a smaller, cheaper place."

"If it's just money, I can help," I offered.

"That's kind of you, dear," he said with a soft smile, "but I need a change. It's hard to be there alone."

The time had flown by. Hugging him in the driveway, I told him I might be gone for a while.

"Be smart, Anna," he warned. "I'm anxious about what's happening. This virus is being politicized. Don't fall for it. Listen, read, pay attention. Be safe," he said and kissed my head.

"You too, Dad. I know you too. Try to stay in the middle. As you say, don't react. Think it through. And please, be safe."

Watching him drive away hurt. We'd had too little time together, but it was more than some had. More than Adam had. All of his family were dead or lost to him.

Adam told us to pack light. The passage between the houses wouldn't occur in a blink. I didn't admit it, but I had assumed we'd jump into a swirling portal and instantly arrive at our destination.

Our packs slung over our shoulders, we met in the living room.

"Follow me," Adam directed. He stopped in the entry way, turning the house alarm on, then descended the stairs to the basement.

"Wine cellar?" I guessed, distracted by the realization that we wouldn't be leaving through the hidden hot tub room, as I'd supposed.

He smiled back at me, taking my hand, but said nothing. I could feel his nerves. Which was rare. He was usually completely self-possessed...or out of control. His nervousness spread through the group.

Half of the basement was devoted to Mr. Seacrest's extensive wine collection. The other part was divided into a large rec room, two ensuite bedrooms, a half-bathroom, and an enormous laundry room.

Gathered in the rec room, we looked around, trying to spy the super-secret location of the portal.

"Okay, let's get going." Adam turned toward the short hallway separating the two bedrooms.

"Um, Adam?" Meg said, stopping him. "Could you tell me what's going to happen? I'm really freaked out. I think knowing will help cool me down."

"Yeah, sure. Okay. You need to follow me through. Once we're on the other side of the gate and in the portal, you'll need to keep your hands to yourself. Don't touch anything. The path will look rocky. It is, in a way. It's hard to describe," he said apologetically. "I've been through five or six times. Each time it got easier – and shorter – because I stopped touching stuff."

"I'm with you," Corey said, moving next to Meg.

"That's a good idea," Adam approved. "Everyone should take a buddy. So, it's Corey and Meg. Finn and Suzanne. Ewin, you go with Anna. I'll lead."

"Do we need to hold hands or anything?" Corey asked, slipping his hand into Meg's.

"It's not strictly necessary, but a good idea. At the very least, you'll be less likely to touch anything." Adam turned toward the little hallway, but hesitated. He looked back and asked, "Any last questions?"

"How long will it take? Does it hurt?" Meg asked.

"It's hard to say. Maybe under an hour, if we're lucky. Could be longer. It is cold and damp. It'll grow colder at the end. I've never been through with anyone but my uncle. He's been through so much, it doesn't - didn't – faze him. But," Adam said, remembering, "despite the chill, I find it *interesting*. Let's leave it at that. So, no, it doesn't hurt if you don't touch anything. Got it?"

He turned back once more, examining our shoes. Apparently satisfied, he finally led the way.

At the end of the short hallway between the two bedrooms was the large laundry room, which housed three industrial-sized washers and dryers. No doubt Mr. Seacrest had installed them for those times when large parties had visited him.

I scanned the room for the portal. I felt nothing. It felt and smelled like a laundry room. Maybe a little stale from lack of use, but certainly nothing out of the ordinary.

Adam bent his head to me and whispered, "Are you wearing Werden?"

I nodded, pulling the neck of my sweatshirt to the side, revealing the chain. "You asked me to," I whispered back.

He gave me a nod and then turned to everyone else. "See you on the other side. Anna, pull the door closed when you're through."

And with that, Adam opened the door of the first dryer and stuck his head in. And then his entire body disappeared.

"I suppose we know where the portal is now," Finn said, grinning with a nervous energy. "Ready?" he asked his partner.

Suzanne went right in, followed closely by Finn. Both disappeared.

"Corey, Meg? You guys ready?" I asked.

"Ready as I'll ever be," Corey said. Amazingly, his big body fit through the dryer. Meg followed on his heels.

"After you," I said to Ewin.

Unlike the rest of us, Ewin seemed genuinely unconcerned about journeying through a magic portal. I guessed that's what came with age. He'd seen a lot. Maybe too much, if this didn't thrill him.

I took one last look around and exhaled, pushing my body through the metal dryer, reaching back to close the glass door. As soon as the dryer door locked in place, the lights in the tunnel went on.

Chapter Sixty-Two

"It's natural phosphorescence. And don't touch," Adam repeated.

I didn't know who he was answering, but he could only be referring to the glowing stones lining the craggy walls. The portal was nothing like I had expected. Of the many scenarios my mind had conjured up, from swirling ether to black holes and shooting stars, a muddy tunnel pitted with luminescent gems had not been among them.

"You weren't kidding about the cold. It's freezing," Meg said, pulling her arms inside her sweatshirt. The air felt only slightly cool to me.

"Everyone in?" Adam asked, looking around. "Anna, you closed the door tightly?"

"Well, I closed it," I said, turning around to check. But it was gone. There was no door, just shimmering mud.

"Where is it?" I asked in confusion.

"We're long past L.A.," Adam answered.

Corey looked around. "But we haven't moved."

"Did you expect to walk all the way to Crimson Hall?" Adam said dryly. Corey was too dazzled to care.

"So how do we get there?" Finn asked.

"Follow me," Adam instructed.

"So, we are walking," I heard Corey whisper to Meg.

After a while, we came to a sharp bend in the tunnel. Taking the turn, we were jerked to a stop, like a conveyer belt reaching the end of its track.

"Talk about whiplash," Suzanne muttered.

There was another jerking motion, like the start of an elevator ride. The popping in my ears was proof I wasn't imagining the change in altitude.

"Colder still," Ewin said to himself.

The altitude leveling off, our surroundings began to change, the mud drying up. Within a few minutes the ground beneath our feet turned hard, smooth, and slippery.

That's when things got interesting. Though we walked on solid ground, I had the sensation that my stomach was about to drop. It was like the moment just before a roller coaster dives. Air about to be squeezed out of my lungs, stomach about to drop… but not yet. An extended moment in time before the bottom falls out.

The disorienting feeling affected us all. All talking stopped as we were entranced by the feeling of perpetual suspension.

"Three, two, one," Adam counted down. "There." And just like that, the feeling of falling ended. "How is everyone?" There were no audible sounds of distress, so he continued. "We're about to get to the canal. Watch your footing on the bank unless you want to get wet. And, remember –"

"Don't touch anything," Corey finished for him, giving us a moment of much-needed levity.

"Right," Adam smiled. "When we get to the bridge, be mindful of the tree roots."

Moments later we came to a slight right bend in this zigzag tunnel, bringing us to the bank of a canal.

The pathway narrowed, with a sharp drop off into the water on one side. We were now in single file, Adam at the lead. Up ahead, a short bridge came into view. It was made of the same material as the wall of Mr. Seacrest's hot tub.

Though the bridge was barely twenty feet long, it wasn't until Adam stepped on the bridge that an enormous willow appeared. It was as if it wasn't there and then simply was. The bridge merged into the trunk, almost as if it were a root. The tree was so massive that I couldn't see past it. It rose

284

straight up, highlighting the seemingly infinite height of the tunnel. As I gazed up, I thought I glimpsed the night sky.

The tree engulfed the bridge. Long ago, someone had taken an axe to the center of the trunk and opened a path to the other side. It was a tight, unpleasant squeeze through the center of the willow, taking much longer than I imagined it would. I hadn't been concerned at all, until now. I wasn't sure why, but I knew it wasn't just the uncomfortably narrow passage affecting my nerves.

My answer came moments later as I finally emerged from the tree, facing a stone staircase. I knew this place. I'd been here before.

"Good job, all. That was just under two hours. Guess I'm a good teacher," Adam laughed. He took off his backpack and handed out bandanas to everyone but me. "Anna and I will lead you through this last part. We're almost to where we want to be. We must pass through the Family library. It's important that you ignore anything you feel or hear while there. It should go without saying, but I really cannot emphasize this enough - don't touch anything in there. In fact, once your blindfold is in place, hold the hand of the person in front of you and behind you. Keep your eyes shut, and we'll go slowly."

I noticed Adam was fidgeting with his new ring. From the bottom of the stairs, I watched as Adam slowly put his ringed hand *through* the door.

Chapter Sixty-Three

The click of the library door unlatching was unmistakable. As soon as it opened, my mind went right to the spot where I knew the silver comb and mirror set was. Adam whipped his head around to me, his eyes penetrating mine, clearing the haze in my head.

"Anna, listen to me. Stay clear of it."

How did he know of my obsession? I'd never told him about the comb set. About how, on occasion, I dreamed of it. How I longed to sit in front of my floor-to-ceiling mirror at home, fresh from a hot shower, and pull the comb through my hair.

"Anna, get it together," Adam snapped.

"Hey," Corey protested, reaching for his blindfold.

"No, no. It's okay," I assured him. "I've been here before, and there's something in there that has my name all over it. It's incredibly hard for me to resist." I was shocked by the yearning I felt. I realized that the longer I'd been away, the intensity of my desire to have it had grown exponentially. "Let's just go."

And so we did. I wanted to run through the library, but that wasn't possible as Adam and I guided the blindfolded.

I concentrated on keeping my friends safe. I watched their movements. Looked for what might be calling out to them. With every step we came closer to getting out.

Up ahead, Adam swore and stopped. "Did you move it?" he asked, knowing full well I hadn't been in the library. Couldn't have been, even if I'd wanted to.

He left the front of the line and came back to me. "The silver set is to the left of the entrance. That is not where it belongs. How was it moved?" he asked, looking for answers I didn't have.

It was taking everything I had to fight my insane desire to touch that stupid comb. But like an itch that can't be scratched, the urge just intensified. It wouldn't let me go.

"You can do this," Adam coaxed. "There's a reason my uncle left you Werden. Use it."

I had been hoping Adam would escort me out, shielding me from this danger since he was now the keeper of the library. He was at home here, full of an ease I'd never seen from him before.

But as was his way, he trusted me to dig down deep and figure it out on my own. He would not baby me. I would have to suck it up.

As soon as the mirror and comb set came into view, the most amazing thing happened. It looked…ordinary.

In my mind I'd built it up as being exceedingly beautiful and precious, full of power. But as I drew closer, I saw that the silver was slightly tarnished, the set smaller than I remembered.

Unthinkingly, I reached out to pick up the mirror. Something so ordinary, and honestly, kind of shabby.

Adam caught my hand. I looked up to see that the others were out of the library, on the other side of its door. "Do. Not. Touch!"

I was shocked and hurt by his reaction. I had just been interested in the change. I'd just wanted to look at it, to show myself it held no power over me.

I pulled my hand back, but he wouldn't let go. "It's a trick, love. Whatever it told you is false. It has your name," he said, gently, laying my hand over the place Werden hung on my chest. "Feel that?"

Adam's hand on top of mine, my fingers warmed with the power of Werden, clearing my mind and showing me the trick the silver set played. I wished I took Adam's advice and sought Werden's help sooner.

Not letting go of my hand, he led me out of the cursed library.

"Can we take these off now?" Meg asked, touching her blindfold and swaying on her feet.

"Not yet," Adam said, rushing to the front of the line. "We're almost out."

I had only been to the library once before. While entering had been quite a production, leaving it had been straight forward. Now, as we rounded up the stairs and took curious turns, I couldn't help but wonder if Adam was trying to hide the entrance to the library from those who would search for it in Crimson Hall.

As we climbed higher, I felt the people in the Hall. Ewin stopped and I smacked into his back.

"Okay. Blindfolds off," Adam said. "We're here."

Chapter Sixty-Four

We were in the hall of remembrance. Greeted by Adam's Aunts, there was a brief discussion about procedure. The small, make-shift council agreed it was prudent to move Finn and Corey out of the Crimson Hall compound during the coronation.

Meg wanted to stay with Corey, but she'd be safer with us. When she protested and Corey took her aside, I realized something. They weren't secretly dating, as I'd thought. They were *friends*. Close friends. Somewhere along the way, I'd been replaced. And I hadn't noticed.

The moment of epiphany was pretty awful. It was beyond selfish to expect his undivided attention when he didn't have mine. I'd just kind of thought he would always be my person. But life changes. And time has a way of marching all over us.

Adam shook me out of my mini-implosion as I watched Corey leave. "Anna, the ceremony's about to begin. We need to get changed."

It was a timely reminder that, oh yeah, my boyfriend was about to be crowned King.

I followed Adam through the Hall until we arrived at his bedroom. Seeing his door, my spirits lifted. This was as far as I'd gotten when, long ago, Adam had brought me to Crimson Hall in a dream. I'd been so upset when my alarm had woken me before I got to go inside his room. Now I was here, and this was not a dream.

We stepped into the turret room, and I relished my first glimpse of Adam's personal space. His bed was in the middle of the large room, facing the roaring fire in a stone hearth. Though I hadn't found the journey as cold as the others, I felt the chill that had set in begin to thaw as the fire warmed my back.

His room had a simple wood desk, clean lines. A hand painted chest with the First Family crest sat under the only window. The most notable feature by far was the lack of bare wall space. Every inch was covered with weapons and war tapestries, a testament of horrors through the ages.

We had been raised very differently.

I slowly walked around his room, taking in the surreal décor.

"This was Melinda's room." His smile reached his eyes.

"It was?" I couldn't imagine growing up with this room as my refuge.

"And before that, it belonged to my uncle Vincent. He was a weapons enthusiast. It's a lot, I know," he laughed.

"Ever think about redecorating?" I asked as I came to a particularly gruesome tapestry.

"Never thought about it," he shrugged. "But, when you're done touching all the things in my room, we need to get downstairs."

"Oh, okay." I was disappointed. I could've spent all day in his room, looking at the objects that were important to him. "Where am I staying?" I asked, tracing a pattern on the tapestry.

"All First and Second are here for the funerals and transfer of power. The Hall is full," he said with studied nonchalance. "We'll have to bunk together."

My heart stopped. I was glad I was facing the wall so he didn't see the hot flush that crept over my cheeks. It had been a while since Adam and I had been alone with anything but heartache and suffering.

He took my hand and pulled me closer. "I promise to be on my best behavior," he teased, his breath sweeping across my collarbone.

"I hope not," I whispered, kissing him slowly.

Chapter Sixty-Five

Our little moment was interrupted by Millicent poking her head into the room. "We're ready for you," she said, her smile dropping as she looked us up and down. "You, get ready," she said, pointing at Adam. "And you," she turned her sights on me, "come with me."

I followed her, winding through the hallway, up one staircase and down another. We passed the Hall of Remembrance, where pictures of their beloved dead hung. Flower wreaths were draped on the new frames. I stopped in front of Mr. Seacrest's portrait.

"We'll save our grief for another day," Millicent said quietly. "Today we hail our new king."

I looked at what she was wearing. Still sporting my stretch pants and neon tennis shoes from the journey, I was definitely not dressed for this. "I haven't changed."

"Do not worry about your clothes. None of us have dressed for the occasion."

She wore a tailored navy suit with wide cut pants and a crisp white shirt, unbuttoned just enough for her solid gold sunburst necklace to stun. She was incredibly put together, from the top of her perfectly blunt cut bob, to the tips of her pointy-toed tan pumps.

This was an everyday outfit for Millicent? She looked like a boss. A powerful, kick-ass boss. I looked like I was ready to pick up garbage on the side of the road. I should've changed instead of gawking in Adam's bedroom.

She ushered me into the expectant crowd. Hundreds had gathered, lining the dirt and gravel courtyard in the front of Crimson Hall. Millicent went off to attend to other business. I stood in the crowd.

I heard all kinds of interesting things as I waited. This was a larger gathering than had been expected. There were whispers of a possible attack on Crimson Hall by the Fourth. Given as evidence was the sighting of a couple of Fourth walking openly in the city. I had no doubt this was Corey and Finn.

What I found most interesting was the talk of the new king. There had never before been a new king for the First and Second Families. It had always been Adam's father. And when he'd died, they'd had just a queen. Most in the crowd only remembered ever having a queen, not being old enough to know anything else. With Queen Cora gone and "Queen" Maggie a traitor to her people, it was up to Adam to lead the way in these new times.

The people around me knew Adam. Most had watched him grow up. He'd been mischievous in school, until his sister had been killed. Then he'd entered the war and earned his people's respect as a soldier. But he'd been far too reckless and fearless to be seen as a leader. With his mother the eternal ruler of the Families, and an older sister, there'd never been any expectation that he would *need* to be. The jury was out on whether he would rise to the occasion.

Behind me, I heard whispered complaints that the new leader would be another First, rather than a Second. Then their conversation turned to me. I wasn't surprised people knew who I was, but it was shocking to realize just how little truth they knew, and yet how much they were willing to gossip and wildly speculate. They certainly didn't know much about me, or they would've kept silent.

I heard nasty musings from many, but only one lone soul in the crowd openly sticking up for me.

"She killed James and Sarah. She's responsible for the death of your father," a woman behind me said to her partner. "She's a witch, and she has Adam under a spell."

"She may be a witch, but she broke the curse," the woman's friend reasoned. "My father's mind had been coming apart. You know that. Same with James and Sarah. Who knows what would've happened if she hadn't worked her magic?"

"If there's anything I know, it's that there's always a price to pay," the woman insisted. "Will that burden fall to us?"

If they only knew the price I had paid and would continue to pay. But they would never know. I finally realized the full meaning of Iris's warning. The people I had helped would and could never understand the burden I would bear, the isolation and suffering. I would constantly be questioned, misunderstood, distrusted. My powers would forever brand me a witch.

Chapter Sixty-Six

I felt her presence before the crowd bristled. Suzanne. She was greeted warmly by a few, warily by most. We locked gazes and I hoped she would rescue me from these unfriendly faces. Instead, she took a place near the front, just behind Millicent.

Feeling the general hostility towards me in the crowd, I gingerly worked my way to the back. The ceremony began. This had only taken place once before, when Adam's parents were chosen to lead the First and Second Families hundreds of years ago. Maggie had never been officially sworn in. Her weeks-long reign had been self-appointed.

The current First and Second council leaders lined the circular entrance to Crimson Hall. The huge wood door guarding the entrance opened, revealing Adam standing in the center of the arched doorframe. One by one, the members of the council approached him. Adam bowed as each council member handed him a small present and bowed in return. They exchanged words that were too hushed to hear, and then returned to her or his place, flanking Adam.

When the last council member had returned to his place, Adam walked out into the middle of the courtyard.

He hadn't told me he was going to give a speech. A small child ran up to him and offered a bouquet of flowers. He thanked the flower bearer and turned toward the crowd, resolved. I knew he didn't want this new position, but here, among his people, I felt the weight of the responsibility he had to shoulder. I felt bad when the thought *better you than me* floated through my brain. But it was true. I couldn't imagine being in his place, nor would I ever want to be. Increasingly, I desired to stay out of the public eye.

"I never considered the possibility we'd be here. My mother, our queen, dead. My sister, Maggie, traitor. You have decided to keep the line of authority in my family. While this is not a position I sought – In fact, I cast a different vote – I will always serve the Families.

"This is a new era. The old ways are gone. Our founders are dead."

Someone from the crowd shouted, "Long live the King!"

Everyone in the crowd held hands and lifted them high, repeating, "Long live the King!"

"My mother ran the Families with a long view. She kept us safe. She kept us strong. She also began using the tactics of the tyrannical Fourth to further her ends. Those ways died with her.

"This is a new age. This age produced the long awaited Fifth, who is among us today." Murmurs erupted from the crowd. Adam extended his arm for me to join him. I wished he had given me some warning. I had been enjoying being an uninvolved bystander. Nevertheless, I went forward.

"Anna broke the curse. She allowed our parents to finally be at rest. Because of her, the tide of war has turned. We will win, we will rid the world of the Fourth. To facilitate this new world, we must be willing to change. We will lead the way, dragging the Fourth down forever!"

Cheers came from all around. I felt like he was rallying the troops before battle.

"To this end, as my first official act, I am instituting a new form of government. I will share the power of my seat. There are Four Families, and it is with all Families that the end will be brought about. I will speak for the First. Millicent Seacrest will speak for the Second."

Millicent, standing to his right, but in the shadows, was stunned. Adam motioned for her to stand next to him. She composed herself, quickly rising to the dignity of her new position.

"Anna is a Second and Third mix," Adam continued. "She is the only living Third we know of. Her unique heritage and abilities will make her an invaluable member of this new government. Is there any dissent?"

A man somewhere in the crush called out, "How can we trust a Third?"

"Jacque, you are right to question a Third among us. But Anna is unlike the Third you have known. She is a restoration of the original line, before the massacre. You have my word that she can be trusted. I understand that may not be enough to ease your fears. I ask, as your new king, that you make a leap of faith and give Anna the chance to prove herself."

Jacque receded, and an older woman asked a similar question. Then another. And another. This went on for some time. Adam answered all questions authoritatively and with an amazing reservoir of patience.

But the real challenge was yet to come. "This new leadership team will not be complete if we don't have a member from every Family," he said carefully.

Some were slower than others, but I watched as understanding dawned on their faces. A Fourth. Adam was talking about giving a Fourth a measure of power over them. Bodies started shifting. Murmurs began rising.

"You have fought with her. Some of you have housed her. I trust her with my life. I trust her with our mission," he said persuasively. "Our mission is her mission. She is a victim of the Fourth's viciousness. She paved the way for the old ways and prejudices to die. Who present will vouch for Suzanne Browne?"

Millicent was the first to back Adam. "I will vouch for her."

One after another, those assembled chose to throw in their lots with Suzanne. The look on her face was heartbreaking. She was pierced through by their acceptance, something she'd never known, had never thought possible. But her hard work and quiet commitment to the demise of the Fourth was known far and wide. It had taken just a moment of reflection for the civic-minded Family to confirm in their minds what Adam had already seen. She was perfect for the job.

"Meet your new leaders," Adam called, his voice ringing out over the crowd. "Together we will run the remaining Fourth to their graves!"

The cheers and applause were deafening. I felt like I was witnessing mob mentality in action. And I didn't like it.

"Or to the police," I couldn't help adding to Adam's rallying cry.

The Families fell silent, Adam's jaw clenched.

With all eyes on me, I wanted to plead for law and order, to make them understand that vengeance isn't justice. When it came down to it, I couldn't be a part of murder. I couldn't kill the Fourth invaders at Mr. Seacrest's L.A. home, and I wouldn't condone the slaughter of anyone.

"This very meeting is evidence that one's Family of origin doesn't prove allegiance or behavior," I implored. "As some of you know already, Finn Varga, son of Dane and Lillian, is staying in the village. He is our ally. Suzanne is our ally. My friend Corey, who happens to have Fourth blood, has fought for us. You – I mean we – can't keep killing people just because of their origin. Times have changed and so must we."

"That's too far, Adam Lewis," a council member called out. "Keep her in line or I will."

If Adam had been mad at me, his anger evaporated with that threat. But Ewin beat him to the punch. In a few bold strides, he was in the face of the council member. "Stand down, William. I'll take you out myself if you ever make a move against her."

For every person who voiced opposition to Adam's new shared governance, there were surely more who were quietly opposed. Had he started a new kind of war with the changes he was making? Would I prove to be too polarizing, leading to infighting? Only time would tell, but we would face any challenges that arose together.

Adam motioned for Ewin to step back. "William, you have been preaching the need for change. With increasing technology and surveillance, it's harder to cover our tracks. The most powerful Fourth were wiped clean in one stroke because of Anna's sacrifice. But in addition to the gift she's given to our cause, she also brings the insight of the outsider. She has shown me how to work better, smarter, together. She is from their world. Suzanne has lived and fought with the Fourth. Millicent is the oldest living Second. Many of you helped to raise and teach me. This is our future. You are our future. Together. Listening to new ideas. The old is dead, but we are alive." Adam paused, taking the temperature of the crowd. "Let's eat!"

The spell Adam cast was a spectacle to behold. The training from his mother, his lessons and experience fighting battles, living in the public eye with the band and on the small screen, all of this made him uniquely suited to win today. To usher in a new age for his people.

Chapter Sixty-Seven

As the virus raged on through the continents, we continued to work. Suzanne made Finn her second. Together they led teams to root out Fourth nests and chipped away at their strong holds. Millicent took control of the day-to-day running of the Families at Crimson Hall, and the Family spread throughout the world.

Corey and Meg went back to the States to wait out the virus together. They agreed to house sit the L.A. estate and the cats Adam had inherited. Katie and Andrew joined them. Safety in numbers was still the best policy. And if they needed anything, we were just a portal away.

This left Adam and I to address our number one mission, carrying out Mr. Seacrest's last request: the dismantling of the Family Library.

Cain sent his sister Sophia to help. She was experienced in disposing of cursed objects. She had the knowledge of what could be kept and what had to be destroyed. She brought a team with her, along with disposal equipment. Every morning for months, Adam and I donned hazmat suits and went to work in the once-private library. It was difficult, meticulous work, yet soothing in its predictability.

By my request, the first items incinerated were the silver comb and mirror. I was relieved by their disposal, but I still couldn't shake my longing for them. Sophia said that's the way it is with some of the curses. Once it gets you, even if the object is obliterated, the call remains. That's why they are so insidious. Their reach is long. The curses are never about the objects. The objects are conduits to darkness and wraiths. My longing would probably always remain. An after-image, permanently burned into my psyche.

Our spring and summer were spent clearing the library and pretending on social media. We both worked on *Ghost House* promos, and Adam and his band played some virtual gigs.

Ghost House was on indefinite hiatus, as was all filming on TeenTV. In fact, all television and film studios were in a holding pattern until the virus could be brought under control. The traditional arts were suffering.

Adam and I hit a sweet spot in our relationship. We'd become a team, working seamlessly together. His sweetness and patience endeared him to me even more, if that was possible. We now emitted a perpetual visible glow when in proximity. I secretly loved it, and the accompanying low-level hum. Adam knew I did – so much for secrets around him – but worked to figure out how to make it stop. The Hall tolerated us, but it wasn't practical if we ever hoped to leave Crimson Hall's grounds.

At night, I read, wandered the Hall and adjacent forest, and tried – unsuccessfully as of yet – to visit Adam in his dreams. Every night, when the last person in the Hall drifted off into lovely dreamland, I faced my new condition. I investigated the Serpent Star embedded on my wrist. I poked at the stones in my mind. I took meticulous notes about my energy, what drained me, what filled me up. I observed what made me spark. I experimented with releasing energy, even exploding a few unfortunate trees by accident.

My problems were legion. I literally couldn't sleep if I wanted to live. I could barely touch or be touched by others, which meant Adam and I couldn't marry in the traditional Family way since I'd become an unpredictable weapon. I carried a scent that unnerved my producer Sylvia and might have similar effects on others once I was back in the world. I was a leader of a people I didn't understand. I was plagued by the intrusive, recurring memories of Adam, Suzanne, and Andrew that occasionally assaulted me without warning. And Adam and I were not fit to be seen together in the outside world unless we figured out how to dim our glow.

As the summer drew to a close, though, I knew one thing for certain. I couldn't figure out how to make peace with my sleeplessness on my own. When the virus subsided, when we were free to move about, I would seek out those like me.

And yet, I was content. These were problems, yes. But they were just stumbling blocks. I had what was most important: love, family, and self-acceptance.

THE END

Acknowledgements

I finished **ROSE STAR GHOST HOUSE** during the first summer of the pandemic, 2020, though I had started it in the spring of 2017. I have never worked on a book so long!

In my mind, **THE FOUR FAMILIES** is a TV series and each book is a season, without end in sight. When I realized I did need to draw all (or most of) the threads together, I didn't know what that meant. I wrote and rewrote parts of this book until I found the truth of it. And then it was as if it was there all along. The figure hidden in the marble slab.

This explains the three years it took to finish the story. The gap between the summer of 2020 and the fall of 2024 is due to a change of careers from teaching philosophy to opening my own business in workplace conflict resolution, coupled with the brutal business that is book publishing.

I came back to **ROSE STAR** (which was called Serpent Star Ghost House for years until months prior to publication) periodically, but it wasn't until my sister, Melinda Hill, who teaches middle school in Seattle, kept gently nudging me for book 4 of the series on behalf of her students. Without this steady encouragement, you would not be reading this. Thank you, Melinda, and your wonderful students, for giving me the gift of encouragement that helped me finish and publish the last book in **THE FOUR FAMILIES** series.

Thank you, Jennifer Newton, for being the best editor ever.

Thank you, Christopher, Judah, Leo, and Thomas, for giving me so much love and support. I love you forever and beyond.

Thank you to the sweet community of readers who kindly read through this book to catch the remaining typos my dyslexic brain won't let me see. Thank you, Stephanie Richardson, Stephenee Carsten, Heidi Batchelor, Mandy Hinson, Taylor Janusz, Jolene Dretzka, Whitney Pope-Adams, and Cathren Bennett-Britt.

Lastly, a shout out to all the people in the world working for peace. Do you want peace in your life? I encourage you to develop and practice your conflict competency skills so you can address conflicts early, often, swiftly, and justly. Conflict is not the culprit: unmanaged conflict is the problem.

Conflict is normal and expected in this life. Let's deal with it!

 Merry Brown is the author of the YA series **THE EXILED TRILOGY** and **THE FOUR FAMILIES** as well as **HOW TO BE UNPROFESSIONAL AT WORK: TIPS TO ENSURE FAILURE** and **THE FOOD ADDICT: RECOVERING FROM BINGE EATING DISORDER & MAKING PEACE WITH FOOD.** In addition to writing, Merry is a speaker, philosopher, workplace mediator, host of **Conflict Managed,** a weekly international podcast about toxic work environments and how to fix them, and the founder of **Third Party Workplace Conflict Restoration Services LLC.** She lives in northwest Tennessee with her family.

Find her social media links at more at her Linktree: https://linktr.ee/3pconflictrestoration.